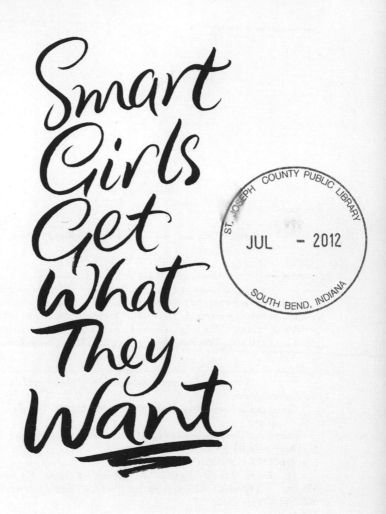

Smart Girls Get What They Want

by SARAH STROHMEYER

BALZER + BRAY
An Imprint of HarperCollinsPublishers

Balzer + Bray is an imprint of HarperCollins Publishers.

Smart Girls Get What They Want
Copyright © 2012 by Sarah Strohmeyer

Library of Congress Cataloging-in-Publication Data
Strohmeyer, Sarah.
    Smart girls get what they want / by Sarah Strohmeyer. — 1st ed.
      p. cm.
    Summary: Three sophomore best friends use their brains—and their wits—to
find happiness in high school.
    ISBN 978-0-06-195340-8
    [1. High schools—Fiction. 2. Schools—Fiction. 3. Best friends—
Fiction. 4. Friendship—Fiction. 5. Interpersonal relations—Fiction.] I. Title.
PZ7.S52152Sm 2012   2011026094
[Fic]—dc23   CIP
                                                                              AC

Typography by Michelle Gengaro-Kokmen
12 13 14 15 16 CG/RRDH 10 9 8 7 6 5 4 3 2 1
❖

First Edition

For Anna

Prologue

Before Bea, Neerja, and I got everything we wanted from high school—the adoration, the fun, the fame, and the super-hot boys—all we did was study. Think hamsters on a wheel running round and round, scribbling notes, cramming, sweating through exams, writing papers, and then starting all over again every Monday morning.

It was okay until the beginning of tenth grade, when we began to wonder if our hard work would ever pay off. I mean, with three more years of school, with SATs, APs—even PSATs—yet to take, it seemed like it would be an eternity until we blew this Popsicle stand. I didn't know how much more I could bear of stupid stuff like gym class and mandatory assemblies and having to overhear conversations in homeroom about how wild the parties were that we missed.

Maybe we were being a bit unrealistic, but we had this hope that if we could just get into the Ivy League, everything would be set. We dreamed of Gothic libraries and leafy green quads and romantic dorms with fireplaces and guys who were not only cute but also smart and charming and, quite possibly, British. In college, we believed, we'd finally find our people.

At least in the meantime we had each other. Bea, Neerja, and I have been best friends since kindergarten, when I broke the rules by bringing a Dorothy doll to class. Back then, I was so into *The Wizard of Oz* that every day after school, I'd dress up in a blue-and-white checked pinafore and skip around the house carrying a basket with a stuffed dog, running away from an imaginary witch. My grandmother had seen Dorothy in a toy store on Newbury Street and bought her for me on a whim, what she called a *cadeau d'amour*—a love present.

I loved Dorothy madly. I loved her braids with the blue bows, her tiny black plastic Toto, and, especially, her removable ruby-red sparkling slippers. They were so cool that I couldn't wait to show them to my class, even though, technically, we weren't supposed to bring toys from home. I was sure my teacher, Mrs. Metzger, wouldn't mind, however, since it was only a doll and, besides, *it was Dorothy.*

But as soon as I showed her to a couple of girls, Mrs. Metzger ordered Dorothy into my cubby, bellowing, "We do NOT bring in our toys, do we, children?" All the other children loudly and gleefully agreed that no, we do NOT bring our toys from home.

I was so surprised and embarrassed and, strangely, suddenly homesick that I almost burst into tears as I reluctantly crossed the room and, with all eyes upon me, did as Mrs. Metzger ordered. That's when I felt someone pat my arm, and I turned to see Neerja's pixie face with her tiny nose and big, dark eyes smiling up at me, radiating waves of warmth and kindness, and I knew I'd found a true friend.

That would have been enough. But then, something even more wonderful happened.

When we were getting ready to leave for the day, I went to get Dorothy and found her shoes were missing. Who would have taken her fabulous ruby slippers? Neerja went to tell Mrs. Metzger, but Mrs. Metzger, feeling validated, I suppose, put her hands on her hips and said, "I'm sorry, Gigi, but that's what happens when you bring in toys from home. That's why we have rules."

I can distinctly remember her smiling down with approval at her pet, Bea Honeycutt, who wore her long red hair in prissy pink ribbons and was so verbally gifted that she was excused each afternoon to join the second graders for reading. I hated Bea at that moment, hated her for being perfect and for not ever doing anything wrong.

Which was why I was so astonished when she looked up at Mrs. Metzger, made a face like, "Are you crazy, lady?" and promptly marched over to Trina Gregoranis's backpack.

"She has them," Bea said, pointing accusatorily—a favorite gesture of hers that I would later come to know and love. "I saw her take the shoes."

Tina immediately started to blubber that she would never take Dorothy's shoes, but Bea wasn't the type to stand around listening to a bunch of lies. Despite Mrs. Metzger's protests about respecting each other's privacy, space, blah, blah, blah, Bea zipped open the top pocket of Tina's pack, removed the shoes, and placed them in my hands.

"There," she said, nodding. "I told you."

Our gazes clicked. Bea's eyes were bright green. Sassy. And I could tell she wasn't half the goody-two-shoes I'd thought she was. She was, at most, a goody-one-shoe.

"Thanks." My fingers curled around the tiny slippers. "You wanna play in the sandbox with me tomorrow?"

"Sure. If I get the dump truck."

The wooden dump truck was my favorite, and I usually managed to call first dibs. So it was a big sacrifice on my part to say, "Okay. And Neerja can come too." Which was easy, since Neerja didn't care about dump trucks; she was a water-wheel girl.

From that moment on, we became the best of friends, united in our defiance of meanies and our love of each other and all things sweet. Sometimes I ask myself if we worked so hard in school just to prove to our old kindergarten teacher that even girls who occasionally break the rules and draw outside the lines and kill themselves trying not to laugh out loud in class can also be the best students.

Like Parad. Our hero.

Parad is Neerja's older sister, a tall, slim, dark-haired goddess who graduated Denton High with a 4.0 average and 2400 SATs. All through our childhood, Parad would tell us to study hard so we could "get whatever we wanted." She made studying seem really regal, you know? Like by earning A's, we'd be academic royalty.

But I didn't really understand what she meant by getting whatever we wanted until one March 31st, the day the Ivy Leagues, at 5 p.m. sharp, email their acceptances—or rejections.

That chilly spring evening, we sat in the white-carpeted hall outside her bedroom where, behind locked doors,

Parad hit refresh on her laptop over and over while we waited for news. Neerja's parents, the Padwamis, were downstairs pretending to be busy making dinner, though they, too, were on pins and needles.

Finally, at 5:11, the bedroom door opened and Parad emerged with red-rimmed eyes. We sucked in our breaths. All clattering in the kitchen stopped.

"Brown, Harvard, Yale, no," she said, biting her lower lip, trying—as we'd later learn—not to smile. "Princeton, yes. With a full scholarship."

A shout went up from their mother, who dropped a plate. We dashed downstairs and found her parents high-fiving and moonwalking, as the elderly are wont to do. Neerja and Parad hugged and screamed, and so did Bea and I.

I knew then that my one goal was to be like Parad. I wanted to click on the March 31st email and see the famous YES! from the Princeton dean of admissions. I wanted to be chosen out of 30,000 applicants, to be part of a select group of brilliant students, to have all the headaches of testing and class standing and applications behind me. I wanted the quads and the libraries and the best education in the world. And, hot damn, did I want the cute, smart guys.

But mostly I wanted to be able to get what I wanted. Like Parad.

It wasn't until months later, while helping Neerja's sister pack for college, that we learned sometimes what you envy about people is only on the surface.

Sometimes even the most perfect people hide the darkest secrets—as Neerja discovered when she peeked under her sister's bed and found what Parad wanted no one to see.

The truth.

One

The day before Parad left for Princeton, I'd been feeling super sorry for Neerja, who was stuck at home packing while her older sister hit Bed Bath & Beyond for the mother lode of college supplies: mini fridge, cool pink plastic shower caddy, matching bedding—with the weird extra-long sheets colleges apparently require—lamps, fluffy pillows, and nifty wall hangings. Those were in addition to the shiny new MacBook Pro and upgraded iPhone she'd been given at graduation.

It was like their parents couldn't do enough for Parad now that she'd made the Ivy League. They let her drive their new Mercedes, with the creamy white interior and voice-controlled sound system, and never asked her to babysit the eight-year-old twins, Shiva and Shari, who we secretly nicknamed Thing One and Thing Two. That was Neerja's job now, and every weekend she had to bag our get-togethers because the Padwamis were going out and Parad was off tooling around in the Mercedes with her best friend, Karla, while Neerja had to play endless games of Pretty, Pretty Princess with The Things.

So that's why Bea and I were over at the Padwami pad on that fateful muggy August morning. If Neerja was relegated to sorting Parad's books and folding her underwear, then the least we could do was bring her an iced Frappuccino and do the heavy lifting. We'd already lugged several plastic milk crates of Parad's junk downstairs when Neerja looked under her sister's bed and found a navy leather-bound copy of *The Zenith*—Parad's yearbook—stamped with her name in gold right on the front.

"That's weird," Neerja said, opening it with a frown. "Parad said hers hadn't come in yet. They were back ordered."

Ding! Ding! Ding! Immedietskie, bells went off in my head.

All the seniors got their copies weeks before graduation so they could pass them around and let their friends sign incredibly hokey stuff, like *Do what I say, not what I did*, and inside jokes like *Bow to Bob, Your Supreme*

9

Overlord. Or *Got pants?* Or initials that made no sense: *IOCHFTS!* Or *Snort farts? Need I say more?* along with eye-rolling recitations of bad song lyrics, and poems from girlfriends to boyfriends and vice versa pledging undying love.

But Parad's page had nothing. Okay, that's not entirely true. A few people wrote creepily formal stuff along the lines of, *You seemed really nice* or *Wish we'd gotten to know each other.* One person actually had the audacity to scribble, *Who are you?* Though most inscriptions were stunningly obvious, like *You were the smartest girl in the class.*

A whopping five wrote, *Remember me when you win the Nobel Prize.*

There was not one personal comment, aside from a long, rambling note written by Karla overcompensating for Parad's lack of social life by listing every single mundane thing the two of them had ever done: *Remember eating paste, sixth-grade Valentines, jumping beans, Buffy, sleeping in on Saturday mornings,* To Kill a Mockingbird, Gossip Girl *Mondays, test crunching?*

It was clear to us then that despite being our personal hero, Parad Devi Padwami, Ivy bound, was, to the class from which she'd graduated number one, a virtual unknown. A nobody.

And, judging from the book's place of honor among

the dust bunnies, it was her dirty little secret.

The realization was like a sudden blow to the solar plexus. It was like learning the tooth fairy was actually our mothers and that they'd been stealing money from our piggy banks to slip quarters under our pillows. All our illusions of Parad's perfect life were shattered.

"Maybe there's more," Bea said as Neerja flipped through the other pages.

Nope. Blank.

We were so saddened and confused by Parad's clandestine nonlife that we hardly noticed the shadow in the doorway until it erupted in a piercing shriek.

"WHAT are you doing?" Parad stomped across her bedroom and snatched the book out of Neerja's hands. "You have no business, no business at all. This is my private property!"

In a burst of anger, she threw the yearbook against the wall, where it made a dent right under her framed Merit Scholar Award. "Out!" she shouted, pointing to the door. "High school doesn't matter. It's a joke and everyone there was totally lame."

We fled and never spoke of *The Zenith* again.

But we never forgot it, either.

For me, Parad's empty yearbook raised a bunch of questions about success versus happiness. I mean, the kids who were having a blast at Denton High weren't near the top of the class like Parad, Bea, Neerja, and me, and that seemed so screwy. Shouldn't the kids at the top *feel* on top?

That's when I made it my personal mission to ensure, unlike Parad, we got everything we deserved from high school, whether that was grades, fame, guys, a totally full yearbook, whatever. I figured this was just a matter of putting our heads together. After all, if we were supposedly so smart, this should have been a no-brainer, right?

My mistake was in not remembering the immortal words of Sir Mick Jagger: You may not always be able to get what you want. *"But if you try sometimes, you might find you get what you need."*

Sir Mick was right. (Of course.) What I wanted was what I needed, though never would I have imagined that what I needed was to be sent to the principal's office, threatened with permanent suspension, and kissed by the hottest guy at school.

None of which would've happened if it hadn't been for, of all things, the AP chemistry midterm.

The AP chem midterm wasn't just any test. It was a paper Weed Wacker that our teacher, Mr. Bouchard (aka Buzzard), used every year to remove all but the highest performers from his class. Anyone receiving an F was automatically kicked down to regular chem. And for those who survived, the test counted for thirty percent of the semester grade. Nice, huh?

Horror stories abounded of perfectly excellent students like ourselves walking into the exams with A minus averages and ending up with C's for the semester because they'd bombed the midterm. Parad's friend Karla to this day claims she would have gotten into Brown if it hadn't been for Buzzard (as if!), and Parad herself ranks his midterm as the Worst Test Ever, even worse than the SATs, because the multiple-choice was so confusing.

So, we studied like crazy, trading notes, redoing our old quizzes, and analyzing Parad's own exam because Parad was the type who carefully saved her tests in color-coded files. (Love her!) We even got Neerja to swallow her pride and call her big sister at Princeton, begging for hints, since Parad had aced everything on the midterm except for the extra-credit question.

Apparently, no one has correctly answered Buzzard's extra-credit questions, ever. Not even Princeton's Patron Saint of Butt Busting.

"Look ahead at the next chapters," was Parad's advice, "because Buzzard wants to see that you're not just parroting back what he taught you, but that you are a true scholar thirsting for knowledge."

Okay. With that in mind, I got a Diet Mountain Dew (not the kind of thirst Parad was referring to, I know) and randomly picked a scholarly-type section—moles—and crammed. But in order to cram, I needed (a) to be in my "pretty clothes"—faded-pink drawstring flannel pj's and my mother's paint-stained MIT sweatshirt—and (b) sufficient nutrition: Reese's Puffs. Also, packets of sugarless gum. Twirling pencil in hair optional.

Three hours later, my hair was a rat's nest of twirling, gum wrappers and empty cans littered the floor around my chair, and there were Reese's Puffs crumbs everywhere.

Even my trusted sidekick Petunia, a five-year-old white-and-brown basset hound with her own eating-disorder issues, was so repulsed by my slobbery that she crawled off my bed and slumped onto the carpet in a heap of disgust.

At midnight, Marmie poked her head into my room. "Still up?" she whispered. "It's almost one."

"I'll go to bed soon," I lied.

Marmie shrugged, not bothered either way. *"Dors bien. Fais de beaux rêves!"* And she blew me a good-night kiss.

Marmie is my French grandmother, very elegant and beautiful with silver-gray hair she pulls into a bun and legs she hasn't crossed since 1964, like the French actress Catherine Deneuve. I don't know who Catherine Deneuve is, but, according to Marmie, if I want to keep my own legs from becoming veiny and gross, I better start crossing at the ankles.

I live with Marmie because my mother spends half the year overseas as a physicist at the Large Hadron Collider in Switzerland, where—fingers crossed!—she's not accidentally creating black holes. You never know. I mean, this is a woman who's baffled by the simple water + eggs + oil + mix directions on the back of a box of Duncan Hines. She always forgets something, either the eggs or oil or both. Let's just hope the same doesn't apply to her handling of supercharged protons.

Don't get me wrong. I admire my mother. She's *extreeeemely* smart. However, she *is* a nerd. When I was just a toddler, she used to let me run around her research lab at MIT like it was the ball pit at McDonald's. Fortunately, MIT labs are only slightly more dangerous than fast-food ball pits—if you don't count lasers and various nuclear devices.

Like my mother, her mother also follows a form of parenting called "benign neglect." The deal is that as long as I appear for breakfast and keep my grades up, Marmie doesn't really care where I go or what I do. It's kind of nice having all that freedom, though, to quote my hero Eleanor Roosevelt, with freedom comes great responsibility.

Responsibility that I'm happy to ignore the night

before a Buzzard midterm.

Two hours after Marmie said good night, I got a text from Neerja asking me to give her a wake-up call since she tends to sleep through most alarms—even smoke detectors. So I texted Bea, who's an insomniac, and asked her to give me a 5 a.m. wake-up call. Then I fell into bed, and in what seemed like a matter of minutes, my phone rang and it was Bea screaming at me to wake up, whereupon I called Neerja, who swore profusely and promptly dropped the phone.

I went downstairs, deposited a frosted blueberry Pop-Tart in the toaster, turned on the water for tea, and waited. When the whistle blew, I poured out a cup, slathered Nutella on the unfrosted side of the Pop-Tart—don't judge me!—and pressed redial.

"What now?" Neerja asked sleepily. As I'd suspected, she'd gone back to bed.

"Why do the good people at Kellogg's put two Pop-Tarts in a plastic wrapper that's impossible to reclose when the serving size is listed as only one? Then the other forlorn Pop-Tart goes stale and starts breaking into crumbs that you can't help but eat even though you know it's pathetic that you're eating stale Pop-Tart crumbs."

"Okay," Neerja said. "I'm awake."

I made her carry the phone to the shower so I could hear the water running to ensure she was physically out of bed. Believe it or not, this is how we get up every week-day morning, the three of us. Not for nothing does my grandmother call us the Queens of Inefficiency.

Pop-Tart consumed, I carried my peppy pink HAPPY BIRTHDAY, GIGI! mug with peppermint tea to the bath-room, took my own shower, and spent the following forty minutes doing my hair and makeup with my chem-istry book propped between the faucet and mirror.

Next to my green eyes, my blond hair is definitely my best feature. So, out of obligation to all the blondes before me (Cinderella, Sleeping Beauty, the many Barbies I have loved and tortured), I tend to spend hours getting it right. You know, so as not to let down the team.

When I was done, not only did I understand the four periodic trends, but I had actually employed two types of heat transference to style my hair—blow-dryer for con-vection and a curling iron for conduction.

Quite possibly, this is what they mean by the term "applied physics."

"Bring it, Buzzard," was my cocky attitude as I headed off to school in my purple-and-gray plaid miniskirt and matching purple flats, my thermodynamically styled hair blowing in the breeze.

It was one of those crisp, late October days that smelled of rotting leaves and woodsmoke and made you want to pull on thick sweaters and bake molasses cookies.

As I passed by haunted house after haunted house, I was glad to be living right outside of Boston, where Halloween decorating is considered an Olympic sport. There's no telling how many hundreds of hours my sick-minded neighbors have invested trying to outdo one another by stringing fake spiderwebs, turning front lawns into cemeteries, and filling flannel shirts and jeans with leaves to create headless bodies that lounged in beach chairs. Made a person feel all warm and cozy to be surrounded by that sort of dedicated fake decapitation.

By the time I sauntered through the big glass doors of Denton High, I was so pumped by the invigorating zing of autumn, not even the usual pre-test pang of anxiety that made my palms sweat and heart race could bring me down. This test was mine to conquer, I reminded myself, as I conducted a quick last-minute note scan, despite Maddie Kildare and Sienna Martin's droning analysis of which white, black, gold, or silver gown they should wear to the Crystal Ball.

To the best of my knowledge, Maddie and Sienna have nothing else to discuss. Every morning, Maddie calls up a photo of the dress du jour on her cell and slides the phone past me to Sienna, who studies it, imparts her professional opinion on why the proposed gown will or will not work—too billowy, too tight around the butt, not tight enough, too white, too cheap, too expensive—before sliding it back.

And every morning I am held hostage to this inane debate and the sliding cell phone because Ms. Andres, our homeroom teacher, insists on assigned seating that places me between Maddie and Sienna as a barrier. Otherwise, Ms. Andres explained once, they'd never stop talking.

Like that's worked.

Mind you, the Crystal Ball wasn't until the week before Christmas vacation. I hadn't even thought about it, not that I had much reason to. I expected Bea, Neerja, and I would go together per usual. Dance a little, eat cake, drink punch, and go home.

Unlike Maddie, who was going out with . . . *everyone*, and Sienna, who was going out with Mike Ipolito, the resident hottie jock, it wasn't like our hopes and dreams were pinned on the one big sophomore blowout of the year.

We had lives beyond high school, thank you very much. We had *futures*.

On my way out of homeroom, I nearly walked past Neerja, who's so tiny, she's often easy to miss. "What's the dress today?"

"Strapless A-line with a ruched bodice."

She squinted her catlike brown eyes, trying to envision the possibilities. "Now that sounds nice. Might be a little over the top for a high school dance, but a lot better than last week's mermaid style in satin."

"Funny, that's exactly what Sienna said."

"Sienna and I have much in common. We know fashion. And we both breathe."

We found Bea by her locker flipping through a stack of crumpled cheat sheets. Normally, Bea's gorgeous golden red hair hangs in natural ringlets. But when she's under stress and forgets to tame it in the morning, her hair tends to frizz out. Today, Bea looked like she'd just stuck her finger in a light socket.

"I know nothing. I feel like I didn't even study. Could have spent last night watching TV."

"That's what you always say." We turned into Buzzard's class. "And, like always, you'll do fine."

She did. We all did, as a matter of fact. I even got the extra credit thanks to Parad's tip.

Buzzard had tried to trip us up with a question about Avogadro's number—6.022×10^{23}—which we hadn't studied. Fortunately, I happened to know that Avogadro's number represents the number of particles in one mole of any substance.

Final grade: 105%. The only downside was that I ruined the curve.

"Hate you!" teased Bea who, with a 92, wasn't too bummed. Neerja, pulling in a 95, was also super psyched. It was a great day for grade grubbers everywhere.

Until Mr. Bouchard called me to his desk. And Sienna's boyfriend, Mike Ipolito.

Bea has a term for Mike—"idiot savant"—because he's the only hard-core jock who's also in all of our AP and honors classes—a mystery, since he's kind of the class comedian who rarely, if ever, studies.

Actually, not that much of a mystery. Mike's one of those guys who really knows how to turn on the charm when he needs a favor, like when he has to copy your homework or borrow notes from the class he skipped. It's an unfair exploitation of lucky genes that graced him with an impressive height and athletic build, longish brown hair that curls ever so slightly under his ears, smoldering brown eyes, and a smile that asks, *What, me worry?* As if he's our own Alfred E. Neuman, only cuter.

I must confess that I used to have a major crush on Mike back in middle school, before I knew better. Each time he'd come up to me in class and stand a little too close and look down at me with that burning gaze of longing, I'd talk myself into thinking things were different, and I'd fork over whatever he wanted. Mike would smile and say, "Thanks, Einstein," before walking off, and I'd do a mental head slap for being such a fool—again.

I was wiser now, though come to think of it, he had sat pretty close to me during the midterm.

Uh-oh . . .

Mr. Bouchard scowled in fury behind his wire-rimmed glasses. On his desk, two tests lay facedown, one wrinkled hand on each as if to keep them from blowing away. "I find it more than a coincidence," he said with a low growl, "that you two sat next to each other and you were the only ones to correctly answer the supremely difficult extra-credit question."

My immediate reaction was, *Wow. Mike's gonna be in a lot of trouble.*

But then, Buzzard rotated his predatory eyeballs in my direction and said, "Ms. Dubois. Would you like to explain yourself?"

Me?

That I was somehow at fault for being the victim of cheating made my jaw drop, and then my jaw dropped even more when Buzzard overturned the papers and, in a shot of panic, I saw that my *105% A+ Excellent!* had been CROSSED OUT in red and replaced with *0=F!*

What the . . . ?

"Aw, man!" Mike exclaimed, gaping at his own test, also reduced to an F. "What did you do that for?"

"What did I do that for, *man*?" Buzzard repeated mockingly. "I did that because you two were in cahoots!"

Mike laughed. "Cahoots? That's a word you don't hear too often. Cahoots. I like that. I don't give two hoots about cahoots."

What was wrong with him? Didn't he realize that thanks to his cheating, not only had we essentially gotten ourselves booted from Buzzard's class down to regular chem but that per school rules we would be automatically grilled by the principal and, quite possibly, suspended? All because he'd been too lazy to study his butt off like I had.

"You two were sitting so close to each other during the midterm, I was going to separate you," Buzzard was saying. "However, I decided to give you the benefit of the doubt and assume you would each act honorably. My bad, as you kids say. A choice to cheat is never honorable."

Cheat? I could feel my blood boiling somewhere deep down and rising up my arms and neck, bursting onto my cheeks. The whole class had now stopped their lab experiments and were whispering about us, *about me*, the goody-two-shoes who'd ruined the curve, now revealed as nothing more than a low, lying cheat, blushing in embarrassment.

"Mr. Bouchard," I pleaded, grateful that despite my panic I'd remembered to use his correct name. "You've got it all wrong. I didn't cheat. I would never cheat. That you would suggest I had after all the studying I did is *outrageous!*"

"Lighten up, Einstein." Mike's brown eyes twinkled merrily. "Ain't no thang."

"Cheating is indeed a *thang*, Mr. Ipolito," Buzzard said. "It is a grave academic offense. Should our principal concur, she will write a letter of no confidence that will be attached to both your transcripts. No teachers will write you recommendations and no college worth its salt will admit you."

Oh. My. God!

Mike shrugged. "I'm not too worried. I met with the lacrosse coach at Amherst over the summer and it's almost guaranteed I'm getting a full scholarship there. I scored over a hundred goals last season."

I couldn't believe he was being recruited by one of my dream schools simply for throwing a little white ball into a net. Seriously, the level of unfairness in this world is unreal. First, I'm wrongly accused of cheating. Then I find Mike Ipolito has already gotten into Amherst.

Where's the justice?

"Anyway, Gigi and I didn't cheat, did we, Einstein?" He threw his arm around my shoulders and gave me a squeeze, thereby confirming Buzzard's suspicions that the two of us were "in cahoots."

I broke free, but the damage had been done. Buzzard circled the F's, pushed back his chair, and picked up the black phone by the whiteboard to call the principal, Dr. Fiona Schultz. If our old principal, Mr. Watson, were still in charge, I would have been in the clear because he knew my record. But Schultz, being brand-new, didn't know me from a hole in the wall. Without academic street cred, I was cooked.

There was a brief conversation with the school secretary, Mrs. Wently, and then Buzzard hung up. "The principal will fit you both in immediately after school. You're to appear in her office at two thirty on the dot. Don't be late."

Mike gave me a wink and reached over to turn up the corners of my mouth with his two fingers. "Don't frown, Einstein. You're so much prettier when you smile." Then he strolled back to his desk as if nothing had happened.

Two

"He already got into Amherst, legit?" Neerja was shocked.

"I'm telling you, we're going about this dream school stuff all wrong. We should just join the field hockey team and watch back-to-back *Millionaire Matchmaker* while waiting for our full scholarships." I slid my thumb under the strap on my bag and shouldered my way toward the cafeteria.

Because of the double-period honors and AP courses, our lunch break is ridiculously early—at 10:30—an unappetizing time most days and absolutely impossible today, since my stomach was tied in knots thanks to the adrenaline rush from getting so angry in Buzzard's class.

I couldn't imagine downing anything more than a cold iced tea. Okay, maybe a cinnamon raisin bagel, and possibly cream cheese. But that was it. Unless they had Rice Krispies bars. . . .

We slipped in line and Bea took out her phone to scroll through her text messages. "Mike's dreaming if he thinks he's already admitted to Amherst. The coach might have talked to him, but that doesn't mean squat. He's only in tenth grade and he still has to take his SATs and graduate and not be busted for cheating."

At the very word, my pulse started revving. Bea put her hand on my arm reassuringly. "Calm yourself, cowgirl. We're going to get you out of this. When you meet with Schultz, I'll go with you and act as your consigliere."

"My counselor?"

"Legal counselor." She glanced up from her phone. "*Consigliere*'s Italian for lawyer. Didn't you ever see *The Godfather*?"

"No way. Too much blood and bullets."

"Don't be ridiculous. There can never be too much blood and bullets." She pulled down a water-splattered blue plastic tray. "Anyway, I just did a quick Google search and it turns out Schultz went to Wellesley and wrote her thesis on misogyny in academia." She grabbed an apple and tossed it to me. Then she tossed another to Neerja. "Imply that you're the victim of sexism and you'll be instantly acquitted. Ga-run-teed."

"That's not true, though," I said. "Buzzard accused Mike of cheating too."

Bea gave me a look. "May I remind you of the Salem witch trials and the persecution of intelligent women through the eons? We are owed, Gigi, if not for this, then for centuries of male tyranny."

"I think you're worrying too much, and with all due respect to you, Bea, I don't think there's any sexism involved." Neerja crunched her apple. "Buzzard flipped out because he's never had two students get his midterm extra-credit question. Like Mike said, ain't no thang."

Bea was incredulous. "You're taking Mike's side? He's the enemy."

"He's not the enemy. Mike's okay."

Two truths about Neerja: She never said an unkind word about anyone, not even the cattiest girls at school. And she was, had been, and would forever be madly in love with Justin Crenshaw.

Justin was so cute he was almost pretty, with crazy-long eyelashes and super-smooth blond hair that he constantly flicked into place. Unfortunately for the cumulative IQ of the universe, what Justin possessed in looks he lacked in brains, which was possibly why he seemed oblivious to anyone but himself—including Neerja.

We stepped into the main part of the cafeteria and Bea

went bug-eyed.

"*Who. Is. That.*"

She lifted her chin to the window where Mike was chilling with B.K. Evans, Smitty Chavez, Jim Mullet, and Parker Forbes, the core members of the Man Clan, so nicknamed by Bea because they always wore plaid shorts—even in the snow. Most of the Man Clan were lax players and sworn bros, except for maybe Jim, who was Denton High's rep to the school board and number one in the senior class, and, therefore, potentially interested in more lofty pursuits than waxing his lacrosse stick.

"It's only the Man Clan," I said. "So what?"

"Not them." Bea pushed me to the right. "*Him.* In the shirt."

There were a lot of guys in shirts. Most, in fact. What was . . . Oh. Oh my. Yes, who *was* that creature?

I leaned forward a little and squinted since I happen to be slightly nearsighted and too vain to wear glasses as often as I should. The subject in question was behind Mike, about the same height, only his hair was jet black and he was in a gray T-shirt under a white button-down, unbuttoned and rolled to the elbows.

This was what Bea meant by *shirt*. For reasons we girls could not fathom, guys in our school only wore T-shirts. Never button-downs, even though they looked so much better in a collar. Bea used to say the buttons were too complicated for their unevolved brains, like laces used to be when they were boys and had to wear shoes with Velcro straps. But obviously this . . . well, this *Adonis* possessed the required dexterity.

"His eyes are so blue. I can see them from here, how blue they are." Bea's freckled face had gone pale, almost to alabaster as she nervously fingered the green beads at her neck.

I snagged Neerja as she passed by to drop off her tray. "Hey, do you know who that new guy is with the Man Clan?"

Neerja followed our gazes. "Oh, him. He was in my homeroom this morning and Henry says he's from California. I think his name is Will something."

Will from California. Figured. He looked like a Will from California. All positive energy and lean, tanned arms. Wait until he suffered through a cold, gray New England winter; then we'd see about the levels of his melatonin.

"Henry says he's super smart." Neerja nibbled what was left of her apple. "And that's saying something, coming from Henry."

Too true. Henry was Henry Filomen, Neerja's next-door neighbor and closest guy friend, though with his brown hair cut in the shape of a bowl and preference for white ankle socks, you could understand why Neerja didn't like him *that* way.

Henry wasn't smart; he was a genius. He was already taking calculus as a sophomore. So, if Henry said Will from California was smart, then he was, and that was good news for Denton High since we seemed to be somewhat deficient in the smart guy department.

"Hey, Gigi," a buttery voice whispered in my ear. "Checking out your future boyfriend?"

Ava Wilkes. Had I not been ogling the new kid, I would have seen her making a beeline for me across the cafeteria and managed to escape. Now it was too late. I was trapped.

Feigning ignorance, I switched my attention to squeezing the rock-hard chilled cream cheese from the annoying metal packet onto my raisin bagel. "We were just looking for a place to sit."

"Oh, please. You guys never eat here. You're always heading off to your chichi honors lounge. You think I don't remember?"

The flimsy white plastic knife practically broke in two as I pushed the gobs of cream cheese around the bagel while trying to avoid Ava's black-lined eyes.

Ava was such a different person from the girl I'd known in middle school, when we used to do impressions of Mrs. McKay's nasal voice in her seventh-grade English class. Back then, Ava was goofy and silly and mega boy crazy. I was still best friends with Bea and Neerja, of course, but with Ava it was plain old pee-in-your-pants-laughing fun.

Almost every Friday night we'd get together for a sleepover. We'd make chocolate chip cookies and experiment with our Sephora samples and deconstruct *Us* magazine, drawing mustaches on Angelina Jolie and doodling long blond hair extensions on Justin Timberlake. Ava had always been a terrific artist, but I had no idea she was a tortured one too, until last semester, when she gradually began to change.

Instead of her preferred pretty watercolors of sunsets and beach scenes, she started sketching lots of "serious" charcoal self-portraits and distorted reflections. Then, as if to live up to the reputation of her artwork, her appearance became equally urbane.

First it was the thick black leggings paired with heavy boots and tweed jackets she'd picked up at used-clothing stores. Later, she took to wearing a thin red, tan, and gray striped scarf wrapped multiple times around her neck and dyeing her once-dirty-blond hair a dark brown that she'd either wear straight behind the ears, pushed up in a messy bun, or pulled back in a severe ponytail. She even gave up wearing makeup aside from the menacing black eyeliner.

Perhaps it's no coincidence that Ava's metamorphosis happened soon after she started going out with Rolf the

German exchange student, who was even more into total annihilation than she was, if that were possible. It was Rolf, I'm sure, who convinced her to drop her honors and AP classes, just as he'd talked her into loving raw yogurt, muesli, and Turkish espresso.

To this day, Bea claims Ava adopted a slight European accent, but I think that was just her imagination.

After Rolf returned to Hamburg, we tried to pick up our friendship again, but by then Ava was too worldly and sophisticated for *Us* magazine and chocolate chip cookies. We had nothing to say to each other. Not really.

Now, the best we could manage was superficial conversation, and it was always awkward. The thing was, I missed Ava. Or rather, I missed the person she *used* to be.

"There's a smudge of charcoal on your cheek," I said, hoping she'd get off the Will topic.

"Personally, I think he's just your type." She casually swiped at the black mark, only making the smudge bigger. "You need a guy who's smart and centered. All the other guys around here are flakes."

She was right about that. I dumped the cream cheese packet in the trash. "Not going to happen."

"Why? Because he has a girlfriend?"

Will from California had been in school for about two hours and already Ava had conducted an intensive background check. If modeling for the cover of *Teen Angst* magazine didn't work out as a career choice, she could get a job with Homeland Security.

"How do you know he has a girlfriend?" asked Bea, eavesdropping like she does. "If you're getting your information from Facebook, forget it. Anyone can put up anything. Gigi's currently married to a dog."

"Well, not any dog," I said. "Petunia."

Ava, who'd always been slightly jealous of my friendship with Bea, snapped, "If you hung out more instead of scurrying off to classes or the library or the honors lounge, you'd know this stuff, Beatrice." Turning to me, she added more softly, "You should go for Mike. Sienna tells me it's totally over with him."

My teeth sank into the bagel as I made eye contact with Bea over the cream cheese. *"Mike?"*

"We were just talking about you two and why a Little Miss Perfect like you would let him see the answers on the midterm. That's when we heard about the crush. It's so obvious. Why didn't I see it sooner?"

Is this what people thought, that I *let* Mike see my test on purpose because I had a *crush*?

Neerja threw out her apple core. "Gigi doesn't have a crush on Mike."

Bea said, "Who told you she did?"

Ava pointed across the room toward the windows, where Mike and Will were slapping each other on the backs. At the exact same moment, both of them looked over at us and grinned. There was a flicker of victory in Mike's smile as the bite of bagel slid halfway down my throat and landed in my stomach with a thud.

No, he is not telling people—he is not telling the NEW GUY—that I let him copy my test. No, he is not.

"Oh, crap. There's Obleck," Ava said, as the assistant principal strolled into the cafeteria wearing his trademark short-sleeved yellow shirt. "He caught me skipping first period and now he wants to *talk*." She ducked behind the trays, narrowly avoiding his sweeping gaze as she inched toward the door. "Talk to you later, Gigi. Text me, okay?" And with that, she slid around the corner and disappeared, right before Obleck turned to check the hall.

Bea blinked. "She is sooo weird."

"Uh-huh." I wanted to drop it since I wasn't really in the mood to get into the Bea/Ava feud right now, not with the million other things on my plate.

Like Mike telling everyone I'd let him copy off me because I had a crush. Next to that, Ava was as harmless as a little kitten.

With long, sharp, black, pointy claws.

There are crises—like this one—when I really wished my mother lived in this hemisphere.

I know girls my age aren't supposed to get along with their mothers, or so I keep reading, but for Mom and me that's not the case. She's always been pretty good about being there for me, even when she's calculating proton collisions on the other end of the phone at the Large Hadron Collider in Switzerland.

Mom has this amazing ability to listen without interrupting, but still letting you know she understands. When I miss her so much it hurts, I remember a night on our deck after dinner last summer. Her bare feet were propped on the redwood railing, and her graying hair blew about in the breeze as she leaned back, eyes closed, a glass of wine in her hands, saying nothing as I analyzed my constant obsession—why guys don't like smart girls.

I don't care what everyone says, it's true. I don't know if guys are intimidated or immature or in awe or whatever. But I do know I'd like an honest answer, for once, instead of flimsy excuses that are supposed to make girls like us feel better.

When I was done with this latest rant, Mom lifted her head and said, "Be patient, Gigi. You haven't even started living."

Then she told me her own ugly duckling story about how she used to (it's so quaint when she says "used to") be a nerd in high school obsessing over *Dr. Who, Star Trek* and *Star Wars,* and anything with a star besides *People* magazine. No one understood her except for a close group of friends from math club and the science fair. All that changed when she went to MIT and found people just like her, including my father.

My father was also a geek who won massive grants to investigate string theory but found it difficult to remember on which side of the street to drive.

They were, to put it in my mother's parlance, like "inert elements," both bright individuals with "negative bonding capabilities." In the end, they went their separate ways while maintaining a deep and abiding affection. Though, apparently, in her absentmindedness, my mother forgot to tell him she was pregnant.

To recap: I am the product of two brilliant inert elements with negative bonding capabilities, one who was a *Dr. Who* fan girl, the other who consistently drove into fire hydrants.

And, somehow, this is supposed to make me feel better.

Three

Thanks to my incredible superpowers of invisibility, the bogus rumor of my crush on Mike hadn't traveled past the adoring fans of the Man Clan. Or so it appeared, because no one said anything to me in English, and Will from California seemed totally blasé when Mike introduced me as his "coconspirator in crime" on the way to Latin.

"Heard about that," Will said, smiling at me shyly. He was even cuter up close, if such a feat were possible.

"There are two sides to every story," I said, since I wasn't sure what story Mike had relayed.

Will shrugged. "You know what they say. It's not cheating unless you get caught."

I was busily formulating a witty reply when Bea, ever

the budding attorney, leaped to my defense. "*Gigi* wasn't the one who cheated. Right, Mike?"

Mike just kept walking in his long strides, that half smile playing at his lips. "How should I know? Ask Gigi."

"Excuse me?"

He turned and grinned, like he was loving this. "You know what they say about goody-two-shoes like you, Einstein?"

"No, what?"

"Watch out for the innocent, because they're the ones who—"

Bea interrupted again. "But you're telling people Gigi let you copy off her test because she has a mad crush on you?"

"*Bea,*" I hissed, giving Will a what-can-you-do-about-crazy-friends look. Honestly. Did she have to add the word *mad*? Did she have to put it in the present tense?

Look, I love Bea for the way she always takes my side, no questions asked. But being the daughter of two lawyers, Bea's mind is kind of . . . warped. There are no gray areas in her world, no ifs or maybes or mistakes. There is only right (hers) or wrong (theirs). And with her flying red hair, snapping green eyes, fiery temper, and crackerjack wrestling moves, she is more than happy to illustrate the difference.

"Can we talk about this later?" I suggested.

She held up her finger and kept the pressure on. "Just how big is your ego, Ipolito, that you would go around assuming that you're the center of the universe, the object of our undying desire?"

"Undying desire?" Mike gave me the eye. "Oh, Einstein. And here all I thought you cared about was grades."

Great. Now Will's first impression was that not only did I cheat, but I was a love-starved, brown-nosing geek. "I don't have a crush and I don't care about grades," I explained to Will, my cheeks growing warm. "Not that much. Grades, I mean, not Mike."

Mike said, "I'll get you a shovel so you can keep digging."

Will averted his eyes, as if stepping into an open sewer were more preferable to being swept up in this mess. "It's okay."

"No, it's not," interjected Bea. "It's slander. A classic case of the guilty seeking acquittal by trashing the victim's character. Tell Mike, Gigi. Tell him that you do not have and have never had and never will have a crush on his sorry self."

"What she said."

Mike only laughed. "'Methinks the lady doth protest too much.'"

"Methinks that is the only Shakespeare line thou doth know."

"Ooooh. Ouch." He slapped his hand over his heart. "Geesh. You really know how to hurt a guy." Laughing, he stopped at Room 201—French—and nodded to Will. "You in this class?"

Will gestured across the hall to Room 203, where Bea and I were headed. "Nah. I'm in Latin Two."

"And we're late," I said.

"Dude. Why would you take Latin? It's a dead language people haven't used for centuries. It's . . . useless."

"Hey, Mike!" Sienna slipped out of French and gave him a hug. They stood like that for a while, a happy couple who'd been together since the summer of eighth grade, before breaking apart. Sienna whispered something in his ear that made Mike laugh as he slid his arm around her waist and they went into class.

It didn't add up.

If Sienna told Ava they were over, then why did they seem anything but?

"I thought you said you were late." Will had the door to Room 203 open, waiting.

"Oh, sorry," I said, rushing in. "Thanks."

"No crush, huh?" He let me go ahead of him. "Yeah. I can see that."

Mike was right about Latin in one respect: it was true people no longer spoke it. But it was hardly dead, because it's used constantly by anyone who speaks the French, Italian, Spanish, and English languages. In fact, the word *language* comes from the Latin word for *tongue—lingua*.

This is why I love Latin, because Latin words are like mini mysteries waiting to be cracked. For example, why would *calculus* come from the Latin word for *stone, calx*? And if *lunatic* comes from the Latin word for *moon—luna—*does that mean there's some truth behind the old wives' tales about werewolves and craziness?

Luckily, our teacher, Ms. Fay, is so thrilled that anyone's willing to study her "dead" language that she's a super easy grader. Also, once a week, she brings in traditional ancient Roman foods—grapes, figs, or pomegranates, plus some cheese and bread—and we sit around drinking "ambrosia"—peach nectar—while discussing a topic about Roman life and earning points for incorporating as many Latin words as we can remember.

This afternoon, the topic is *manus* ("hand" or "fist"), from which come the words *manipulate* and *manhandle*, which means "to move roughly," but which until I took Latin I thought meant "being handled by a man."

Manus was also the law that governed ancient Roman marriages, in which a woman forfeited all rights—and all property—to her husband when they married. Total rip-off.

"Even if a husband ditched his wife, he got to keep her

property," Ms. Fay said, biting into a fig. "He could leave her completely destitute and at the mercy of strangers."

Bea went, *"Propudium!"*

"Excellent, Bea. Three extra points to you!" Ms. Fay made a mark on her planner.

This is how Bea jacked up her Latin grade, by swearing—a mutual interest she shared with the ancient Romans, who loved nothing more than to hurl insults, often, weirdly, by calling people mushrooms. (*Fungi!*) As if being a chlorophyll-challenged life-form were the lowest of the low.

Will, I noticed, contributed nothing to our discussion about the sexism of Roman marriage. He sat quietly, arms folded, listening. When the bell rang, he got up and walked out without even touching his fig. There was something about him that projected deep unhappiness, I decided. Or was that what made him so attractive?

"Ready?" Bea wiped bread crumbs off her table and dumped them in the trash. "We should be off to see the wizard."

Schultz. Right. I took a deep breath and exhaled. This was my opportunity to set the record straight, to get back the 105% I had earned. As long as I kept my cool and stuck to the point, Schultz, I was sure, would see my side.

On our way to the principal's office, we met up with Neerja, who was outside the drama department with

Lindsay Maybury, Henry, and Justin. The Love Rectangle, Bea and I called them, since Henry was madly in love with Lindsay and Neerja was madly in love with Justin, even though Lindsay mostly ignored Henry while Justin, like I said, was in love with himself.

"Awkward turtle," Bea murmured, cringing as Lindsay pulled out her phone just as Henry came over to talk to her. "If only he learned how to communicate like a normal person instead of being obsessed with math, maybe ditched the white ankle socks and got a different haircut, he'd have half a chance. We should get Neerja to say something to him."

"She can't. She's afraid of hurting his feelings."

Bea rolled her eyes. "So Henry suffers a broken heart because Neerja's too polite. Yeah, that makes sense. And nice guys wonder why they finish last."

"Hey!" He gave us a cheerful wave. "Listen, don't worry, Gigi. I have it on good authority that Schultz is a pushover who doesn't believe in suspensions."

It wasn't the suspension I was worried about, it was clearing my name—and that zero.

Justin said, "Who's getting suspended?"

"Not me," I said.

"*You?*" Justin took a step closer. "But you never do anything wrong."

"Guess there's a first time for everything."

"Aiight." Nodding in admiration for my hidden rebelliousness, he checked me up and down, like he hadn't really seen me before.

While he tried to find something cool in me, I tried to find what Neerja saw in him. Was it The Hair that he constantly flicked into place? Was it his long eyelashes that curled at the ends? Perhaps it was the narrow leather-cord necklace at his throat or the way his oversized Adam's apple bobbed when he swallowed.

No. It was something else. Something intangible. *Total unattainability.*

That's what drove Neerja crazy.

"So what bad-ass thing did you do, exactly?" he said with a flick. "Getting suspended is really hard-core."

Bea took me by the shoulders, pushing me slightly down the hall. "She did nothing wrong. Come on, Gigi, you don't want Mike to tell his side of the story first."

"Mike?" Justin turned to Henry.

"Ipolito," Henry clarified. "Mr. Bouchard accused them of cheating on his midterm."

"Holy . . ." Being criminally associated with the coolest guy in our class clearly had upped my cachet. "You and Ipolito, huh?"

I glanced over my shoulder and shrugged, and couldn't help being pleased when Justin's jaw lowered just a little.

* * *

Although my official consigliere, Bea wasn't allowed to accompany me to my meeting with Schultz, nor was Neerja, because they weren't my parents or legal guardians—another reason why friends should have the right to adopt one another after age thirteen.

"Don't offer any more information than absolutely necessary," Bea advised as the school secretary, Mrs. Wently, directed me to the principal's inner sanctum. "Stick to the question."

"Keep your head up!" Neerja called behind her. "Remember, it's Buzzard who's wrong. Not you!"

That was easy to forget, considering the way Schultz acted when she met me at her office door, frowning and seemingly disappointed already. "You're a few minutes late," she said, checking her watch and going back to her desk.

It wasn't my fault, I wanted to say. Ms. Fay let us out late. However, I decided now was not the time for lip.

Schultz wore black pants and a purple cardigan with a chunky necklace that matched the colors in the half glasses hanging from a chain around her neck. Unlike my grandmother, she kept her silver hair cropped short, with big silver hoops at her ears, like she was trying to make up for lost femininity.

"Please give me a moment, Genevieve, while I get organized."

I didn't see how that was possible, I thought, sliding into the wooden chair across from her desk. Even her wastebasket was alphabetized.

When our old principal, Mr. Watson, owned these digs, his desk had been piled high with papers and folders and various flimsy awards for questionable achievements, such as Best Bowler 2009. There was always a half-eaten blueberry muffin on waxed paper, and a partially dehydrated cup of coffee, and a bowl of Atomic Fireballs, too, that he handed out as lovely parting gifts just for stopping by.

That was the great thing about Mr. Watson. He liked kids. He even set out to learn all our names within the first week of freshman year and would make a point of standing by the front door every morning, welcoming us with, "Hello, Gigi/Neerja/Bea! Another wonderful day in paradise, eh?"

I used to think he was way too goofy, but sitting across from the serious Dr. Schultz in her pristine office with charts and graphs and diplomas on the walls instead of family photos and awards for World's Best Dad, too goofy was beginning to look pretty darn appealing.

There were no Fireballs on Schultz's desk, only a

miniature zen garden with white sand and pebbles and a tiny rake. Also, a small red teapot emitting fumes of chamomile and a paperweight that read NOBODY CAN MAKE YOU FEEL INFERIOR WITHOUT YOUR CONSENT—ELEANOR ROOSEVELT.

That made me feel sort of better since anyone who loved my hero couldn't be all bad.

However, the sight of an opened file marked IPOLITO, MICHAEL S. did not. It was Bea's opinion that a distinct advantage fell to whomever got to meet Schultz first. Somehow, Mike had managed to beat me to the punch, the stinker.

Schultz topped his file with mine, put on her glasses, read a bit, then took off her glasses and said, "I'm very surprised by the circumstances that brought you here, Genevieve. A girl with your commendable accomplishments"—she pinched the corner of my transcript—"a four-point-oh average in all advanced classes, recipient of the Junior Honor Society award three years in a row, The Denton High Outstanding Freshman Scholar Award, The American Legion Good Citizenship Award . . . on and on. Well, I can't remember the last time I reviewed a sophomore's academic record that was this impressive."

I let out a long sigh and relaxed. Bea and Neerja had so called this, Schultz instinctively aligning herself with me. Even though we didn't have the personal relationship that Mr. Watson and I had had, Schultz would only have to review my transcripts to realize that someone like me had no reason to cheat.

Clasping her hands, she leaned forward, her eyes liquid pools of gray, and in an earnest voice she asked, "Is it too much, dear? The pressure."

I blinked in confusion. No idea where she was going with this. "Excuse me, Dr. Schultz. What pressure?"

"From your parents. Your peers. Yourself. When the bar is set beyond our reach, often overachievers like you"—she smiled to herself—"*and me*, will do whatever it takes to grasp it, to experience the rush, the high, if you will, of success."

That tea. Maybe there was more in there than just chamomile. "There's no pressure from my parents, Dr. Schultz." Heck. Marmie could not have cared less, and Mom's attitude about high school was that the grades were all inflated and you really didn't begin to learn until college. "My mother and grandmother aren't worried about my grades, just as long as I'm not totally screwing up."

"I see. So then this drive comes from within." She chewed on the end of her half glasses, thinking. "You know, sometimes, Genevieve, the pressure we place on ourselves is far worse than the pressure placed on us by others. I think this is particularly true for girls. The fear of failure combined with the need for approval can often lead even the brightest young women to make the darkest of choices."

Her words packed a more devastating punch than Buzzard's accusation that Mike and I had been "in cahoots." For some reason, Schultz was under the impression that *I* had cheated off Mike.

"I don't know where you got that idea, Dr. Schultz." Answer: Mike Ipolito. "But I didn't copy from Mike. If anything, Mike copied from me."

"Really. And you have evidence to support such a serious allegation, I suppose."

"It's impossible to prove a negative, Dr. Schultz. In this country, we have to prove our guilt, not our innocence, unlike France and Mexico, where Napoleonic Law requires the opposite." Got that from Bea. Score!

"Genevieve, I'm not asking you to prove your innocence. I'm asking what evidence you can produce to show that you understood the extra-credit question and answered it correctly." She paused and added, rather snarkily in my opinion, *"On your own."*

"Because I know what a mole is. Not just a little furry thing that makes tunnels in our lawns and is mostly blind, but a mathematical number. And not just any number, Avogadro's number—6.022 times 10^{23}." As often happens when I'm put on the spot, I started babbling, drowning in the sea of my own excess verbosity.

"And you bring up moles because . . . ?"

"Because that was the extra-credit question." Okay. Maybe I should have started with that. "The point is, I didn't have to cheat. Unlike some people."

"Meaning Michael Ipolito."

I arched an eyebrow. "If the shoes fits"—and is not too expensive—"wear it."

"You assume that Michael wouldn't know what a mole is."

"We didn't study it in class. Buzzard—I mean, *Mr. Bouchard*—usually makes the extra-credit question about something we haven't learned yet. Has to do with us being chemistry scholars, according to Parad. That's how I knew to read ahead, though Avogadro's number was just by accident. I would have answered it right even if I hadn't talked to Parad. Because, like I said, or maybe I didn't, of the mole party."

Schultz gave herself a slight shake, as if she didn't even want to know who or what constituted a Parad. "Genevieve, I'm not permitted under law and school policy to discuss the private record of another student, but what if I told you—in a hypothetical sense, of course—that someone like Michael was, shall we say, equally academically gifted."

"Mike?"

Un-freaking-real. Somehow that con artist had managed

to wrap our new principal—with her Wellesley degree and her PhD and her expensive clunky jewelry and zen garden—around his little finger, just like he did all the teachers and his coaches, and anyone from whom he ever needed a favor. Just like he used to do to me in middle school.

"Look, Dr. Schultz. There's something you don't know about Mike. Those grades? Those AP and honors courses? He got those because he gets people like me to do his work for him." I took a deep breath as I tiptoed to the edge of pushing my luck. "With all due respect, Dr. Schultz, he even managed to manipulate you."

Her lips went pale. I hadn't just pushed my luck. I'd shoved it over a cliff.

"All right then." She closed my file and winked. "You've stated your case very clearly. Now, I plan to take this under advisement, discuss my recommendations with Mr. Bouchard, and meet you bright and early at eight a.m. You'll come to my office instead of homeroom so we can dispense with this matter before your first class." She stood.

I stood, unsure. Then she extended her hand and we shook.

For a second, it seemed like she was about to say something. Her lips twitched, her grip tightened. I thought she was going to reassure me that everything would be okay and that I was in the clear and that my 105% would be restored immediately.

Instead, she let go and waved me to the door. "Good night, Genevieve. Go home. Do your homework and get some rest. Remember, tomorrow is another day."

The way she said that kind of sounded like a threat.

Four

It is a universal rule of high school that teachers heap on the most homework Thursday nights. I blame their unbridled thirst for revenge.

For example, tomorrow I have to turn in a five-page paper on *Jane Eyre* for English, fifteen lines of Latin, a worksheet of chemistry equations, and end-of-chapter questions in Algebra II. Times like these, I have to outline my night starting with chemistry (from 5 to 6), Latin (to get it out of the way, from 6:15 to 7:15), a Netflix break for about 45 minutes, and then math (9 to 10) and, finally, my English paper (10:15 to whenever).

It's one of those timetables that looks good on paper and is absolutely worthless in reality. I'd barely finished my chemistry when Marmie casually mentioned that she'd forgotten to go to the grocery store so we had to do a "kitchen surprise" dinner.

A "kitchen surprise" dinner means I root around the cupboards and fridge until we can pull together an edible meal of questionable nutrition. Tonight, it was a bag of frozen peas and carrots, veggie burgers (no rolls, though, because we didn't have any), basmati rice, and a couple of cherry tomatoes, plus a snack-size Snickers.

For Marmie, who's French and therefore physically dependent on fine wines, fresh vegetables, soft cheeses, and homemade bread, "kitchen surprise" can plunge her into a deep funk, and it did. She had to make herself a cup of hot chocolate and go to bed early, just to recover.

Then, right as I was settling down to do my algebra, Bea called to deconstruct my meeting with Schultz; though, let's face it, this was major procrastination on her part since I'd already told her everything, right down to how Schultz hesitated at the end as if giving me a heads-up that she was on my side.

"I'm still bothered by what Mike said." There was a crunch on the line as Bea bit into some celery. Bea was on a diet again. She's always on a diet. "You know how I feel about members of the Man Clan, but even so, he doesn't seem like the type to rat you out to the authorities."

I lined up my paper and pencil and turned to the chapter

questions. "There was nothing to rat. I didn't cheat."

"You know what I mean. Underneath his jock exterior is a semi-okay guy, I have the feeling."

"A semi-okay guy willing to sell me down the river."

"True that."

Having wrung the last drip of gossip from the Mike/cheating/Schultz issue, Bea got back to work and I attacked a bunch of polynomials, inventing stories about their love lives to keep myself entertained.

This is a trick I often use to spice up the otherwise dry existence of integers. *X* and *Y* are much more interesting when they're trying to hook up, especially when you think about how everyone's always out to isolate them.

Take, for example, Pythagorean triples, the method used to find the sides of a right triangle if you're given only two positive numbers. The formula is (*n2 - m2*), *2mn*, (*n2 + m2*). Pretty basic. Pretty dull.

Now think of *n* as a girl and *m* as a boy. At first the powered-up girl and the powered-up guy are apart (*n2 - m2*). Then they get together (*2mn*). Then they're a power couple (*n2 + m2*). What happens after that is for them to deal with. There's always a chance *m*'s not that into *n* and they go their separate ways. One up the *y* axis and another across the *x*, bumming around up and down, never quite grounded as when they were a couple. It's what they call tragic.

It's also what they call precalculus.

I don't mind math. In fact, I find it relaxing, a change of pace from all the reading. I can play music, pet Petunia, even chat on Facebook, which was what I was doing with Neerja when up popped a message from Mike:

Mike: Hey. How'd it go

Me: You creep

Neerja: Justin said I should audition for the play

Mike: ????

Me: Romeo + Juliet?

Me: You told Schultz I cheated off U

Neerja: Justin said I'd make a good Juliet. And that he'd make an awesome Romeo ☺

Mike: Did not

Me: Did too

Me: U would!

Mike: It was u who told S that I cheated off UUUUU!!!!

Neerja: Too scared to try out. What if I bomb?

Me: You lie

Me: You won't. Want me to try out w/u?

Neerja: Seriously?

Mike: She set us up.

Me: What day?

Me: Who?

Neerja: I have to check

Mike: Schultz

Me: No way!

Me: Sure

Neerja: You're the best

Me: No YOU'RE the best! And you'll be the best Juliet, too!

Mike: Yo. Einstein. Read my wall.

I am one of Mike's 4,956 friends or something on Facebook. In contrast, I've got exactly fifty-two, one of whom is Mike because it's a convenient way for him to contact me about upcoming homework and put in the latest request for a favor.

Anyway, if I hadn't been in a state of deep procrastination, I probably would have thought twice before drifting over to his page and reading his latest post. What a mistake.

Attention, People of Earth. I, Michael Simon Ipolito,

officially state that I did not cheat, copy, plagiarize off

Gigi D and ditto for her, too. Peace. Out.

It wasn't his refreshingly well-spelled post that made my heart fall. It was the comments that followed:

- Gigi D who?

- Dude. You got caught cheating?

- Sounds serious, man.

- What's a Gigi?

- G.G.D.

- Gigi sounds like a dog.

- Probably *she* is!

You know, contrary to popular belief, the primary quality most desirable in a secret agent is not James Bond's ability to woo dangerous spying women, but the ability to blend into the crowd, to remain anonymous and easily forgotten.

It was obvious from reading the comments to Mike's post that my vocational calling was to quit school and join the CIA. At least there my powers of invisibility would be rewarded with free world travel and, probably, a really cool car.

Don't get me wrong. I am so past the adolescent angst about popular kids, blah, blah, blah. To me, that is *très* middle school. But I have to admit, reading those comments hurt because aside from the ignorant ones about my name, what sucked was the realization that despite being number one in our class, a lot of people I went to school with had no idea who I was.

But then up popped this:

She's hardly a dog, dude. More like a fox.

It was from California Will.

I might just be up to fifty-three friends.

With only a few hours of sleep under my belt thanks to working late on the *Jane Eyre* paper and then tossing and turning about my morning meeting with Schultz, I got up early, woke Bea (for once!) and Neerja, and then proceeded to make myself head-to-toe babe-i-licious. Skinny jeans. Scoop-neck tank top in black with my own hand-beaded silver jewelry. Hair conditioned, blown dry, and shined to perfection. Makeup impeccable. And, to top it off, on my feet were the Frye boots Bea and I found for a pittance at One More Time, the used clothing store in Cambridge.

They made the best sound—*clump, clump, clump*—when I walked to school that morning, head held high as I hooked a right into the office.

"They're waiting for you." Mrs. Wently was in Denton High's colors—red T-shirt, black capri pants—instead of her usual more flattering skirts. Friday was school spirit day. Also dress-down day. The combination often made for some alarming fashion statements among the faculty.

I passed through the inner sanctum to Schultz's private lair. Sure enough, there was Mike's backpack thrown on a hard plastic chair and, when I opened the door, there was Mike in his soccer jersey—38 Ipolito—sharing a hearty chuckle with Schultz like they were besties. At the sight of me, they both stopped laughing.

Skin from a snake, I tell you. The guy could charm skin from a snake.

Schultz cleared her throat. "Have a seat, Genevieve."

"Genevieve, huh?" Mike grinned.

"The patron saint of Paris." I pulled out the chair next to him, flipped my fabulous blond hair, and crossed my legs. Catherine Deneuve be damned.

He gave me the once-over, his eyes taking in my top, the jeans, and the boots. He flashed me the thumbs-up.

Schultz cleared her throat. "I'll get right to the heart of the matter. You two have been accused of collaborating during a midterm exam. Specifically, you've been accused of conspiring to answer the unusually difficult extra-credit question."

There were those silly words again. *Conspiring. Collaborating.* As if I had been an equal partner in this crime.

"After reviewing the exams, discussing the events with Mr. Bouchard—who knows his students better than anyone—and conducting personal interviews, it is truly impossible for me to determine with any degree of certainty that the two of you definitively cheated."

"Yes!" Mike raised his hand to high-five me, but Schultz shook her head. "Not so fast, Michael. I'm not quite finished."

He lowered his hand, wary.

"What I find far more disturbing than the possibility that two students compared each other's answers on one relatively insignificant question, is my discovery of the underlying crack in the foundation of the Denton High School community that, left in disrepair, will undoubtedly expand into a dangerous fissure resulting in a total collapse of society."

What?

Mike said, "English, please."

Schultz swiveled in my direction with a glare that iced my body. "Genevieve. When I played devil's advocate and asked why you copied from Michael, you swiftly turned the tables and accused him of copying off you because you seem to assume that he is not up to your par academically."

Mike caught my eye. "Nice one, Einstein."

My cheeks went hot. "Sorry," I murmured.

"And, Michael." It was his turn. "When I posed a similar question to you, asking why you copied off Genevieve, you immediately became sarcastic. If I recall, your exact words were"—she picked up her notes and read—"'Yeah, I would have copied off her except I can't see that high. I guess you don't know that Gigi and her friends are above us all.'"

I could not believe he thought *we* were above *him*.

"You said that?"

"Chill, princess. It was a joke." He shrugged. "Anyway, Dr. Schultz, I thought what we told you was confidential."

That was an excellent point, actually.

"Only where your individual transcripts are concerned." Schultz folded her arms and regarded us with disappointment. "Perhaps you can understand my deep distress. Cooperation and respect are the cornerstones of civilization. They are far more important than a genius IQ. If we cannot work together in cheerful harmony, then there is no hope for the human race."

Mike gave me a look that read, *Bit dramatic, that.*

I replied with an almost imperceptible nod of agreement. Never trust a principal with a zen garden on her desk.

"So, after a thoughtful exchange with Mr. Bouchard, it is our agreement that the two of you should learn to truly collaborate on a project that will require equal contributions to assure success."

"More work?" Geesh! We already had a huge project due in English and another for American Studies. Plus, knowing Mike, he'd slack off, so, let's be honest, most of the responsibility would fall on my shoulders. Again.

"Yes. More work, Gigi. Mr. Bouchard proposed an interesting presentation of the periodic table of elements with visual aids. May I suggest PowerPoint? Wonderful program."

A presentation? The mere suggestion caused an all-too-familiar flush of anxiety to rush from my heart and up my chest. Reflexively, I pulled my shirt to my chin so Mike and Schultz couldn't see my embarrassing reaction.

Here's the bottom line: I do NOT do presentations. Seriously, I have a physical reaction to getting up in front of the class, like I'm almost allergic. It starts with the flush and soon I'm breathing hard and my voice gets shaky and my heart goes haywire and I get dizzy and wobbly and . . . Well, most of my teachers know better than to make me speak. I could practically get a doctor's note, if I wanted.

Under his breath, Mike said, "Total CYA."

"What was that, Michael?" Schultz pursed her lips.

Mike lifted his chin. "I said, you look lovely today, Doctor. Burnt umber is definitely your color."

Schultz fingered her amber beads and took a sip of tea to compose herself. Oh brother. Once recovered from Mike's flattery, she said, "Mr. Bouchard informs me that he's already scheduled your presentation for the week before the Thanksgiving break or, as we in the faculty think of it, the end of the first-quarter marking period."

I was speechless. That was impossible. Absolutely impossible with our schedules.

"It's the playoffs!" Mike exclaimed. "I've got practice

every night after school and we're up against Belmont next weekend. I can barely get my regular homework done."

"Which is why you have a partner. Genevieve will help."

Thanks, I wanted to say, unable to resist adding, "So what else is new?"

She ticktocked her finger. "Ah, ah, ahhh. That's exactly the attitude we're trying to change, Genevieve. Michael is your partner and, as such, will contribute his fair share. Isn't that right, Michael?"

Mike, hands on his knees, staring at the floor, said, "Uh, yeah. Right."

"Now, let me just be clear. If you don't collaborate equally, those zeroes will remain on your midterms and, therefore, on your first-quarter grades."

"And the letter of no confidence in our files?" I asked.

"No longer a concern."

Whew! Well, at least that was something positive.

"However, I'm afraid each of your transcripts will include a letter noting you were referred to me for cheating but that the charges were never validated." She smiled with regret. "I'm so sorry. I thought it was a little harsh myself, but apparently it's a new school policy the board passed just last spring, before my arrival."

"School policy?" That was outrageous! "But it's our

first offense. And . . . we were innocent! What's the point of a letter like that?"

She blinked rapidly. "It's your track record. If you're accused of cheating again—either here or in college—the institution will consider it as part of a pattern of behavior."

I couldn't believe how unjust this was, as if the school were intentionally setting us up to fail.

"Can we go?" Mike blurted. "I've got class."

She checked her watch. "Oh my. You'd better run. You only have two minutes before first period."

When she said that, the bell rang, and Mike, doing nothing now to hide his full-blown anger, yanked open the door, grabbed his backpack, and stormed out.

Not me. I was frozen in place, glued to my chair by the unfairness of a stupid school policy that cruelly penalized students for nothing—and would force me to get up in front of the class. "Dr. Schultz, if Brown or Williams or Stanford see that I've been referred to you for possibly cheating"—the very idea was bringing me to the edge of tears, either out of anger or self-pity or possibly both— "it'll trash my chances on the spot. Isn't there anything you can do?"

"All I can do is include my own letter of explanation, which I plan on writing as soon as you and Mike complete your project." Then, seeing my tears, she added sympathetically, "We're not asking that much, Genevieve. A simple presentation. You and Mike should be able to do it in a weekend."

"Uh-huh." Obviously, she'd never witnessed Mike in un-action. Or me standing up in front of a class. "Well, thanks for everything."

"Genevieve!" She stood as I opened the door. "You said 'we.'"

I gripped the doorknob. "Pardon?"

"Just now, when you said you were innocent of cheating. You said 'we' were innocent."

"Did I?" I hadn't even noticed.

She beamed. "Don't you see how important that is? Already you're thinking cooperatively."

"Sure." I smiled and left before my tongue got the better of me and shot back a nasty reply. Outside Schultz's office, Mike was leaning against a file cabinet and chatting up Mrs. Wently. So much for being late for class.

I breezed past them, but Mike stepped in my way. "Hold on, Einstein. I want to talk to you." Leading me toward the copy machine in the corner, he said, "How *are* you?"

Mike was doing the human koala bear thing, his brown eyes deep pools of sympathy, meaning he was about to ask me for another favor. Like I didn't know what. "Look, Ipolito. If you're going to try to talk me into doing all the work on this periodic table thing because your soccer playoffs are so important, you can save your breath. You heard what Schultz said. This has to be a *collaborative* project."

He rubbed my arm. "I know, Einstein, I know. I'm not going to stick you with this whole BS. Right now, I'm more worried about you."

"Why?"

"'Cause you looked really upset in there, like you were about to cry or something."

"Oh, please." As if. "I was so not about to cry."

He stuck out his lower lip and cocked his head for maximum koala-ishness. "Now, now. You can tell your uncle Mikey. Is it that you've never been called down to the principal's office before? That you're afraid your pristine perfect reputation is ruined forever? That you're letting down your saintly namesake?"

That almost made me laugh. "It's not any of those things," I said, readjusting my backpack and noticing that Mrs. Wently had maneuvered her chair so she could eavesdrop. "It's the part about getting up in class. That's what got me upset." I hadn't planned on telling him this, but I hadn't planned on him caring, either. Then again, who knew if his caring was genuine or manipulative. "The thing is, Mike, I totally suck at public speaking. It makes me sick. Literally. Like barfing sick."

He studied me a bit, as if trying to figure out if this was legit. "Well, if that's all it is, relax. I'll do the talking for us."

"Really?"

"Sure. You do all the work and I'll do all the talking."

Oh no. Oh no, no, no. "I'll kill you, Mike Ipolito. I swear I will."

He punched me on the arm. "Lighten up. It's a joke. Sort of. Come on. I'll walk you to chem."

Slinging his arm across my shoulder, he escorted me past Mrs. Wently, pausing briefly to remark that nothing lifted his spirits more than seeing her wearing Denton High colors on school spirit days.

Mrs. Wently went redder than her shirt. In fact, she actually giggled.

Five

The Shady Acres Cemetery is a quiet place of towering oaks and crumbling old tombstones at the top of the hill behind Neerja's house, and it's been our tradition since sixth grade to sneak up there and look down at the twinkling lights of Boston and dream of when we'll live in the big city, with our own apartments on Commonwealth Ave. and no parents to tell us what to do.

They keep the graveyard dark at night, and because it's a popular shortcut, Neerja's parents have forbidden her from going there after hours, which was why we had to leave from my house in our pj's and sweatshirts, taking with us only my harmless basset for protection.

Petunia loved it here—though she preferred the

daylight hours when she could bark at squirrels. Not that she would actually chase a squirrel, mind you. But somewhere in the depths of her doggie brain, she believed that by barking, she was in a general and meaningful way contributing to the community rodent roundup.

"Schultz is right, unfortunately." Bea slid behind the LUCY B. EDELMAN headstone to escape a swirl of blowing dead leaves. "I went online this afternoon when I got home and found the newspaper articles. The school board just totally overreacted after that cheating scandal. First they fired Mr. Watson, and then they passed this superstrict policy to overcompensate, and now it's you who has to pay the price."

Funny how that cheating scandal, such a big deal when it happened, had almost slipped my memory.

Last spring, two seniors, Derek Kirkpatrick and Kyle Remsen, broke into the school office, took cell phone photos of the master answer keys to a bunch of finals, and then mass-emailed them to ten to fifteen of their closest friends, the numbnuts. As if stupidity were not its own reward, they forgot to remove their sending email addresses, so it took the administration five minutes to find the culprits.

Derek and Kyle were barred from graduation, and anyone else who used their answer key received zeroes on their finals. Meanwhile, panicked parents started loudly complaining about technology they didn't understand and how kids were using it to commit plagiarism daily thanks to the "interweb." I guess this was how the new policy came to be.

I couldn't help but find it a teensy-weensy bit ironic that I, who'd never cheated aside from exchanging homework with Neerja and Bea, would pay the punishment of a nasty letter in my permanent file, whereas Derek and Kyle got off pretty much scot-free. Last I heard, they were at UMass, partying away.

"There has to be something Gigi can do to clear her name," Neerja said. "I mean, a letter of explanation from Schultz might help, but . . ." Her voice trailed off as she leaned down to help Petunia push her rolls of fat onto ARTHUR JAMES LITTLE. With several whines and scratching of toenails against the granite tombstone, chubsy-wubsy managed to extend her stunted legs over the edge and climb onto the smooth surface, collapsing with as much exhaustion as if she'd just scaled Everest.

Neerja ripped open a bag of Skittles and, holding it out of Petunia's reach, poured me a handful. "If the policy's new, maybe it can be overturned or something."

I took the bag and passed it to Bea. "Neerja might be right. Did any of your research say anything about that?"

"Sure. You can always go to the school board and ask them to amend it," Bea said, helping herself to just a few.

"I mean, I don't know if they'd change the policy, but it'd be worth a shot. You'll probably have to stand up and talk into the microphone, though."

Bea and Neerja were well aware of my phobia because they'd been in my second-grade class when I delivered the oral report on ladybugs. Mike wasn't there because he was in Mrs. Arend's room next door. I think.

Anyway, the report started off okay. I managed to keep my jitters in check even though my voice was shaking, until I got to the part about how ladybugs apparently taste nasty to predators, and suddenly I turned toward the blackboard and threw up my lunch. Not any lunch, *lasagna*. All the kids went "Ewww" and pinched their noses and pushed back their chairs. Only Bea and Neerja were brave enough to lead me to the bathroom so I could wash out my mouth. Mr. Ritter, the janitor, came in and scattered black stuff on the vomit, and my teacher, Mrs. Cafferty, sent me to the nurse, who took pity and called my grandmother, though I was fine.

I didn't have a virus. It wasn't the school lasagna (for once). It was just that I freaked. To this day I can remember the sour sensation of anxiety building and building and building until, finally, I had no choice but to explode. Seriously, if you've ever thrown up, especially in front of your whole class, you'll do anything to guarantee you never do it again.

Bea, on the other hand, LOVES to get up and speak. And she does it brilliantly, too.

"Can't you go to the school board for me? You're the budding lawyer."

"Wouldn't have the same impact." Bea nibbled on a raspberry candy, hoping to make it last. "You've got to tug at their heartstrings with your personal story. They need to know that once upon a time you were a straight-A student with a clean record hoping to go to an Ivy League school."

"*Once?*" I asked, not liking the sound of that.

"That's right. Now, instead of graduating summa cum laude from Brown or whatever and going to Oxford and becoming a famous author with a cute British husband and adorable blond children all living in some castle on the moors, you're going to end up in the streets, homeless and alone and unloved, eating dog food out of a can. On Christmas. All because they insisted a letter be included in your file saying that you'd been referred to the principal for cheating back in tenth grade."

Wow. I didn't know it would be that bad. "*Homeless?*"

"Totally, dude."

We sat in shocked silence listening to the wind in the trees, gently blowing away my future.

Finally, Neerja, in an attempt to be encouraging, said, "But I'm sure you'll be loved, Gigi. We will always love you, and as the Beatles said, all you need is love."

"And a can opener," Bea added. "For the dog food."

I was about to noogie her when from the bottom of the hill came the faintest sound of shuffling leaves. Footsteps. Petunia lifted her head and listened, the hair on her back rising in a line of alarm. My girl was on the case.

"Did you hear that?" Neerja hissed. "Someone's coming."

It didn't help that when she said this, the breeze picked up, howling through the branches. I shivered and rubbed my shoulders. "Maybe we should get out of here."

"So the ax murderer or whoever he is will see us running?" Neerja's eyes were round white balls in the dark. "No way. It's better for us to stick to the shadows."

We kept still as the footsteps got closer. I reached for Neerja's hand and Bea reached for mine. We held our breath and waited. The footsteps got louder and louder. Definitely male and definitely coming straight toward us. Two dark figures loomed, and from the base of Petunia's throat came a low growl.

"Hey. Whassup?"

The white ankle socks were a dead giveaway.

Neerja let go. "Henry?"

"Hey, Neerja," another voice said.

"Justin." Neerja sighed in relief. "I'm so glad it's you."

She meant this in more ways than one.

"Next time, how about a shout-out." Bea shook her head at the sight of our two ghosts in hoodies—Henry grinning like a happy idiot and Justin shaking his head so the breeze wouldn't mess with the preferred direction of his overgrown bangs. For a while, there was a story going around school that Justin got his hair professionally straightened and styled for about $170 a month. I've always wanted to ask him if that was true.

"So, so sorry," Henry gushed. "I should have thought of that, how you guys might get scared. Geesh. I'm so stupid sometimes."

Justin, without sharing a shred of Henry's guilt, said, "Why are you guys hanging out in a cemetery? Don't you have anything better to do on a Friday night?"

Petunia moaned and dropped her head.

"By 'better,' I suppose you mean being at Maddie Kildare's Eve of All Hallow's Eves blowout," Bea said, omitting the fact that we hadn't exactly been invited to said blowout. "How was it, Justin? Everything you hoped and dreamed?"

"*Hmmm.*" This was Neerja's secret signal to Bea to *shut up*.

Neerja did *not* want Justin to know that we knew he was going to be at Maddie's party. It was bad enough that Neerja always just happened to bump into him between classes.

"Eh, the party was kind of lame." Justin leaned against a tall tombstone topped by a hulking angel.

"Mega lame," Henry confirmed, sitting next to Neerja and giving Petunia a pat. "There was no one there."

Neerja poked him playfully. "By no one, you mean Lindsay."

"Busted." Justin pointed a finger at his friend and laughed.

"Fug you, Crenshaw," Henry said, ripping grass and throwing it in Justin's direction.

Justin wiped grass off his sweatshirt. "Chillax, dude. All I'm saying is you should take action. Like ask her out."

"Too weird. We hardly see each other anymore now that I'm in AP classes." Then, probably to get Justin back for the busted comment, he added, "Not that you would know, Crenshaw."

Justin went, "Hah! Loser. That's what you get for being a genius."

Neerja sighed since she and Henry shared the same predicament. "Been there, doing that," she said under her breath.

Henry gave her a squeeze to let her know he understood. For years, he'd been listening to her complain about being ignored by Justin and assuring her it was simply a matter of time until his friend saw the light. After all, if Henry was friends with Neerja and Henry was friends with Justin then, logically, Justin would be friends with Neerja. According to Henry, their eventual relationship was dictated by the transitive property.

But Neerja didn't want to be "just friends" with Justin, and she was tired of waiting for the transitive property to jump-start her love life.

In the meantime, Justin, per usual, was clueless to her feelings, being far more interested, for some reason, in Henry. "So how do you know Lindsay, anyway, if she's not in any of your nerd classes?"

"From middle-school chorus and . . ." He paused.

"Gymnastics," Neerja finished. "In elementary school the three of us were in Miss Vicki's All-Star Tumblers."

Henry dropped his head into hands. "Ugh. I wish you hadn't said that."

"Ballet?" Justin let out a snort. "Dude, you were in *ballet*? Did you, like, wear a pink tutu and stuff?"

"Not ballet, *gymnastics*," Neerja stressed, jumping to his defense. "And he was really good, too. Miss Vicki still talks about his sixth-grade spring performance on the rings. She said she'd never seen a boy that young do the Iron Cross."

"Ooooh." Justin flapped his arms. "Look at me. I'm twirling on rings."

"Shut up, Justin!" Bea barked. "Men's artistic gymnastics

is an authentic sport that goes all the way back to the ancient Greeks. It requires incredible strength and is definitely not for sissies."

"Thanks. I'll stick to soccer."

"And drama." Okay, it was kind of a snarky comment, but it was what Justin deserved for giving Henry grief.

"Hey, lay off drama," he said with another flick of his bangs. "Until the middle of, like, the last century, women weren't even allowed to act in public."

"Uh, you're off by a few hundred years there, Shakespeare. Try 1660, after the Reformation of Charles the Second." Bea snorted as she often does when making an exceptionally pithy point. "But thanks for playing."

Neerja quickly changed the subject before Bea and Justin came to blows. "Speaking of drama, I've decided to take your advice, Justin. I'm going to audition for *Romeo and Juliet*."

"You are?" Bea said. "I thought that was still up in the air."

"Not after Gigi said she'd try out with me."

Bea said, "Since when do you act?"

"Since Neerja said she wanted to audition."

"But you hate getting up in front of people. It makes you . . ."

I gave Bea's finger a quick twist to send the message

that this had nothing to do with me and everything to do with Neerja and Justin.

"Owww!" Bea shook her hand. "Okay, I get it."

Justin said, "Get what?"

"Get why Henry needs to try out," Bea said.

"Me?" Henry said. "I can't act."

Neerja nudged him. "Yes, you can. Remember when we were little?"

"It was the Three Little Pigs, Neerja. In our backyard. That was hardly acting."

"You had me fooled. You were such a scary wolf, I was mad afraid of you after that."

Henry lifted his hands like claws and leaned over her. "I'll huff . . . and I'll puff . . . and . . ."

"Boring!" Justin drew a hand across his neck. "Okay, so back to Henry. Why does he need to try out?"

"Because Lindsay's auditioning for the play too," Bea said. "I overheard her this morning in homeroom."

"Really?" Henry said, perking up.

"Perfect! That'll give you a chance to be with her, Muscles." Muscles was Neerja's pet nickname for him. "You know, Parad used to say there was nothing more romantic than acting in a play together—all those rehearsals, late-night hours, baring your soul on stage."

"Baring what?" Justin said.

"That's why so many actors fall in love shooting

movies," Neerja prattled. "I assume you've heard of Brangelina and Bennifer."

"And, coming to a theater near you soon—Jeerja," Bea quipped.

"Who?" Justin seemed to be having particular trouble keeping up tonight.

Bea said, "*Neerja*. I was going to say she should do what she can to push Henry and Lindsay together during rehearsals."

"Absolutely. That's a fantastic idea." Neerja gave Henry a hug. "I'll be like the nurse in *Romeo and Juliet*, joining two star-crossed lovers."

"Wow," said Henry. "Awesome. And I'll help you with *you know who*."

"Who?" Justin said again.

"Talking about *Dr. Who*, J. You know how we nerds love our *Who*."

"*Who*? How did you two get on *Who*? We were talking about the play."

"What?" Henry said. "I dunno. Guess that's the problem with us geniuses, the way we go off on tangents and miss half of what's being said."

"Got that right," Justin agreed. "It's like I have to explain everything to you at least twice, Filomen, 'cause you're always in la-la land. Seriously, you should try harder to stay with the program or maybe start popping some Adderall or whatever."

Henry scratched behind his ear. "Yeah. I'll work on that."

I thought Bea was about to bust a gut, the way she was bent over, shoulders shaking.

"Black Ops?" Justin said.

Henry pushed Petunia off his lap. "Sure. Why not?"

They said good-bye and we watched them trudge down the hill toward Henry's house, a trail of leaves in their wake. When they were gone, Neerja let out a high-pitched squeal. "Beatrice Rachel Honeycutt, I was about ready to kill you. Jeerja. *JEERJA!*"

I nearly rolled off the tombstone, laughing. "That is so your new nickname."

Neerja balled her hands in fists. "It is so not."

"Relax, girlfriend. Justin's super cute, but he's not the sharpest tool in the box," Bea said. "That's the upside to dating cute-but-dumb guys. You can insult them right to their faces and it goes straight over their heads."

Six

I've decided Halloween when you're sixteen pretty much epitomizes the concept of adolescent purgatory.

On the one hand, the kid in you can't believe the days of harassing neighbors for sugar loot have swiftly come to an end. And yet, the prospect of beating aside four-year-olds for the last Giant Pixy Stix on the block seems somehow wrong.

For years, Neerja, Bea, and I have managed to deal with this moral dilemma by getting together to watch *The Blair Witch Project,* which is good for a laugh because inevitably Bea, hopped up on a mega-mix bag of Tootsie Rolls and Starbursts, will yell, "Follow the river. Follow the river, you idiots. Seriously, just how stupid are you?"

I'd so miss that this year.

This year, because Halloween fell on a Saturday, the day before her brother's birthday, Bea's parents were taking her and George out to dinner at Legal Sea Foods. I'm sure this is exactly how Bea's brother wants to celebrate the big two-oh, by listening to his father bicker with a waitress over the price of oysters instead of going with his friends to a Halloween party on campus. But, when you're Harry Honeycutt's kid, you tend not to disagree.

Neerja, meanwhile, was stuck babysitting The Things while her parents, attired in matching clown suits, attempted to cheer up/frighten to death Dr. Padwami's elderly patients. After that, the whole Padwami clan was off to a party of doctors—which left me to celebrate Halloween alone, with Marmie.

Anyway, with nothing much to do, I was updating my status on Facebook from "in a relationship with Petunia Dubois" to "it's complicated," when Mike's chat screen appeared at the bottom of my page.

Mike: U going to Ava's party?

I thought, *Ava's having a party and she didn't invite me?*

Me: Nope
Mike: Aren't u 2 friends?

Me: Guess not

Mike: U can come w/us

Right. Just what I wanted, to tag behind Mike and his equally tall and beautiful girlfriend, Sienna, as the slightly irregular but intelligent third wheel? Um, pass. Though it was thoughtful of him to ask, I'd give him that.

Me: Thanks, but I have plans

Mike: OK. Bye!

I logged off and lay on my bed, staring at my ceiling as I fought an existential crisis.

See, this is the problem with Facebook. If I hadn't gone on, I would have remained blissfully ignorant about Ava's party. I might even have had fun by myself knitting the scarf I was making my mother for Christmas and watching *Blair Witch* and teasing the cute trick-or-treaters. But now, I couldn't shake the insult of total rejection.

Ava and I might not have been as close as before her Rolf days, but at least she could have included me in her first-ever Halloween party. Apparently Mike thought so too, otherwise he wouldn't have asked me so casually *Aren't u 2 friends?*

Exactly.

The doorbell rang again, sending Petunia into a crazy

tailspin of barking and baying at the latest round of trick-or-treaters. It was the Brezinski brothers dressed up as ninja warriors/pirates/*Star Wars* Stormtroopers. They lived three doors down and their front yard was dirt from all the damage they'd inflicted on the grass by digging, scraping, and wrestling like maniacs.

I held out the bowl of candy and they whined in unison, "Not Reese's Peanut Butter Cups. EVERYONE gives out those."

All righty then. I put the bowl back on the table, crossed my arms, and said, "Trick."

Stuart Brezinski, the youngest of the gang at about age six, said, "What do you mean, trick?"

"It's trick-or-treat, right? So you guys have to do some tricks 'cause you dissed my treats."

The oldest, Marcus, gave him a light punch. "Come on, Stewy. Let's go."

But Stuart was intrigued. "Like magic tricks?"

"Like egging her house," his other brother, Andrew, said. "Toilet-papering her car."

"I dare you."

Their faces lit up. Even under their masks, you could tell their greedy eyes were shining with delight at the prospect of actually being encouraged to commit minor acts of vandalism. Now, *this* was Halloween!

They hopped off our front steps and ran down the

walk, heads bent together. I had to laugh at their evil glee. What a bunch of little thugs.

"That's a bit dangerous, don't you think?"

I hadn't even noticed Will standing there in a red-lined black satin cape, hands in jeans pockets. I'm not a diehard vamp fan, but IMHO guys should wear capes 24/7. With his jet-black hair, he looked like an Edward Cullen fantasy come to life.

"Don't you think you're a little old to be begging for candy?" I said, my blood suddenly pulsing as I remembered his comment on Mike's Facebook page. "Or is this how they do things in California?"

"This is how they do things in Massachusetts when you have a seven-year-old brother who's new to the neighborhood." He nodded to his left, where a vampire in miniature was skipping toward him down the sidewalk. "I'm waiting at the end of the street to give him a sense of 'independence,'" he said, making air quotes around the word.

I couldn't help but be touched. I also couldn't help but wonder if he'd been invited to Ava's party too. Bet he had. "That's very sweet."

"That's what big brothers are for. By the way, I forgot to ask Mike. How did it go with Schultz?"

"We were acquitted. That's the good news. The bad news is we have to do a project together and we still get letters in our permanent files saying we were referred to the principal for cheating."

He made a face. "That's not right."

"Word."

The miniature vampire came to a skipping halt and, after flashing me a questioning glance, tugged on Will's cape. Will kneeled down and let him whisper into his ear. This was too darned cute.

"Ah," Will said, smiling. "So my man Aidan here"—he ruffled his brother's hair—"would like to know if he could use, um, your facilities."

It took me a second to define facilities. But then I got it. "Oh! No problem."

I waved them inside, trying to remember if I'd removed the spare emergency Tampax from its place of honor on the top of the toilet tank. I'm kind of lazy about leaving that stuff around, seeing as we don't get much call for menfolk in these here parts.

"But you have to be careful," I said to Aidan. "There's a killer basset inside."

Petunia howled and Aidan shrank into Will.

"She's kidding." Though Will himself didn't seem so certain. "Right?"

Petunia howled again. "You'll just have to take your chances."

Aidan seemed pretty scared when he went through the vestibule into the house, until he saw my fat, elongated, stub-legged dog, a mass of wiggles and wags, so incredibly overjoyed to see a real live kid approaching her with a bag of chocolate that she was drooling.

"Bayooooo!" Petunia bayed happily as Aidan shyly extended a hand to pet her pointed head.

I took his candy bag and placed it high on the bookshelf out of her reach. If dogs could curse, Petunia would have rattled off a blue streak.

Will leaned down to pet her. "What is this thing? It almost looks like a dog, and yet it's totally distorted."

"That, my good man, is an eating machine. Hamburgers. Cookies. Entire chickens. Spare auto parts. Doesn't matter, she'll eat it, especially if it's coated in sugar." I gave her a kiss. She smelled like corn chips.

"Her ears are long." You could tell Aidan was dying to touch one.

"And soft. Go ahead. She loves to have her ears stroked."

He did so gently. "Why come they're so long?"

"Supposedly, so she can sweep more smell toward her nose. But really it's so she'll be able to collect the last bits of food from her bowl." And I showed him how Petunia could easily suck on their ends.

Aidan chortled. "I want a dog like this."

Petunia bayed in approval.

Will said, "I thought you wanted to use the bathroom."

"Oh, yeah, right." And hopping up, Aidan followed my directions to the end of the hall.

"Close the door!" Will yelled. Then, as way of explanation, said, "We live in a house of men."

"Oddly enough, I live in a house of only women. My grandmother, mother, and me."

He smiled, his teeth a blazing white. Which was when it hit me that this guy, who was by far the hottest member of the male species I'd ever seen off a screen—J.Crew looks, square jaw, gorgeous bone structure, and those eyes—was also standing in our kitchen, where I frequently whipped up my disgusting creations, like pizza-bagel egg sandwiches with hot sauce and salsa.

"Can I get you anything?"

"Nah, thanks. I snuck some of Aidan's candy." His gaze drifted to Marmie's half-open bottle of wine and leftover cheese and bread from dinner. "So, where's your father?"

Adults cringe when they hear this question because they feel sorry for me, the half-orphaned child. But having known nothing but a brilliant absentee dad with zero directional sense, it's really no big deal. I find it kind of funny.

"My parents broke up before I was born, though since they're both scientists, I've long held suspicions that I'm indeed an alien."

Will laughed.

I said, "And your tale of woe?"

"Mom's in L.A."

"Oh. Okay." Kind of odd. "Permanently?"

He stroked Petunia under her flabby chin. "We don't know. My parents separated last year when Dad got this offer to teach at Tufts. Mom didn't want to shut down her interior decorating business in California and Dad wanted to return to the East Coast, so we're doing a test run. Can the three Blake men survive on their own?"

Already I had a million questions. Why didn't he and Aidan stay with their mother, for starters. But I didn't think it right to ask, considering we'd talked maybe twice.

Will stood, shook Petunia hair off his cape, and lowered his voice. "Aidan doesn't know this, but actually it was Mom who wanted the break. From *us*."

Geesh. That was harsh. I mean, my mother also lived thousands of miles away, but that was because she worked as an internationally renowned nerd, not because she was in need of some "me" time. "I'm sorry."

"That's L.A. It does weird things to people sometimes. Dad and I are hoping that she'll snap out of it."

The toilet flushed and I decided it might be wise to change the subject. "And how's Aidan liking Boston?"

"So-so. He really misses our home and his buddies. He hasn't been sleeping in his own bed since we got here, so he's been sleeping with me."

A vision of Will Blake in bed popped into my head and I blushed, rushing back to the safe, neutral subject of his brother. "Is that a good thing or a bad thing?"

"Mostly a bad thing. He kicks constantly and tends to wake up with the sun. Then he drags me out of bed to watch cartoons. I'm seriously sleep-deprived."

I could not be held accountable for my actions if someone dragged me out of my bed at dawn to watch cartoons. "May I just be so bold as to say that sucks?"

"You may. But if sleeping with me helps Aidan adjust, then it's worth it. That's one reason why I'm going to Denton instead of a boarding school—so I can be here for him. That said, I'm majorly bumming about leaving L.A. and . . ."

Here comes the part where he mentions a hot girlfriend.

". . . anyway, it's kind of weird going to a school where you don't know anyone and you're used to being in a place where it's always sunny and warm and you've got tons of friends. It's a serious culture shock."

"I bet." *And the girlfriend . . . ?*

"I'm trying to get psyched about being here. I know Boston's an awesome city with lots of history and funky hangouts and—"

"Let me give you a tour!" I had no idea where that came from. I'm not normally in the habit of boldly asking out strange boys. Okay, to be technically correct, *any* boys. It's just that Will really got me with the story about his mother, and Aidan not sleeping. Or, maybe, Will really got me with his blue eyes and that sexy jaw. "I'd be happy to show you around."

"For real?" He looked taken aback, and I remembered what Henry said about Lindsay, how it's awkward to ask out someone you hardly hang with. "Well, you know . . ."

Fortunately, the powder room door opened and there was a brief sound of water being turned off and on as my hero Aidan emerged to save my self-respect. "I'm done!" he boasted.

"We can take Aidan to the science museum and the aquarium!" I slapped my thigh like this was *exactly* what I'd had in mind. "Has he ever seen a seal before?"

"We, uh, lived in California."

Moron. "Okay, then a lobster. I bet he's never seen a live New England lobster."

"Restaurants? You know those tanks?" He wiggled his fingers to imitate lobster crawling.

"I've never seen a moray eel except on The Discovery Channel," Aidan said. "They're mega poisonous."

"*Wicked*," I corrected. "Now that you're in Massachusetts, young man, your preferred hyperbolic adjective is 'wicked.' As in, Petunia is a wicked fat dog. Or, Gigi, you're a wicked gorgeous creature."

Aidan gamely played along. "Moray eels are wicked poisonous."

"Atta boy. Actually the moray isn't that bad, though all eel blood is poisonous to humans—a fact that won Charles Richet a Nobel Prize for determining that you could die from an allergic reaction to a toxic substance. Isn't that fascinating?"

Aidan was blunt. "Not really."

Ah, the refreshing honesty of youth. I switched tacks. "However, if you want to see something really cool, there's a thirty-foot octopus named Truman in the aquarium's center tank."

"*Awesome!*" Aidan clapped. "I love octopi. Do they have blue-ringed? Those are my favorite."

"I don't know. We'll have to see."

Will gave Aidan a slight push toward the door. "Great. I'll text you and we can work it out. Weekends are kind of"—he nodded in the direction of Aidan, who was on tiptoe, trying to reach the bag of candy—"hard."

"Gotcha." I fetched the bag and hooked my finger around Petunia's collar so she couldn't follow them home. Aidan toddled out the door and Will hung back, letting him go. Taking my elbow, he looked deep into my eyes and said, "Thanks. That was really nice of you. Means a lot."

I got all warm, though I tried to act like it was nothing.

"Sure. It'll be fun."

"For me, too." He smiled and then jogged to catch Aidan from crossing the street alone. They waved good-bye and turned the corner as I shut the door and realized something. Now I knew why Halloween takes a backseat as you grow up, because there are so many sweeter things to look forward to than Snickers bars.

Like Will.

Not so much that giant octopus.

Seven

Ava was waiting for me when I got to school Monday. Okay, I couldn't prove she'd been waiting specifically for me, but when I turned up the sidewalk, there she was by the concrete planter. Either Mr. Obleck never found her or their talk didn't take because she seemed in no hurry to get to class.

"Gigi! Just the person I wanted to talk to," she said, wiping off her hands and zipping up her black portfolio. "How are you?"

"Okay." Although Halloween had worked out in the end, seeing Ava rekindled the hurt feelings. You could tell she knew that, too, because immediately she started telling me how great I looked in my new black skirt.

"You have the legs to pull it off. You're so lucky." She

popped open a box of cherry-flavored Sucrets. "Want one?"

She knew I couldn't resist cherry. "Sure. Thanks."

Ava dropped one into my outstretched palm. "Now, what if an innocent child were to come across this?"

"Bubkes." I had to laugh.

It was an old joke of ours, a reference to first grade, when the secretary of our elementary school confiscated Ava's Sucrets because she hadn't brought a note saying she was allowed to eat cough drops. The secretary actually called Ava's mother at work and said, "What if an innocent child were to come across one of your daughter's cough drops? Then what?"

To which Ava's mother, a bit of a rebel herself, replied, "Well, Jeanine, my guess is probably bubkes."

We latched on to the word *bubkes* like it was the funniest word ever. For two solid weeks everything between us was "bubkes," and as we walked into school that morning, I realized it was stupid stuff like this that I missed about Ava. *Bubkes.*

"I guess you probably heard about my Halloween party," she said, yanking open the front door.

I had to give her credit. At least she came out and said it. "Yeah. Why didn't you invite me?"

"Because . . ." The door shut behind us so we were alone in the foyer. "Because I knew you wouldn't like it. You wouldn't fit in."

Translation: I was not much of a partier. "Still, you could have asked. I'd have asked you."

"Oh, really?" Her attitude seemed to shift with her hip. "Like you ever invite me along when you're hanging out with Bea and Neerja."

"I *used* to, but you turned me down so many times I didn't see the point. Besides, aren't we too boring for you now?"

She closed her eyes, as if counting for patience. "Anyway, seems to me your Halloween turned out all right. A little bird told me one of your trick-or-treaters was Will Blake."

How did she know? "Yeah. So?"

Ava licked her lower lip. "You like him?"

I was about to issue the standard nondenial denials, but she knew me too well. "Don't even try it, Dubois. I know you do. The question is, does he like you?"

Schultz and Mrs. Wently were marching down the hall, coming to monitor the tardies. Ava glanced at them, then me, and casually leaned against the door. "Look at you. Look how terrified you are about being late."

We had only seconds to go. It wasn't an issue of being terrified; it was an issue of being forced to do detention. "Stop it." I tried to reach the door, but she inched over to block me.

"Not until you tell me what's going on with you and Will."

"Nothing's going on with me and Will. And what do you care?"

"I don't. I'm just curious. New guy skips my party to spend Halloween with you, a person wonders."

Schultz rapped her knuckles on the glass. "You're keeping the door closed," she barked—as if we didn't know.

Ava grinned, daring me to make a move. "Why don't you and I leave right now? Just blow off homeroom and first period. What will happen? Will the world as we know it come to an end?"

Schultz rapped on the door. "Open this!" she shouted through the glass.

"Could be fun." Ava raised a brow. "A change of pace from the rat race."

For a flash, for one crazy second, I wanted to turn and run, to see the shocked expression on Schultz's face as Ava and I headed across the parking lot to wherever it was she went when she skipped class. But this, I knew, wouldn't solve the problem Parad faced of being an unknown. This would just make me a slacker.

There was a clunk as Mrs. Wently leaned on the door and shoved it open, sending Ava flying. "There," she said, smoothing down her flowered jumper. "Now, if you don't mind, girls, you have exactly one second before the bell rings."

Schultz studied Ava and me as we moved past them into the lobby. I could tell she was trying to understand our connection and why I would be hanging out with someone who repeatedly violated school rules when I was supposedly a good student who never, for example, cheated.

It didn't help that in homeroom I was forced to overhear Maddie and Sienna rehash the "sick" Halloween party at Ava's house and what a blast it was and all the wild stuff B.K. and Parker did. How student rep Jim Mullet, the straightest guy in the senior class, Mr. Upstanding, actually poured gas on the bonfire and everyone nearly got burned to a crisp. And how the fire department would have come if Parker Forbes hadn't called his uncle, who called someone in the police department and told them it was under control. It was insane!

Where is a deus ex machina when you need one?

Then they returned to sliding Maddie's phone back and forth, debating the merits of sequins versus seed pearls and off-white versus ivory, while I finished my assigned reading in *Jane Eyre*, though I'd already gone way past the required chapter since I had my doubts about this dude Rochester and what was up with his attic.

Suddenly the phone stopped under my nose. "Hey," Sienna said. "Aren't you the girl who was caught cheating with Mike?"

Took her long enough to get that.

Maddie snapped her fingers. "Yeah. It was definitely her."

Dog-earing *Jane Eyre*, I said, "I'm not 'the girl' and I'm not an 'it.' I'm Gigi and I've been sitting between you two in homeroom for eight weeks, not to mention going to school with you for almost eleven years. How hard is it to remember my name? I remember yours."

Sienna wrinkled her nose, like she'd just smelled something bad. "Don't get so pissy. *You're* the one who doesn't talk to us. You're always reading or doing homework, pretending like we don't exist."

Really? "No, I don't."

Maddie said, "Uh-huh."

"Einstein!"

The three of us turned to the doorway, where Mike was in the hall, waving.

I pointed at the clock. Five minutes until the bell for first period. He could wait. Anyway, what was it with everyone suddenly trying to get me to cut class?

"Hi, Mike!" Sienna trilled.

He flashed her a smile and then put his hands together in a prayer, squeezing his eyes tight as if his life depended on me meeting him then and there. *Puh-leeze,* he mouthed.

"I think he wants something," Sienna said. Then added with slight surprise, "I think he wants you!"

Oh, all right. Gathering my stuff, I slid past Mrs. Andres, absorbed in grading papers, and met Mike in the hall.

He immediately pinned me against a wall. "Einstein. Oh, Einstein. Oh, beautiful beacon of academic excellence. You are my only savior."

I remained unfazed. "What?" I slipped underneath his arm and headed toward chem.

He quick-stepped to my side. "Look, I met with the coach this morning and he's wicked pissed. That letter in the file saying we'd been referred to Schultz for cheating? It's major, major bad. It might kill my chances of getting a scholarship to Amherst."

"Hello? And you're just realizing this?"

"I thought it was bogus. You know, like getting a warning from the cops for speeding. But I was wrong." He was so upset, he began running a hand through his longish dark hair. "I feel bad because you're going down too. I blame myself for this, Einstein."

At last a confession! "Finally."

"I mean, I can't help it that you're madly in love with me and just had to show me your answer."

"Mike Ipolito!" I quit walking and faced him, furious.

He was laughing himself silly. "Gotcha."

I gave him a shove. "You didn't even meet with the coach, did you?" I pushed him again. "You're not worried at all about Amherst, right?"

He held up his hands in surrender. "Easy, Einstein. I'm just having fun. How did that rumor start, anyway?"

"Like you don't know."

The first bell went off, doors flew open, and we had to brace ourselves against a stampede. Mike said, "Didn't come from me. Where did you hear it?"

"Ava."

He winced. "The woman in black. Man, she threw a boring party. You should be glad you didn't go."

"That's not what Sienna said." Though I was secretly glad. "I understand Jim Mullet nearly set Ava's house on fire."

"Yeah. That was kind of, um, interesting." He shrugged and slung his pack over his shoulder as we walked toward Buzzard's room. "So, when do you want to work on this project?"

"After school sometime this week. Soccer practice is winding down, right?" Since no one expected them to make it past the semifinals.

"Yeah, but then I've got ski team drylands."

"Sounds like a T. S. Eliot poem."

To my surprise, he picked up on the reference. "That's

The Waste Land. Awful pun." He elbowed my side. "And when it comes to drylands, April's not the cruelest month, November is because we have to train for our first Alpine race in the beginning of December—without any snow. We get, at the most, two practices on manmade crap if we're lucky. Hey, you don't ski, do you?"

"Why should I when you make it sound so appealing?"

"Because Coach is looking for girls. We're two short of an official girls' team, which means the four senior girls can race, but their scores won't qualify. Sucks to be them."

The only person I knew who skied was Bea, but her parents were dead set against her joining the team after her brother got into a snowboarding accident that nearly left him paralyzed. Now, just mentioning skiing or boarding or, God forbid, racing sends them into a tizzy.

Still, Mike's suggestion might just solve Bea's Parad problem. What better way to make a name for herself than by saving the girls' ski team?

"How about Sunday?" Mike was saying.

"Huh?"

"Sunday to start the project. I'll come by your house sometime in the afternoon."

The second bell went off. "Sure. And we should talk about going to the school board and appealing the cheating policy. I don't think those board members had any idea how stupid that policy was when they voted on it."

"You're my hero, Einstein." And without seeming to give it any thought, he absently squeezed my arm and strolled into chem.

That afternoon, in the downstairs girls' room, Neerja finished filling in her lips with professional red lip color, dramatic makeup left over from Parad's stash when she was acting in Cambridge community theater.

"I'm not sure Drew's ready for a Bollywood Juliet," Neerja fretted, maniacally brushing her hair.

Drew was our drama director, a thin, highly excitable English teacher who wore striped sweaters and tended to throw hissy fits during dress rehearsals.

"Are you nuts?" I said. "Who *wouldn't* want a Bollywood Juliet?"

"According to Parad, every high school drama department. That's why Parad stuck to community theater and didn't even bother auditioning for school productions."

"Parad never tried out for a play in high school because she was scared to bomb in front of her class," Bea said. "Nothing against your big sister, but you're the perfect Juliet, Neerja. You're innocent and sweet and Drew is *not* going to love you unless you quit stalling and try out." She yanked the hairbrush from Neerja's hand. "Now, go break a head."

"A leg, you mean," I said, laughing.

Bea said, "Whatever."

Good old Henry was standing by the auditorium doors waiting for us. Or, maybe he was waiting for Lindsay since he was all spiffy in a new North Face jacket and a shaggy haircut he must have gotten over the weekend. Gone was his bowl of brown hair along with his trademark white ankle socks. He wore dark jeans, a wide navy-and-white-striped Henley, and sneakers. He looked totally normal, not at all like a math geek. Even the calculator that usually peeked out of his pocket was missing. A first.

"Wow, Henry," Neerja said. "You look so . . . *kempt.*"

This cracked them up. Sometimes being around Neerja and Henry was like hanging out with identical twins who've developed their own language.

"Lindsay's supposedly on her way," he said, leading us to a bunch of seats in the third row, an empty one next to Justin reserved by Henry's backpack.

"Thanks," Neerja whispered, sitting.

I sat one seat over from Henry in case Lindsay arrived, though the chances of her sitting between us were slim. The theater was surprisingly empty considering it was *Romeo and Juliet.*

Justin said that was because with football and soccer season ending and basketball and hockey starting up, it was hard to get students to commit to the play. Plus a lot of people thought Shakespeare was dull and old-fashioned, as opposed to the spring musical, which was fun. Last year it was *Grease* and it was so popular, Drew had to turn away over fifty kids who didn't get parts.

Yes, I could see how playing Danny Zuko, a semi-illiterate motor head, would pale in comparison to playing a passionate Italian who professes his undying love in alternating iambic pentameter.

"There she is," Henry hissed as Lindsay walked in with Marissa Brewster.

Lindsay was the quintessential gymnast—petite, muscular, and slightly hyper. She tended to wear her hair in a messy knot at the top of her head, possibly to make herself seem taller. Not only was she super-friendly and cheerful, she didn't seem to possess the slightest inkling of insecurity. She was happy and smiling wherever she went.

She glanced briefly at Henry, waved merrily, and sat in the first row.

Henry let out a sigh. Neerja turned around and whispered, "I'll bet she doesn't want to appear too obvious."

So much so, I thought, that she sat two rows away.

"People, people." Drew bounded onstage and started clapping for our attention. "A couple of ground rules for you newcomers and then let's get started." He proceeded to explain that because of the incredibly short practice time—only twenty-seven actual days—we should leave now if we couldn't give *Romeo and Juliet* our full attention. Also, he seemed very eager for us to understand that we were not to show up on his doorstep or have our parents call to complain or—God forbid—drop out of the play if we ended up with a small part.

"There are no small parts," he said. "Just small people."

This was not entirely true, as I whispered to Henry and Neerja. There must also be small people with small parts. "Think Munchkins."

Henry laughed.

Not Neerja. All this talk about giving "one hundred and ten percent" and not dropping out and small parts versus small people was spiking her anxiety. I could tell because she started twirling her hair and crossing her legs and jiggling them. If she auditioned in this state, she'd end up as some nonspeaking member of the chorus instead of the nurse or the mother or even Juliet herself.

Or, worse, she wouldn't be cast at all.

"Don't think about it," I said to her as everyone made their way to the stage for warm-ups. "Don't think about Parad or Drew or . . . Justin."

She bit her lip. "It's harder that he's here. What if . . ."

"Shhh. The only 'what if' you should be thinking

about is what if you can't get enough tickets for your huge family for opening night." But not even poking fun at the 1,456 members of the extended Padwami clan could get her to crack a smile. "I know. Pretend you're in your backyard with Henry that summer you acted out 'The Three Billy Goats Gruff.'"

"'The Three Little Pigs,'" she corrected.

"Pigs. Gruff goats. Same difference. The point is, put yourself *there*. Not here. And you'll do fine."

During warm-ups we did so much bending and stretching and mirroring that I was beginning to wonder if I'd accidentally wandered into a yoga class.

Finally, that torture was over and we were allowed to return to our seats while Drew called students to the stage. Since this was going to be slow going, I decided to get a head start on my chem homework and pulled out Mr. Buzzard's questions for the end of the chapter: *1. Describe the bonding process of ionized atoms.*

This, I knew from my reading, was a trick question since the electrons around atoms that have been ionized are free floating and, therefore, too wishy-washy to bond. I like to think of ionized atoms as the cute and popular guys of the nuclear world. Witty and zippy, but hard to nail down in a permanent commitment.

I'd just finished explaining why ionized atoms can't bond when I heard Drew calling my name. Uh-oh.

Couldn't he call someone else first? Perhaps someone who, you know, knew how to act.

Neerja crossed her fingers. "You can do this."

No, I couldn't. Already I could feel my stomach churning as I climbed the few steps up to the stage. The lights were so bright. The audience was so dark. Thankfully, I hadn't eaten lunch. This was why.

Drew handed me a script. "Gigi, I'd like you to start with Lady Capulet."

Okay, Gigi. Focus. Concentrate on the reading. The scene is the night before Juliet sneaks off to marry Romeo. Her mother thinks Juliet's agreed to marry Paris and can't figure out why Juliet's up and rummaging around her closet. Simple enough. Play the nagging mother.

Breathing deeply, I tried to straighten my posture and channel an Italian noblewoman. The butterflies would have to calm down. This was for Neerja.

"Whenever you're ready, Gigi," Drew said.

"What?" I announced. "Are you busy . . . ho?"

"Ho?" laughed someone in the audience. It might have been Justin.

Drew said, "There's some punctuation you might want to follow, Lady Capulet. Makes all the difference between Shakespearean English and, shall we say, a rap song."

Rereading the line, I definitely understood his point. "'What, are you busy ho?'"

He winced. "The 'ho' is supposed to be an exhortation. As in, let's get a move on. Not 'ho' as in the urban slang 'ho.' Once more, please."

I did it again, but my voice shook so much that Drew said, "Is this your first time onstage?"

"Kind of."

"Well, try to relax and read the line again."

"Can we just drop the ho?" I suggested. "We could substitute something else. An 'or not,' perhaps? Like, 'Are you busy . . . or not?' Or maybe cut it out altogether."

Drew blanched and reached for his bottled water, taking a good healthy swig. "Dear lord, no. It's Shakespeare. We don't substitute or cut the greatest poet in the English language." Swallowing hard, he added, "You may go back to your seat, Gigi. Thank you."

This always happens. Once I start public speaking, teachers cut me off and send me back to my seat. Though I'm not going to lie. It was a huge relief to get off that stage.

"Good job." Neerja forced a smile.

"No, it wasn't. I blew."

"You didn't. You just brought your own . . . *interpretation*."

It was a lie, but I didn't care because my acting flop had soothed Neerja's jitters. She'd quit twirling her hair and was visibly relaxed as Lindsay read her part. Few things take the edge off your own nervousness like realizing you can't go lower than your stupendously sucky friend.

Hey, somebody's got to set the bar low.

Next up was Henry, who pulled off a pretty impressive Friar, and then it was Neerja's turn. I quickly reached over and unraveled the knots in her hair. "You're going to hit it out of the park. I just know it."

Henry came up the aisle and stood at the end of our row as Neerja slid out. "Tell you what. Halfway through, I'll have you paged to the office so you can escape."

She punched him on the shoulder. "Don't you dare, Muscles."

"And Justin Crenshaw." Drew shielded his eyes to scan the audience. "Justin, I'd like you to read Romeo."

Oh my god. It was a Neerja Padwami fantasy come true. Her as Juliet. Him as Romeo. Henry gave a knowing wink.

"Romeo!" Drew cupped his hands to his mouth. "Wherefore art thou, Romeo?"

Justin ran up as Neerja rocked on her heels, the script behind her back. Justin joined her, panting.

"Neerja Padwami," Drew said, reading over her questionnaire. "You're not, by any chance, Parad Padwami's sister, are you?"

You could see Neerja shrink. All through school, teachers had been asking her if she was related to Parad Padwami. And always they said the same stupid line, which Drew promptly repeated.

"Well, if you're half as talented as your older sister, you'll do very well. I remember seeing her play Scout with the Cambridge Players and she was simply arresting."

Then Drew explained they were going to read the same passage Lindsay had just read, the garden scene, and instructed Justin to give Neerja the lead-in.

Justin read, "'When he bestrides the lazy-pacing clouds and sails upon the bosom of the air.'"

This was Neerja's cue to utter the most famous line in Romeo and Juliet: "*O, Romeo, Romeo. Wherefore art thou Romeo?*" But all she did was open her mouth and cough.

We waited.

Drew stroked his chin. "Something caught in your throat, Neerja?"

Neerja shut her jaw and shook her head.

"She's scared," Henry said under his breath. His fingers tightened over the armrests.

He was right. I knew that look. I knew that *feeling*. Neerja wanted to speak, but she was afraid that whatever she said would be so wrong Drew would automatically reject her. It was safer to say nothing at all.

"Once more, Justin, please." Drew nodded encouragingly at Neerja.

Again, Justin read the line and again the same reaction—Neerja froze. Eyes wide. Mouth opening and closing like a hooked bass. She'd been spooked. Maybe it was Drew's comment about her being Parad's younger sister or maybe it was that she'd never auditioned for a play before or maybe it was . . .

Justin.

Yes. From the way she was gaping at him, I knew that had to be it and that Neerja would never get through the garden scene if she had to pledge her love to a guy from whom she was hiding her mega intense crush.

Pulling out my cell, I quickly texted Bea in the library, Henry's off-the-cuff remark to Neerja having sparked an ingenious idea.

Call Justin 2 the office. ASAP.

One second later, Bea texted back: Y

Splain later. Now!
Ok. On it.

I tapped my fingers, counting the seconds. If Bea didn't act fast, Drew might dismiss Neerja before she got a chance to audition.

"What's going on?" Henry asked, gesturing to the phone in my hand.

"Something. Just be ready to take Justin's part, okay?"

It might already have been too late. Drew was asking Neerja if she'd like to try one last time and Neerja was hesitating. I had to create some sort of distraction, a noisy disturbance that would buy us time. I couldn't yell "Fire!" because, as Bea's always telling me, it's illegal to yell "Fire" in a theater, though she never said anything about yelling . . .

"Mouse!" I screamed, hopping out of my chair and then onto it. "A mouse!"

"A mouse?" screamed Lindsay.

"It was right by my ankles. It ran over my foot. I think it's headed toward you."

Lindsay also jumped on her chair. Henry looked up at me like I was insane. "There's no . . ."

I glared at him. Hard.

"Oooh. I think I saw it," echoed Marissa Brewster, who got down on her hands and knees and started crawling in the aisle, searching. "Here, mousy, mousy. I won't hurt you."

"People! People!" Drew called from the stage. "May I remind you that I specifically asked for quiet during auditions."

"But there's a mouse!" Lindsay yelled. "It's crawling around our ankles. It could bite us and give us rabies."

Highly doubtful.

"JUSTIN CRENSHAW. PLEASE COME TO THE

OFFICE FOR AN EMERGENCY PHONE CALL.
JUSTIN CRENSHAW."

Yes! Finally. Though . . . *emergency* phone call. Shoot.
She might have gone too far.

"What do I do?" Justin asked Drew.

Drew shrugged. "What can you do? Take the call."

Throwing down the script, Justin jumped off the
stage. Drew turned his attention back to Neerja. "And
how about you? What would you like to do?"

"I don't know," Neerja said. "I lost my Romeo."

I gave Henry a poke. "Read for Justin."

"Wha . . . ? Oh, yeah." Henry raised his hand. "I can
read Romeo."

Drew blinked into the audience. "Well, Neerja? It
seems we have a volunteer in one Henry Filomen."

"That'd be fine," she said, nodding vigorously. "Henry
and I have acted together before. We're next-door neighbors."

"All righty then. Henry, come on up."

Lindsay, still on her chair, said, "What about the
mouse? Don't we need to call security or the janitor or
the cops or something?"

"Oh, I have the feeling the mouse followed Justin
down to the office," Drew drawled, as Henry picked up
where Justin left off and Neerja proceeded to read beautifully.

Whew. With that crisis averted, I texted Bea: Thnx.

Bea texted back: OMG. In bsmnt boys' room. Come quick!

I stared at the letters, not quite comprehending why she'd be in the boys' bathroom. Y?

To which I received a one-word reply:

hot-o-meter

Eight

Sure enough, on the far wall of the stinky boys' blue bathroom, between a row of disgusting white urinals and the paper towel dispenser, was a crude drawing done in red Sharpie of a meter rating all the girls in the tenth-grade class from *ice cold* to *lukewarm* to *smokin'*. Technically, it wasn't so much a meter as a thermometer, like the Project Graduation one outside our school. Hardly original.

"So you were in the office to page Justin when you heard them talking about this?" I did a quick once-over looking for my name. You know, out of curiosity. Not that I cared or anything.

"Yeah. Mrs. Wently was radioing the janitor, asking

him to clean it off the wall," Bea said. "I wanted to see for myself if it really was as bad as she claimed."

"It's pretty bad. It's going to tick off a lot of girls."

"Not Sienna. I can't believe she's in first place." Bea pointed to Sienna Martin's name, from which rose red wavy lines of steam, as if there was any doubt she was the hottest. "I definitely would have put Phoebe Ballard there."

"Really?" I wasn't so sure. Sienna had those big golf-ball eyes and that thick, brown, straight hair boys seem to crave.

Running a finger down the list, being careful not to make physical contact with the cruddy tile, Bea said, "You know, I don't think we're even on here, you, me, and Neerja. I think they left us off!"

"Good!" Though, privately, I was kind of insulted. Not that I wanted my name to be displayed on the grossest bathroom at Denton High or that I gave one wit about being ranked by mentally challenged Neanderthals. But I had to admit it would have been nice to have been nominated.

Bea, however, was upset. I could tell because she suddenly became very quiet. Bea never shuts up unless her feelings are hurt.

I did a double check to make sure she hadn't missed us. "You know whoever drew this was a total misogynistic moron, right?"

"Right, however . . ." She stood and folded her arms. "It's the Parad yearbook thing all over again. It's like we don't exist, Gigi. We bust our butts and participate in class and get these great grades and yet, we're . . . invisible."

I was trying to summon a reassuring response when the door flew open and Ava stormed in along with Lilla Dimarco and Janelle Colone. "So, it's true." Ava put her hands on her hips and shook her head in outrage. "Those idiots. It doesn't even look like a thermometer. Looks like a test tube drawn by a two-year-old."

Janelle pointed at her name near the low end of *smokin'*. "There I am!"

"That's nothing to brag about," Ava said.

"You're a *lukewarm*, Ava," Lilla said, adding somewhat somberly, "so am I."

"Geesh. Would you listen to yourselves?" Bea threw up her hands. "It's like you give a damn. You're ranked on a freaking bathroom wall. It's degrading and repulsive and maddening." She was so pissed, you'd have never guessed that two seconds before she'd just been whining about being excluded.

"And where are you, Beatrice?" Ava asked.

Bea snapped her mouth closed.

"Apparently we're too hot for the hot-o-meter," I said. "Our hotness is off the charts."

Ava grinned. "Yeah, right. I'm thinking, not."

* * *

Neerja was kind of worried because the excuse Bea had invented to persuade Mrs. Wently to call Justin to the office was that his dog had just been hit by a car—especially since Justin's dog apparently had survived a brush with automotive death mere days before.

But since we figured Justin would never connect the dots, Bea and I were confident it would blow over. At least we hoped. Neerja would have died if Justin found out we'd rigged the whole thing just to get him off stage so she wouldn't be so nervous.

"What's the difference between a monopoly and a trust?" I asked Bea as we spent fifth period in the honors lounge while a miserable autumn drizzle ran down the one window. I was completing our take-home history exam on the Industrial Revolution while Bea procrastinated.

"Monopoly is a board game," she said, flipping through her magazine. "Trust is what you hope you have in your tampon."

Somehow I didn't think that was the answer our American Studies teacher, Mr. Crow, expected.

Bea should have been working on the Industrial Revolution exam too. Instead, she was busy attacking the Hollywood crossword in the back of *Us* magazine, fully aware that the exam was due on Crow's desk the next morning before homeroom. Knowing Bea, she probably wouldn't start it until midnight and, even then, would be finishing the last couple of questions on the way to school. Anything sooner, in her opinion, was for amateurs.

"I was talking to Mike," I began, jotting down my definition for *trust*. "And he said if Jerry Mahoney doesn't get two more girls on the ski team this year, they won't be able to qualify for races."

"Huh." Bea flipped to an article about the new hot color for fall: Spiced Rum. "Since when is rum a color?"

"I almost told him about you."

She slid her eyes sideways. "That would have been a mistake."

"Really?" I put down my pencil. "Mike says the girls on the team now are all seniors. If you start racing as a sophomore, Bea, you could be the captain by next year."

She twirled her finger. "Whoop. Dee. Do."

"Come on, Bea. You're an awesome skier."

"I'm not going to join, Gigi, so you might as well forget it. You know how my parents wouldn't let my brother race Alpine and I'm not even half as good a skier as he was. They sure as heck aren't going to let me sign up, especially not after George's accident."

"Yeah, but George's accident wasn't skiing, it was snowboarding." And, I was tempted to add, with all due respect to her brother's athletic prowess, he got hurt because he'd

(a) lacked experience, and (b) was hot-dogging. From what Bea'd told me, he'd made it over the edge of the pipe and then failed to properly revolve 360 degrees. It was more like 270, and he landed smack on his back.

Ow!

Those first days in the hospital everyone was worried that he'd be half paralyzed. He wasn't, thank God. He's actually fine now because of his one sensible move— wearing a helmet.

Even so, Bea's parents went crazy. The day after the accident, Mr. Honeycutt gathered all the family snow equipment—the skis, the boards, the sleds, even the ice skates—and dumped them at Goodwill. A week later, he filed a lawsuit against the ski area, claiming they should have closed down the half-pipe sooner in the day.

That's why Bea hasn't skied in years even though she was so good when she was younger that her parents honestly thought of sending her to one of those snobby ski schools where kids train for the Olympics and do hardly any homework.

It's a major shame, in my opinion. If Bea were skiing now, she'd be a much happier person.

I was about to tell her I'd join if she did when in walked Neerja. She slid her backpack onto the table with a thump. "I've got big news."

"You got Juliet in the play," I said as she threw herself

on the ratty honors lounge couch.

"No. Cast list doesn't go up until Friday after Drew's left school for the day and can't be reached. I'm talking about Jim Mullet and what happened at Ava's Halloween party."

All I knew about Jim Mullet and Ava's Halloween party was what I'd overheard from Sienna and Maddie, that he'd doused a bonfire with gasoline and nearly set off an explosion. Anyone else would have been ripped a new one, but Jim was one of those squeaky-clean guys who never got caught. Or maybe, as student rep to the school board, he was able to pull some strings. "Don't tell me he got in trouble for that."

"Ooooh, yeah." She blew aside her bangs. "Someone shot him on their cell phone holding a beer and—"

Whhhhzzzz. Bea stuck her pencil in the electric sharpener and blew on the tip. "So what? There's always drinking at Halloween bonfires."

"*And,*" Neerja continued, "the pictures of Jim drinking were texted to the entire universe. Schultz found out this morning and now Mullet's been kicked off the school board. What an idiot, huh?"

"He definitely made a *bad choice*," I said, since whenever kids were caught drinking, our old principal, Mr. Watson, used to say they'd made "bad choices." The phrase was now something of a school joke.

"This is what I don't get about guys like Jim," Bea said. "Why let people take photos of you breaking the law? Might as well turn yourself in for criminal stupidity." She sipped her Coke. "Remember the cheerleader thing freshman year? They actually posted photos of themselves partying on Facebook. How stupid was that?"

"At least they didn't tell someone their dog died," Neerja said.

Bea set her jaw. "Get over it, Neerja."

"No harm done," I said quickly, before those two got into a tiff. "His dog's okay, right?"

Neerja rolled her eyes. "I suppose. Anyway, here's the thing about Jim, the reason I came in here. Mrs. Greene and I were talking just now, Gigi, and we think you should run to take Jim Mullet's place as student rep."

I was shocked. Being on the school board was the last thing on my agenda. Why would Mrs. Greene, the librarian, want me to do that?

"Looks good on your resume," Bea said. "Colleges love that kind of civic involvement stuff. Shows you're willing to be active beyond the school, that you're into the community and all."

"Also," Neerja said, "if you were a voting member of the school board, you could get that cheating policy changed. You could get that letter removed from your file."

"She has a point," Bea agreed.

I couldn't argue with her logic. I'd have a far better chance of changing the policy if I were on the board instead of just another student complaining about unfairness.

On the other hand, being a student rep would probably require the dreaded public speaking and, as usual, simply the prospect of getting up in front of a crowd—especially with the torturous *Romeo and Juliet* audition still fresh in my mind—triggered a wave of nausea that had me reaching for my own Diet Coke. I took a deep swallow and my stomach loosened. "I don't know. . . ."

"*Hot-o-meter.*" Bea twirled her pencil and arched her eyebrow. We didn't like to mention Parad's yearbook in front of Neerja, but I knew Bea was thinking this too. "Nothing ventured, nothing gained."

She was right. It was like I had come to a fork in the road. I could either take the safe, well-lit path that led to an existence of total obscurity or I could risk the dark, rutted road filled with unknowns. The unknown road would mean facing my greatest fear—getting up in front of a live audience—but it could save me from wasting four years of high school too.

Don't think, a voice urged. *Do!*

"Okay," I blurted. "I'll do it. I'll run for student rep."

"Excellent!" Neerja exclaimed.

"On one condition."

Bea cocked her head. "No way."

I shot my finger at her. "Bingo. You sign up for the ski team."

"Wee!" Neerja squealed, giving a little clap. "See, it's all coming together. I'm going out for the play. Bea's going out for the ski team."

"I didn't say that," Bea quickly corrected.

"But they need two more girls to make a team," Neerja said. "It's the perfect opportunity."

Bea narrowed her green eyes. "Wait. Have you and Gigi been talking behind my back?"

"Of course," Neerja said. "We talk about you behind your back all the time, duh."

"Unfortunately," I added, "you've been really boring lately. Which is why you need to join the team so we'll have something to talk about."

"Seriously," Neerja said, "I've been thinking about this a lot. And my conclusion is that the only way we'll get the most out of high school is if we go for it."

The first bell rang. We didn't move. "I could break my leg," Bea said.

"You could break your leg falling down your stairs at home," I said. "Look at me. If I run, I'm almost guaranteed to barf on some podium or faint or pee my pants."

Neerja wrinkled her nose.

"What I'm saying," I went on, wondering where I'd come up with that one, "is nothing worthwhile comes easy." I'd read that somewhere. Maybe on the back of the Pop-Tarts box. "This is probably the advantage of being stupid. Stupid people just do. We tend to overthink. If we could eliminate the 'over' and just think, then we could do, too. Only we'd be smarter doers because we'd be thinkers. Does that make sense?"

We thought about this, not saying a word.

Finally, Bea said, "You know, why not us? We're the smartest people in our class, and there's no reason we shouldn't be ruling this school instead of being locked up in . . ." She looked around the bare room. "Here."

Neerja said, "I'm so sick of here. I want to be out there."

"Me too," I agreed, taking her hand. Neerja reached for Bea's, and Bea reached for mine, so we ended up making a somewhat dorky circle. I could feel our pulses quickening, our hands getting hot, at the prospect of facing bodily injury and total massive public humiliation.

"You guys are my best friends," I said. "The best friends in the world. And I'm pretty sure that if we decide to do something, we can do it with each other's help."

"Dude," Bea said. "So true. I say we go for it. Ski team. Student rep. The play. Gigi's right. Let's not think and, for once, just *do*."

We squeezed our hands together. We could do this. We *had* to. Because high school only comes around once, and I would hate to look back and think I didn't make the most of every moment because I was scared of what other people thought. Other people never think that much about you anyway.

Eleanor Roosevelt said that.

Nine

It was done.

Before Bea could wiggle out of it, Neerja and I dragged her down to the gym, where she signed up for the ski team, and then they led me kicking and screaming (okay, not really, but close) to the front office, where I informed Mrs. Wently that I wished to submit my name as a candidate for student rep. My palms were sweating so hard, they left a mark on the black counter.

She handed me a printout of the Dos and Don'ts when running for a class office. (*DO promote school spirit. DON'T stoop to name calling.*) The election would be as soon as possible, she said, so I should start campaigning now.

"It's great to see so much enthusiasm," she added.

"Who else is running?" Bea asked.

"My lips are sealed. Dr. Schultz will make an announcement at the pep rally. Until then, I've been sworn to secrecy."

"We have got to kick into high gear," Bea said as we left the office. "The whole enchilada. Stickers, lots of stickers, in hot pink with VOTE 4 GIGI in glittering black plastered on every locker. Signs. Freebies. Handouts. By the time I'm through, yours will be the only name anyone will remember."

"I like 'Gaga for Gigi,'" Neerja said. "It has a certain rhythm."

I liked it too. "I'm just surprised people are running for this. As far as student elections go, class president is big, but who cares about being a student rep on the school board? No way would I have been interested if it hadn't been for this cheating thing."

Bea had this one all figured out. "Makes sense. It's a month or so before college applications are due and people are panicking because their resumes are thin." She sniffed. "But don't you worry, Gigi. With me running your campaign, you're gonna stand out like a hooker at a Girl Scout camp."

On second thought, maybe I should get Neerja to take over.

At home, I tried to put my jitters to rest. I helped Marmie make dinner—garlic soup with French bread, a crisp salad, and pears for dessert. I fed Petunia and called my mother in Zurich, though she was half-asleep and could barely mumble "Love you" before hanging up.

As for whether or not I'd told Mom about the cheating thing, the answer was a resounding no. Mom is all for me being independent and on my own until she decides I'm on an unfair playing field that's not tilted in my direction. Then, it's like she turns into a demon. If she had any idea that Buzzard had accused me of copying off Mike and that Schultz refused to remove the letter of referral from my file, she'd be on the next plane from Switzerland with chocolate in her bag and justice on her mind.

This is why sometimes it's better if parents don't hear about every little problem in your life. You know, for their own sanity.

Having finished my Latin and math, I took a quick shower, wrapped my hair in a towel, smeared a nice cooling green mint and aloe mask on my face, and slipped into my pretty clothes. I went downstairs, made a cup of hot chocolate, grabbed my box of Raisinets, and settled down in bed to watch an episode of *Bones* on my computer. This is how I treat myself when I've finished a ton of homework. Raisinets and *Bones*. A killer combination for unwinding and forgetting about school and things like running for student rep and cheating referrals.

Poor Bea, I thought, nibbling the chocolate coating off a Raisinet. Just pulling out her history exam and getting started on explaining the Industrial Revolution, while here I am drooling over David Boreanz.

I picked up my phone and sent her a text:

Raisinets + pretty clothes + Bones = happiness

She sent one right back.

I. Hate. You.

This episode was one of my favorites. Two kids come across what appears to be a spaceship buried in the ground with a dead alien inside. Bones, of course, has her doubts about the alien because aliens—news flash!—don't exist. Bones is, in short, my hero. She is like a one-woman marketing campaign for smart girls.

My fingers tiptoed to the box of Raisinets as Bones became trapped underground. I cannot watch anything suspenseful without my Raisinets, and not from one of those puny grocery store boxes, either. I require the over-size yellow ones you get at the theater for like six bucks; otherwise it's just not the same.

My fingers found the box. I turned it upside down and shook out . . .

. . . nothing.

Dragging my gaze away from the screen, I checked the box again. It was empty, all right. And slightly damp from saliva.

Basset saliva.

"Petunia?" I poked the sleeping thief, who turned out to be a pillow.

As for my thieving basset, she was on the floor, retching. Her head was bobbing up and down and her eyeballs looked like they were about to pop out of their sockets. She was the spitting image of that rubber doll you squeeze.

Some dogs are allergic to chocolate and can actually die. Mine is not. This is because twenty minutes after pigging out, she gets sick.

"NO!" Right on my piles of not-quite-clean-almost-dirty clothes. I was saving those!

Without a moment to spare, I shoved my feet into my blue flats and dragged her by the collar out of my room and down the stairs, throwing open wide the front door as the two of us scrambled into the cold, windy night. The door slammed behind me—of course—and I knew without even trying the knob that I was locked out.

Beautiful.

It was almost 2 a.m., I was in nothing but my ugly pretty clothes, my face was covered in a green mask, the house was locked up like a fortress, and my grandmother, who takes out her hearing aids when she goes to bed, was dead to the world.

Also, this was not something I wanted to mention earlier, but I had yet to start my latest essay on *Jane Eyre*. I know, I know. I should have finished it before watching *Bones*, but in my defense, I usually can crank out an English essay in a couple of hours. Not if I've been sleeping on the front porch clutching a barfing basset on a cold and windy November night, though.

Speaking of which, where was she? I shielded my eyes and peered into the dark.

Petunia was gone.

And I mean *gone*. Hounds aren't like normal dogs that might stray to the end of the block to run after a cat and then turn around. Hounds are born wanderers. If their nose catches a scent and they're off the leash, look out. They may not return for days, weeks, even months—if ever. Don't even talk to me about electric dog collars. Hounds have been known to brave the zap of electricity in pursuit of the elusive rabbit, squirrel, or generic member of the rodent family. (Though technically, rabbits aren't rodents, they're lagomorphs. They have a closer genetic relation to horses than mice.)

"Petunia!" I called softly, so as not to wake the neighbors. *"Petunia!"*

There was a rustle up ahead by the Andersons' compost pile and a white tip of a tail zoomed by. There she went, that rascal, sneaking into the Garcias' backyard. For a fat schlub who can barely lift herself off the couch, she could sure hightail it when she wanted to.

I had no choice but to yank the towel off my head and run after her, my flats slapping the ground as I dashed up the dark and desolate street, wriggling over fences and around kids' swing sets, trying to keep it quiet so I didn't alarm the neighbors. The fronts of my flannels were becoming muddy and grass-stained. The edges of my favorite flats got tinged black with grime. My nose became so cold it started to drip snot, but I didn't dare stop, lest I lose Petunia forever.

Finally, I turned the corner and spied that white-tipped tail of hers slipping under someone's back porch. Now I was presented with an even more daunting challenge since no way was I crawling under a stranger's porch where there could be cobwebs. For where there are cobwebs, there are spiders.

"Petunia!" I hissed as loudly as I could. "Come out of there, now! You are a bad, bad dog."

Click! A light went on upstairs in the old Victorian house. Right above me, the dark outline of someone appeared in the window while every hair on my arms leaped to attention. The homeowner was up and coming down the stairs after me, turning lights on along the way. Dog or no dog, I had to get out of here before I was arrested for trespassing or, worse, spotted with a green mint-aloe face mask.

Thwack!

I didn't know what happened, actually, but somehow I tripped over a rock and fell flat on my back, onto the driveway. The wind was knocked out of me so I couldn't move, though I could see the front door open and someone come out.

"Hello?" inquired a masculine voice.

I couldn't speak. I tried, but I couldn't. Then the porch light turned on and I had to close my eyes it was so bright.

"Gigi?"

Oh no. Please, no. Please tell me I am not lying spread eagle in my ugly pretty clothes on the driveway belonging to Will Blake.

"It is you, isn't it?"

Frankly, I was surprised he could recognize me, considering my sexy disguise. "How about that tour of Boston?" I managed to say as my lungs recovered. "Might as well get an early start. No traffic."

He came down the steps. "No, really. What are you doing here? It's after midnight."

I tried to stall by brushing off the mask that had dried

to flakes. I wanted to appear sane, really, but it was a hard sell considering my face was peeling green. "Petunia took off after a rabbit or a squirrel or maybe the rest of Aidan's Halloween candy and this is where we ended up. She's under your porch."

"It wasn't a squirrel and Aidan ate all his Halloween candy." Will knelt to peer under the porch. "It was a raccoon, I bet. There was a whole nest of them when we moved in." He crawled in a bit and said, "I think I see her. Lemme go get a flashlight."

Two seconds later, he returned with one of those big industrial things that could signal low-flying planes. "I just want you to know," I said, "that I didn't just dress up to impress you. I'm always this glamorous around the house."

He smiled, sort of. "It's okay, Gigi. I didn't even notice." He clicked on the light and directed the beam to the corner.

I bent halfway and looked too. I'm helpful that way.

"You found that flashlight pretty fast. We can never find stuff when we need it at our house. We had a fire on the stove once and my grandmother tried to put it out with spray cologne, which I definitely don't recommend." *Unless you want to end up like Jim Mullet at the Halloween bonfire.*

"Yeah, well, my dad's former military. A place for

everything and everything in its place." He dove in.

Yuck. I couldn't look, thinking of all those spiders. Also, what if there really was a nest of raccoons? Raccoons fell under the category of deceptively cute animals like koalas or pandas that, given half a chance, would rip your lips off with their sharp teeth and claws.

But, somehow, Will managed to emerge with Petunia waddling right after him, her nose going a mile a minute.

"Did you have food?" I asked, amazed, since Petunia never follows me like that unless I'm carrying, like, a whole ham.

"Got a hot dog. Figured it would help." He fed her the rest and patted her head.

"Do you have a leash?" he asked.

"Odd. Along with a spare key, not to mention decent clothes, I managed to forget the leash."

"Okay. I think I can find a rope." In a flash, he was back again, rope in hand. Also, in sneakers and a hooded sweatshirt. "Thought I should walk you home. My dad would kill me if he found out I let you go back by yourself this late at night."

"That is very gentlemanly and also unnecessary, Mr. Blake. I think I can defend myself against the random Denton housewife in her Cross Country Volvo."

"You sure? Because you never know. There could be another raccoon and Petunia could take off and then where would you be? At least with me around you'll have a secret weapon." He displayed a zip-lock bag holding two hot dogs.

Petunia panted in lust.

"You're kind of like the Pied Piper of hot dogs, huh?" I said as we started walking.

"That's a true story, you know. There really was a Pied Piper who played the flute and lured away a hundred and thirty children in the town of Hamelin back in the thirteenth century, and there might be a connection between those kids and Count Dracula."

"Seriously?" My heart did a little dance. Could this be someone who shares my passion for completely useless trivia?

He went on to explain about the children actually being led away either in a children's crusade or to settle Transylvania. "Possibly the Pied Piper might be a metaphor for the plague or some natural disaster that killed all those kids. But whatever, in June of twelve hundred something, those kids vanished."

As intriguing as this theory was, I quit listening because (a) I couldn't believe any guy my age would admit to knowing about the history behind the Pied Piper of Hamelin, and (b) I couldn't believe any guy my age would use the word *metaphor* in regular conversation.

"So, how're you fitting in at Denton?" I asked after

we'd exhausted the Pied Piper topic. "Feeling any better about the move?"

"I guess. It's a lot easier here, that's for sure. Then again, my old school was really top of the line academically, so it makes sense that I've already done a lot of what you guys are doing."

"Which is why you're in eleventh-grade math with Henry Filomen, our resident math genius."

"Basically. Henry's pretty cool."

"Just don't get him started on Fermat's Last Theorem. He can go on forever."

Will laughed and seemed to relax a bit as he shoved his hands into the pockets of his sweatshirt, his strides long and easy. "Loving *Jane Eyre*, though."

Wait. "*You're* reading *Jane Eyre*?"

"Yeah. So?"

"So we were given the choice, *Jane Eyre* or *Grendel*, and most of the guys in the class chose *Grendel* because it's written by a man and it's about a monster and it's short."

"Eh, I've already read *Grendel* and I've always wanted to read *Jane Eyre*, and I'm glad I chose it. I mean, in one way I think she should let her hair down. Live a little, you know? She's so freaking repressed. She deserves true love."

Heart. Beating.

"Anyway, that's why I was up when you came along. I couldn't put it down until I found out if Jane was running off to India with this St. John dude."

Were I Charlotte Brontë, this is the part where I would break into the story and write: *Reader, can you blame me for falling instantly in love? Mr. Blake not only uses* metaphor *in a sentence and walks me home and doesn't mind coaxing my dog from under the icky porch, but he also openly discusses his admiration for the best book ever written.*

"By the way," he said, as we turned the corner to my house, "I've decided to run for student rep."

To be honest, I was so savoring the presence of being with a cute guy who believed Jane Eyre deserved true love that this stunning announcement didn't really register at first.

"I know I've only been here a few weeks, but I was president of my class in L.A. and I think I have a knack for politics. My uncle's a state senator in Oregon and I worked on his re-election campaign one summer. It was awesome."

Gradually I absorbed what he was saying. Will was running for student rep.

He was running against me.

And, it appeared, so was the universe.

"So," he prodded. "Can I count on your vote?"

"What?"

"Your vote. I don't know who else is running—we're supposed to find out at the pep rally. But, as they say, while I have you on the line . . ."

We were at the walk to my house. Petunia sat and attempted to manipulate him with her best red-rimmed sad eyes.

"You can't have my vote." I inhaled a breath.

Will's smile fell. "Why not? Who are you voting for?"

"Me." And I explained about how being on the school board would give me a chance to change the school cheating policy and remove the referral letter from my file. "And Mike's, too," I added, as if that would make a difference.

"Mike, yes." He grinned. "The guy you *don't* have a crush on."

I'd almost forgotten about that. "Yup."

Will glanced away as if lost in thought. A stiff breeze blew back his black hair and I resisted the temptation to reach up and trace the outline of his chiseled features. There were Greek marble statues in the museum downtown, I knew, that could not compare to the profile of Will Blake.

"Well, then," he said, extending his hand. "May the best man win."

"That would be *woman*." I shook it and was surprised

when he held on slightly longer than I would have expected. "Um . . ."

"We're still on for that tour," he said, not letting go. "You promised."

"Sure."

"How about Saturday? Aidan has nothing to do in the afternoon."

"Sounds great. Nothing I'd rather do than spend a Saturday looking at octopi."

"Poisonous ones, I hope, for Aidan's sake."

"Absolutely."

Finally, he let go of my hand, though he didn't let go of his gaze. Those eyes, blue even in this darkness, didn't leave mine for a second. "I like you, Gigi. You make me laugh and you're smart."

Amazing. All my life, I'd been told that if I stuck to my guns and didn't lower my standards, a really great guy would come along and find me irresistible. I didn't believe it, honestly, but now I knew it was true because none other than Will Blake was standing here saying in oh-so-many words that he liked me. And that was after seeing me in my ugly pretty clothes.

"You know who you remind me of, Gigi?"

"Who?" I murmured, hoping it'd be along the lines of a blond Kate Middleton.

"Talia. My girlfriend."

Screeeech. "Girlfriend!"

"Yeah, I know it's crazy." He kicked the curb, obviously mistaking my dismay for incredulity. "Talia's in L.A. I'm in Boston. It makes no sense."

Oh, and her name would have to be something sophisticated like *Talia*. Figured. As it sank in that he didn't like me that way—and that I didn't remind him of a blond Kate Middleton—all bubbly hope inside me went flat. Still, one must not pout or come off as disappointed in such situations. After all, WWKD? (What Would Kate Do?)

"She must be someone great if you're still going out with her three thousand miles away," I said gamely.

"She and I, we're kind of . . ." He was about to say more but, as if deciding he'd already said too much, abruptly switched the subject. "Anyway, if I don't talk to you in school, see you Saturday afternoon."

And without thinking, I automatically answered, "It's a date." Crap. I slapped my hand over my mouth. "I mean, that's something my friends and I say. I'm not saying . . ."

"Actually, I agree. It *is* a date." And brushing his lips against my cheek, he headed home, drawing his sleeve across his mouth.

Guess I should have warned him about the face mask.

Ten

"Tell me, please, that you are not thinking of dropping out of the race for a boy." Bea folded her arms and glared.

I tried never to do anything for a guy, but Will was a special case. "He's new to the school and I'm one of his few friends. I should be supporting him, not trying to beat him, right?"

"Wrong," Neerja said, as we headed down the hall toward the gym for assembly. "Look how you guys got all over my case for being afraid to audition because of"— she scanned the area for signs of Justin—"*you know who.* How is this any different?"

I was about to answer when Bea said, "If anyone gets to drop out of stuff, it's me. At least you and Neerja auditioned together for the play. And you know both of us will help you with the campaign, Gigi. But me? I'm skiing on my own. It's like I've been abandoned."

Neerja and I didn't know what to say to this. It was true, but what could we do? Neerja didn't ski. Period. And I hadn't skied in years, was a total chicken when it came to heights, and was certain to break my neck if I went faster than a turtle. Plus, with all this other craziness going on, like *Romeo and Juliet*, not to mention serving on the school board if I won, when would I have time?

"I'd love to," I began, "but . . ."

"But what?" Bea raised an eyebrow. "But you don't care that I'm the only sophomore girl and no one on the team knows me, that the rest of them are all seniors who've been doing this forever and are the best of friends?"

"Oh, Bea," Neerja said with a sigh.

We turned the corner and ran smack into the end of the line to the gym. Wow. So many people. And the noise! Were pep rallies always this much of a zoo?

We didn't have a clue because it'd been quite a while since the three of us had gone to one. Usually, we avoided pep rallies like bad breath, sometimes hiding out in the honors lounge while Mrs. Greene the librarian plied us with herbal tea and sugar cookies as classmates screamed their heads off and laughed at our mascot—a guy in a rubberized Greek soldier costume.

Like us, Mrs. Greene saw the hypocrisy in taking time out from class to cheer for fake Spartans when we could be learning about the real ones.

I doubted my classmates had any idea how bloodthirsty and brutal the real Spartans were. Sure, they were awesome warriors, but they were mostly awful human beings who took newborn weakling babies from their mothers and tossed them into mountain gorges to die.

And these were our heroes?

"Make way for the team." Our assistant principal, Mr. Obleck, pushed back the line so a wave of varsity players in their red-and-black uniforms could stream in.

"Hey, Einstein!" Mike slipped away from his soccer teammates and jogged toward me. The black smudge under each eye made him look kind of fierce. "The only thing that's riding on this election is that letter in our files and therefore our entire collegiate future, so don't screw up." He punched me on the shoulder. Rather hard, I thought.

"Ow!" I rubbed the spot where he hit me. Bam Bam didn't know his own strength. "Thanks for the encouragement, especially after I told you how nervous I am getting up in front of a crowd."

"Oh, yeah, forgot about that." He frowned, thinking. "Have you tried the old pretend-everyone-in-the-audience-is-naked routine?"

I had. "It doesn't work. It just makes me sicker."

"Good point. There are definitely guys I don't want to see naked either." He grinned. "Girls on the other hand . . ."

My turn to give him a punch.

"Hey! Just a joke."

"IPOLITO!" Mr. Guitterez, the soccer coach, was about to blow his whistle. "Stop chatting up the ladies and get back in line."

"Gotcha!" Mike gave me a small salute and yelled, "Just remember, when it comes to speeches, don't be a boxer, keep it brief!" before jogging with his teammates into the gym.

Neerja said, "I think that's from a Fruit of the Loom underwear commercial."

"*Do* you have a speech ready?" Bea asked.

Instantly, my stomach clenched. "Sort of. I thought I'd go up and kind of wing it." Translation: No. Because every time I sat down to write something, the words refused to come out the end of my pen. "The way I see it, all I have to do is get up and introduce myself and sit down. Like Mike said, keep it brief!"

Neerja's eyes went wide. "Um, I think you're going to need to do more than that."

"Definitely," Bea said. "What about your plans? Your qualifications? Why we should vote for you over someone like Will? This might be the only opportunity to address the whole school."

Will passed by holding up a large poster that looked like it'd been professionally done. I wasn't able to catch sight of the whole thing except for the catchphrase *Yes, We Will!*

Oh God. Bea and Neerja were right. I should have prepared more than just my name!

Another roar boomed from the gym as we entered, and I shot a glance at the clock above the basketball hoop. Almost two. In just a matter of minutes, I would be at that podium smack in the center of the gym floor addressing more than eight hundred people. My heart did a double beat as my throat went dry.

"I can't do this," I whispered to Neerja.

She gave me a squeeze. "Yes, you can!"

Either that, I thought, *or it's* Yes, we Will!

Bea was ahead of us, climbing the steps, when we saw Justin and Henry waving at us. "Did you see?" Henry said as we slid into their row, Neerja strategically squeezing between Justin and me. "The cast list is up."

The blood drained from Neerja's face. "What did you get, Henry?"

He shrugged. "I don't know. J and I were headed down to the gym when we caught Drew sneaking out to his car, leaving for the day. That must mean it's posted."

I noticed Lindsay three rows in front of us hugging and kissing her gymnast friends as if she had something to celebrate. "Lindsay!" I yelled. "What part did you get?"

She spun around, her whole body squirming with glee. "Juliet." She clasped her hands to her chest. "Can you believe it?"

Lindsay was the kind of person who acted surprised whenever good things happened to her—though they always did. Good grades, popularity, gymnastic medals, a lead in the school play as a sophomore. You could tell already that her life would be a breeze.

"Excellent. You see what anyone else got?"

She pointed our way. Neerja's small hand slipped into mine.

"Henry!" Lindsay made a heart with her index fingers. "He's Romeo."

"Henry?" Neerja let go, astonished. I knew what she was thinking, that this was our doing. If Justin hadn't been paged, Henry never would have accidentally auditioned for the role.

Fortunately, Justin seemed none the wiser.

"Dude, that's awesome." Justin raised his hand for a high five that Henry returned rather listlessly. He seemed as flabbergasted as the rest of us.

Lindsay smiled at him sweetly. "We better kick some

booty, huh?" Then another of her friends, apparently just hearing the fantastic news, squealed and clamped Lindsay in a head lock. So that was it as far as pumping her for more info was concerned.

"Well," Neerja said, letting out the breath she'd been holding. "Guess I won't have to push you two together after all. You'll be practicing with Lindsay every single day."

Henry let out a low whistle. "Wow. Lindsay and me, Juliet and Romeo." He ran a hand through his hair. "How did that happen?"

"You must have knocked it out of the park at tryouts," Justin said. "Me? I got called down to the office for someone else's dog."

Bea kicked my foot.

"Oh, I knew I bombed," Neerja fretted. "I'm probably just in the chorus. That's where Drew puts all the people who can't act."

"No way," I assured her. "You and Henry were fantastic. I bet you're the nurse. Or maybe Lady Capulet. You'd make an awesome Lady Capulet."

She let out a low moan. Neerja could get herself really worked up about failing. You should see her when we get tests back, all pale and shaky.

"Tell you what. I'll go find out." Bea dumped her backpack on the bleachers and slid out.

Neerja mounted a faint protest. "No, don't. I don't want to know."

"Don't worry, Neerja. You did fine," Bea said, taking the steps two at a time.

"Find out what I got, too, okay?" Justin asked.

Bea said, "I should charge or something." She worked her way through the crowd and out the door. I could sense Neerja tensing into a knot of worry and was just about to reach for her hand again when Justin beat me to it.

"Don't think about it," he said, holding on, smiling at her sweetly. "Think about me."

Neerja shot me a sidewise glance and a scooched a little closer. "Okay." She bit her lower lip and tried to act normal, though you could tell she was ready to burst.

I nudged Henry, who saw what I saw. Too bad Bea wasn't here to see this.

Justin and Neerja continued to hold hands while standing for the school fight song, which sounded like every other school fight song—militaristic and impossible to sing. None of us could remember the words. Then we sat again and Schultz stepped up to the podium, where she announced that before the pep rally got underway, she wanted to introduce the three students who were running for student rep and wasn't it great that the spirit of democracy was alive and well at Denton High.

No one applauded.

Where is Bea? The drama department was right below the gym. She should have found the cast list by now.

"It's bad," Neerja said as Schultz wound up her speech. "Bea doesn't want to tell me."

"She probably just ran into a friend in the hall." Which was the best, if lamest excuse, I could muster. My cell buzzed in my hand and, without letting Neerja see, I leaned back and checked the message. Sure enough, it was from Bea.

Crap. U got COR-NS.

COR-NS stood for a nonspeaking chorus role, which just shows how far Drew trusted me when it came to opening my mouth. Personally, I was extremely relieved since nonspeaking chorus members weren't required to attend every rehearsal. With my schedule, I needed all the free time I could get.

N got prompt.

Prompt? What was a prompt?

"Prompter!" Neerja covered her mouth. She'd been reading over my shoulder. "That's what I got . . . *prompter?*"

Justin moved his hand from Neerja's hand to her shoulder as Smitty Chavez, a senior, took the podium.

"Hi, I'm Smitty Chavez. And I am running for student rep for only one reason." He paused over the microphone. "To boycott this election."

People started murmuring. Smitty lifted his hand and waited for quiet.

"Listen up! Jim Mullet is my best friend and a standup guy. He has been an excellent student rep for two years. What happened to him this week, the way he got completely disrespected because of a random photo that meant nothing, is total BS!"

A shout went up. Smitty nodded and gave the podium a pound. "That's why I am urging a boycott of this election. If you believe in justice, if you oppose Big Brother prying into our business after school hours, then do not vote a month from now. Show the powers that be we will not be fooled again!"

A bunch of seniors stood and pumped their fists and went, "Whoot! Whoot! Whoot!"

And here I thought I was being selfish by running to modify our cheating policy. Smitty was running out of protest. The gym was now filled with a noise like thunder as the seniors—and Mullet's other friends—stomped their feet.

Mr. Obleck got up, adjusted the waist of his pants, and

scanned the crowd, warningly. Finally, he motioned for Bob, the security guy, to come out to the gym floor. After that, people started settling down. Obleck was not a fan of kids getting out of control.

"I got prompter." Neerja's eyes were welling up with tears.

Justin gently stroked her hair. I'd never seen him be so sweet—or pay so much attention. Neerja had to be loving it. But also hating it, right? It was like when Justin found out I'd been busted for cheating. Suddenly I became a person of interest.

Over her head, Justin asked softly, "Bea say what I got?"

I texted Bea.

She texted back: Paris. I showed him the phone.

He closed his eyes in appreciation but tactfully kept his mouth shut.

"Thank you, Mr. Chavez," Schultz was saying as Smitty returned to his seat. "Such is democracy, students. Candidates run for all sorts of reasons in the real world, too. Of course, some reasons are more honorable than others." She cleared her throat in disapproval of Smitty's speech. "Next up, sophomore William Blake." She smiled broadly and read from a white paper, an introduction possibly written by Will himself. "Now here is a candidate with a positive spirit. William Blake came to

Denton High just last month as a transfer student from California, where he was an AP scholar even as a freshman. An avid lover of lacrosse, soccer, and chess, you may not know Will now, but you will, because wherever Will goes, he will excel."

"Will Will?" joked Henry.

Neerja giggled and lifted her head from Justin's shoulder. "Good one."

I couldn't help but feel a certain envy as Will confidently strode to the podium in an unbuttoned white-and-red-striped shirt that hung loosely off his shoulders, exposing his red spartans T-shirt underneath. Parker Forbes quickly set the *Yes, We Will!* poster against the podium and dashed back to his seat.

"Hey, everybody!" Will lifted one hand casually.

"Hey!" the entire gym shouted back.

He thumbed toward our principal, who was returning to her metal folding chair with the other faculty. "You wouldn't believe how much I had to pay Dr. Schultz to say all that."

On cue, a drummer in the band played a rim shot and Schultz playfully waved him away as Will continued.

"So, um, a lot of you are probably asking yourselves where a guy gets off running for student rep after being at school less than a month. Well, to answer your question, I got off at Logan Airport."

Another rim shot. Laughter at the lameness of his joke. Even Henry smirked.

Will linked his fingers. "No, honestly. Already I love Denton. Everyone here has been so awesome and welcoming. You guys rock!" He held open his arms and, as if rehearsed, Lindsay and her gang yelled, "We love you, Will Blake."

Will said, "See you girls after school."

"Whoooooo!" they trilled in unison.

My cheeks went hot. Neerja, still holding hands with Justin, murmured, "You're far cuter than he is."

Justin winked and said, "Thanks. I know."

Oh brother.

"And I want to do what I can to represent you guys. I'll listen. I'll think. And, most importantly, I'll get your message across to the oldsters, *aiiiit*?" He shot them with his finger. "So, if you can, vote for me, Will Blake. Like they used to say back in L.A., people love me until they get to know me."

Except for the seniors protesting the emergency election, the entire gym went overboard with a standing ovation. Sure, it was a great speech, but still, a standing O?

Dr. Schultz went to the microphone. "Gigi Dubois? Are you here? Gigi Dubois."

"She's here," Lindsay yelled, as I snapped up, realizing

too late that I should have been waiting in the front row like Will and Smitty.

"Oh, it's you, Genevieve," Schultz said, introducing me as just a "sophomore whom most of you know. Genevieve Dubois." She lowered the microphone, gave me a pat for good luck, and the gym went quiet.

Dead quiet.

That sea of faces. So many faces. They became not kids I'd known forever, friends and classmates, but impatient spectators spoiled by Smitty's rousing protest and Will's easy humor. They didn't want to hear me drone on and on about the unfairness of the cheating policy or how, during budget cuts, we needed a representative on the school board to stand up for "non-core" staff like Mrs. Greene, the librarian.

It was Friday. They wanted to start the weekend.

I tried to open my mouth just to say "Hi!" like Will had, but I couldn't. My body shifted into shutdown mode as the seconds ticked. My stomach twisted. My palms gripping each side of the podium went damp. There was the familiar pounding in my head and my heart had decided to simply quit.

At any moment, I expected to be asked to sit down. Or worse, to throw up.

Somewhere in the distance a shout went up. "Vote for Gigi!"

It was Bea standing by the doors. "Vote for Gigi!"

"Go, Gigi!" Mike bellowed from the soccer team. "Go, Gigi!"

But the rest of the gym stayed silent aside from the rustle of my bored audience shifting in their seats. I swallowed hard and managed to eke out, "Hi. I'm Gigi Dubois and I hope you'll vote for me for student rep."

More silence. The imaginary belt around my middle tightened. It suddenly got very hot as I felt the cool trickle of sweat run down the side of my face.

"Thank you," I whispered into the mic, before stepping away from the podium and quick-stepping across the gym floor, my head bowed, my fists clenched. I never wanted to have to do that again. *Never*.

Thankfully, the band started up the Denton High fight song again. The podium was removed and in its place the cheerleaders formed a pyramid. The mascot did a cartwheel.

Mike was in the front row of the soccer players, giving me a thumbs-up while I made it to the safety of the bleachers, where Will was waiting by the steps and chatting with Ava, apparently so embarrassed by my abysmal performance that he acted as if he'd never seen me before in his life.

Eleven

Saturday morning, I pulled the blanket up to my nose and tried to get comfortable, not that this would be easy, seeing as how I was lying on Neerja's floor—on a fluffy rug, but still on the floor—with Bea snoring next to me and Neerja taking up her whole double four-poster bed.

This is the problem I'm finding with sleepovers lately. It's a blast staying up all night chatting with your best friends, but exhausting in the morning—even if I was wide awake. Since there was no way I could get back to sleep, I got up, slipped on my jeans and sweatshirt, yanked my hair into a ponytail, and went downstairs.

The rest of the Padwami household was up. Neerja's dad was in his leather chair by the fireplace reading the

New York Times while her mother was at the counter cutting into a grapefruit. I assumed Thing One and Thing Two were in the family room, from which came the blaring of Sponge Bob's homicidal cackle.

"Ah, Gigi. You're up! Early bird gets the worm." Neerja's mom plunked the grapefruit half in a bowl and handed it to me. "Fresh from Florida. It's the beginning of the season, you know."

I told her thanks and sat at the kitchen counter.

Neerja's mom is very pretty, with dark hair she parts in the middle and pulls back tight into a bun. She often looks not that much older than Parad, especially when she's out of her hospital getup and in her Indian clothes. Today she was wearing bright pink shalwar under a kameez of purple etched in gold and matching pink.

I think it is totally unfair that the rest of us don't get to wear these. I would kill to walk around all day in flowing purple and pink lounge wear.

"And how is your mother?" she asked, pouring a cup of tea for herself.

I told her my mother was still busy making sure a black hole didn't swallow the universe.

"That is good," Neerja's dad said from behind his paper. "I do not want the universe swallowed up by antimatter. At least, not until I beat Jack McCarthy at golf."

This was an example of Dr. Padwami's humor. Dry

almost to the point of nonexistent.

I dug into my grapefruit and noticed Neerja's mother shooting me darting looks.

"Shouldn't you be at the hospital doing rounds?" she asked her husband, checking the time on the stove. "It is almost seven thirty."

My hunch was right. Neerja's mom wanted to dish and preferred to do it without her husband butting in every two seconds asking who was who and who did what. Like a lot of dads I've observed, Dr. Padwami enjoys gossip in theory but, having grown up male, simply lacks the basic skills to effectively participate.

"Yes, yes," he said, folding the *New York Times* and taking a last sip of coffee. "When I get back, tell the girls we are cleaning out the garage. We need to get the bikes and noodles put away before winter comes."

Neerja's mom smiled innocently, but as soon as Dr. Padwami was out the door and we heard his tires crunch on the gravel driveway, she whipped around the counter and pulled up a stool. She leaned so close, her jasmine perfume made me swoon.

"Okay, who is this Justin fellow?"

"He's just a friend of Henry's." Though that status was changing, a shift not lost on Neerja's mother.

The night before, Neerja, Bea, and I had been drowning our sorrows in Dr Peppers and Bollywood—*Jab We*

Met, the happiest Bollywood movie ever with a hero to die for, Shahid Kapoor. (Pant!) And we were dancing to the movie's most famous song—"Nagada Nagada"—which has this powerful drumming that makes it impossible not to move.

Soon The Things joined in, hopping up and down, and then Neerja's parents. So there we were, spinning around the Padwami family room, waving our arms, bumping into each other and the furniture and laughing, when in walked Henry and Justin.

Henry immediately started dancing with Neerja and then the twins and her mother, but Justin just stood in the doorway and gaped, like we were circus freaks. That's when Neerja got self-conscious and claimed to be in need of water. She and Justin went to the kitchen, where they held hands and laughed, and I caught her parents exchanging looks.

"I do not like him." Neerja's mother cupped her hands around her tea. "Why does Neerja?"

"First of all, it's not as if they're getting married." I swallowed a grapefruit section. "For another, you have to admit he's cute, and yesterday when she found out she didn't get a role in *Romeo and Juliet*, he was really nice to her."

Neerja's mother went, "Hmph." She sipped her tea and put down her cup, thinking. "Is he in any of your classes?" Translation: Is he an honors student?

"He's in gym." Part of me felt like I had to defend him, for Neerja's sake. "But being smart isn't everything."

"It should be. You must watch out, Gigi. It is often tempting for intelligent girls like yourself to dumb down just to get boyfriends. What a pity so many boys are put off by a girl's intelligence."

I'd had this same discussion with my own mother so often that listening to Neerja's mom was like hearing a recording of Mom.

"Neerja's young," her mother was saying. "And she does not have much experience with boys. But I know her father and I would feel better if this Justin were a boy *friend* before he became a *boyfriend*. We would like for him to sit down with us so we could get to know him before he starts dating our daughter."

Good luck with that, I thought, as if anyone "dated" these days. Which reminded me of my promise to take Will and Aidan to the aquarium—our own date—and that got me kind of excited.

"Thanks for the grapefruit." I slipped off the stool and dumped the rind in the compost bowl. "I gotta go."

"You won't say anything to Neerja about our talk this morning," she said. "You know *Romeo and Juliet.* It's never good when children find out the parents disapprove."

"No problem. By the way, if meeting smart men is so hard, how did you and Dr. Padwami get together?"

She took a sip of her tea and smiled to herself. "Our parents arranged our marriage."

I must have looked appalled, because she added quickly, "It's not as horrible as it sounds, Gigi. My parents loved me. His parents loved him. They wanted the best for us and we trusted this to be so. And we have been very, very happy, which is more than I can say for a lot of other couples our age. Sometimes—not always, but sometimes—the old ways are still best."

It was insane how worked up I was getting about the date to the aquarium. When I got home, I took a long, hot shower, scrubbed and shaved and exfoliated several body parts, smoothed some shine stuff on my hair, tweezed a few brow hairs (like Marmie says, you pluck chickens and tweeze brows), and minimized pores. With my long blond hair blown dry and curled with the big-barreled curling iron, I was ready for the red carpet.

Only, I had nothing to wear. It was cold and gray outside, a typical November in Boston, which meant jeans, sneakers, a black top, and my mother's MIT zip-up hoodie. Cool and casual.

At noon, I waited for my phone to ring or ping a text from Will telling me when and where we were meeting.

Marmie called up from downstairs and asked what I wanted for lunch and I told her nothing. At 12:15 Bea called and said she and Neerja were headed into Cambridge to satisfy their jelly bean cravings at Hidden Sweets and did I want to come with.

I hadn't told them about Will simply because I didn't want them asking a bunch of questions and leaping to the conclusion that I had a mad crush on him—which, I'll be honest, I kind of did. Far better to calmly mention over lunch Monday that the two of us took his little brother to the aquarium and ease them into the situation.

"Um, I'm going to stay here and brainstorm about the campaign. If I change my mind, I'll call you."

Bea sounded skeptical. "Really? Neerja has a gift card."

A gift card at Hidden Sweets. Chocolate-covered cranberries. Sour worms. Jelly beans galore. I contrasted that with the prospect of being with Will in the dark, dipping our hands into the tidal pool and cradling baby starfish. "I'm good."

"Ooookay." And she hung up.

The noon hour came and went. So did the one hour. I was starting to get pretty nervous since I didn't feel like paying for a full day when we'd have, at best, thirty minutes. At 2:30, I picked up the phone to text him and went on Facebook instead.

You'd have thought I'd learned my lesson on Halloween, right?

Of course, I rationalized that I was going to his page only to send him a message, but once I was there I kind of got lost. I noticed that his last posting had been a comment on the page of a friend in California. I also noticed that while his profile picture was of him—alone—standing on a cliff with what I assumed was the Pacific in the background, his status was: In a Relationship with Talia Caulkins.

If there were 250 photos on Will's page, 150 of them were of Talia.

What I thought right off when I saw her was "mermaid." In nearly every picture, she was in a bikini, rarely the same one: white, navy, polka-dot, sunshine yellow. Seriously, she must have had an account at Bikinis R Us. Her skin was golden without being that scary cancer-causing brown. Her long hair was super blond, almost white, and rippled in gentle waves. And her eyes were as blue as Will's, though hers were big and wide.

There were other photos too. Talia in an adorable pink dress with her arms around Will outside a restaurant at night with friends. The two of them sitting on a garden wall, tackling each other in touch football, on bikes, throwing and catching Frisbees, side by side on skis, squinting at the bright sun reflecting off the snow. Always smiling.

And this girl was smart? No. Totally unfair. You could not be this pretty and smart, too. There were rules!

Googling *Talia Caulkins Harvard-Westlake*, the results came up vastly disappointing.

In .46 seconds, Google informed me that Talia was not only a star center on Harvard-Westlake girls' basketball team but also the recipient of numerous academic awards named after people I didn't know, a budding director who'd shot a film about homeless teenagers, and a leader, apparently, in Harvard-Westlake's community service program. Also, she saved abandoned Easter bunnies.

Wow. *I* wanted to be Talia Caulkins.

"Love you, T!" Will had written that on her wall—sometime between walking me home from Petunia's escape and yesterday morning.

I sat back and caught sight of myself in the full-length closet mirror. What I saw there was a fool, an idiot who'd let herself get so wound up about a boy she hardly knew that she'd ditched her closest friends and spent a whole Saturday waiting for his call. A girl who'd fallen for a guy who was clearly madly in love—for good reason—with someone who skied and got great grades and documented homeless teenagers while prancing around in neon-yellow bikinis.

What had happened to me? I wasn't the type to spend hours conditioning my hair and filing my nails for a boy.

That wasn't the Gigi Dubois I knew. The Gigi Dubois I knew set her sights beyond high school to college, to grad school, to that English castle on the moors.

The Gigi Dubois I knew put her friends first.

Snatching my phone, I called Bea, who answered on the third ring. "Hey."

"Where are you?" If they were still in Cambridge, it'd take me no more than twenty minutes to meet them.

"Just got out of the candy store and now we're waiting for the seventy-three back home."

Shoot. "If you stick around, we can catch a movie in Harvard Square. Or go out for coffee."

"I don't think so. I'm wicked beat," Bea said. "I didn't get much sleep last night."

"Hear ya."

Neerja took over Bea's phone. "Guess who we just saw outside the Harvard Coop. Your competition, Will Blake, and you'll never believe who he was with."

Will was at the Coop? With someone else?

"Your old pal, Ava. And they were holding hands."

Twelve

The first thing I did was unfriend Will Blake on Facebook. The second thing I did was block him.

Then, feeling really low for being such a crappy friend, I texted Bea and told her I was joining the ski team because she was my best bud and this is what best buds do: help each other succeed.

Friends come first.

You rock, she wrote back. Run tomorrow? Training.

Running. Oh, geesh. I hadn't counted on having to do actual exercise.

Sure

OK. After 11. Me tired.

Weren't we all? I thought, tossing aside my phone and crawling onto my bed next to Petunia.

Heartbreak was surprisingly enervating—a word that doesn't sound like it means, which is drained of energy. As flattened as if I'd been run over by a steamroller, I pulled out my worn copy of *Jane Eyre* and resolved to finish it by Monday.

Jane Eyre, once a pure escape to a faraway world, had now been tainted by Will, as were a lot of other things—Petunia, the campaign for student rep, even the few Reese's I'd managed to save from Halloween. Never would I read, pet, do, or eat those things without thinking of him.

Odd how quickly guys can worm their way into your brain—like that bug in *Star Trek II: The Wrath of Khan*. (What can I say? I'm the daughter of a diehard Trekkie.)

Fortunately, sleep is a magical healer and I woke the next morning strangely at peace, listening to gusts of rain blowing the last brown leaves off their bare branches. I lay there until my mother called from Switzerland—part of her usual Sunday routine.

Bea and I put off running on the lame excuse that we were waiting for the rain to stop. However, around three it did stop, taking with it our excuse, and I dug out my running shoes and gray sports bra. (When had I last seen that thing?)

I found Bea waiting for me at the corner, stretching against a telephone pole. We extended this and that. Did a few lunges. Got the old hamstrings limber and then took off.

Running with Bea is kind of like . . . walking. We didn't break any records, for sure. We took our sweet time lumbering up to Waverley Square, where we ordered a couple of iced coffees at Starbucks before heading home as the rain resumed, soaking through our sweats and chilling us to our bones.

"That was fun," I lied.

"Wait til we do it in the snow," she said with a laugh as she headed into her garage.

After dropping off Bea and jogging the remaining four blocks home, my one goal was to jump into the shower, pull on my ugly pretty clothes, and make a fire while Marmie cooked Sunday dinner. Sunday is the one night when she really does it up right, from soup and salad to dessert.

But life, as they say, happens when you're making plans. I had barely pushed open the front door, kicked off my wet sneakers, and shook off the rain, when I heard Marmie in the kitchen talking—to a boy.

Will!

He'd come to apologize, obviously. And he couldn't have picked a worse moment. A furtive glance in the foyer mirror confirmed my fears. Hair matted like a wet rat. Red nose running. Black mascara oozing under my eyes. (Did Bea let me go into Starbucks looking like this?) I ventured a dangerous whiff of my underarm. A locker filled with nasty gym shorts smelled sweeter.

"Gigi?" Marmie called. "Is that you? You have a gentleman visitor."

Gentleman visitor. *Cringe.* Okay. I could go in like this, looking like I just stepped out of *Scream 4.* Or, I could sneak upstairs, wash off the mascara, form my hair into a semi-attractive style, and emerge athletic but composed.

"Be right there!" I called out, sneaking past the kitchen and dashing up the stairs. In the safety of the bathroom, I turned on the hot water and searched for a brush, opening and closing drawers. Finding an old one, I dragged it through my hair as the water got hot. Soap on washcloth. Washcloth on face. Mascara was gone, leaving red marks under each eye. Oh well.

And that's when I noticed the coffee blotch smack in the middle of my sweatshirt. No, that would never do. Flicked off the water, sailed across the hall to my bedroom, quickly surveyed my piles of clothes divided into three helpful categories—Fairly Clean, Meh, Disgusting—and from Fairly Clean pulled out the only shirt left that was decent.

Okay, so it was a faded Barbie pink with white bleach stains. Will would have to deal. Pulling off the stained sweatshirt and tossing it into the Meh pile, I was shaking out the pink one when my door opened.

And there stood Mike, his expression shifting rapid-fire from carefree, to shocked, to embarrassed, to something else I couldn't read. "Einstein!"

"Mike!" I clasped the T-shirt to my chest. Thank God for the excellent coverage of sports bras. "What are you doing here?"

"I, um . . ."

"Will's downstairs."

Mike checked behind him. "He is?"

"Get out of here!" I picked up my slipper and threw it at him.

Mike shut the door and the slipper bounced back to the floor. I wiggled my arms into the T-shirt and opened it.

He was still standing there. "You forgot, didn't you?"

"Forgot what?" Deodorant. Deodorant. Where was that freaking deodorant? I rummaged through my backpack, reaching down to the bottom where it usually hid.

Mike held up a clipboard. Across the top was written

in blue Magic Marker *Periodic Table Project*. "Sunday afternoon? Remember?"

Oh. Crap. I quit looking and sat on the bed. He was right. We'd made plans to meet this afternoon to start the periodic table project for Buzzard. It had completely slipped my mind. And now Will was downstairs, waiting to apologize.

"Okay," I said, sighing, as my brain realigned. "Let me go talk to Will and . . ."

He pushed me back on the bed. "Will's not here."

"But I heard him."

"You heard *me* talking to your grandmother." His smile widened to an annoying grin. "My, my, Einstein. You're blushing. Do we have a thing for the opposition?"

"The opposition? NO!" I batted away his hand. "I was just expecting him to come by. There's some—"

"You blocked him from your Facebook."

Whoa! "How do you know?"

"Because he called to see if I wanted to come over to his house to watch the game today and when I told him I was going to work on a project with you, he said, 'Ask her why she unfriended me on Facebook and how come I've been blocked.'"

You can tell when you've been blocked on Facebook?

Mike tried to move around my room, negotiating the piles of clothes and junk like they were land mines.

"Einstein, I gotta say. This isn't what I expected from the smartest girl in class. My, my." He leaped over my treasured pile of *Us* magazines and landed, rather unsteadily, by a heap of underwear. "How can you live in this . . . *mess?*"

"Territories." I pointed to the relatively clean circle— half circle, technically—around my desk and the path leading to my bed.

"Ah." He sat on my chair, relieved to have found an oasis. "So what's going on with Will?"

"Nothing." *Maybe I* should *get rid of that underwear,* I thought, bending down to shove it under my bed.

"Sure. That'll get 'em clean." Mike was smirking at my under-bed organizational system as I begrudgingly pulled out the pile again. "According to him, you two were supposed to take his brother to the aquarium yesterday."

"Geesh. What else did you guys chitchat about, makeup tips?" I stuck the underwear into my overflowing bottom drawer.

Mike shook his head. "Helpless."

"I have other priorities." And I gave the drawer a push with my leg. "Did Will say why he blew me off?"

"He blew you off? Was this supposed to be some sort of date?"

I must have gone crimson because Mike's face lit up

and he said, "It *was* a date. And you got stood up and now your innocent genius heart is broken." He did that pout thing with his lower lip. "Poor Einstein."

"Don't be silly," I said, not meaning to sound so defensive. "It was just that we'd made plans. I'd cleared my schedule for yesterday afternoon and then I didn't hear from him. It was rude and I'm pissed. That's all."

I definitely was not going to tell Mike about Neerja and Bea seeing Will with Ava, not after his gleeful reaction about our so-called date.

"Let me get this straight." Mike leaned forward, elbows on both his knees, suddenly much taller in my blue-and-white bedroom than at school. "Because you went all crazy and for no good reason blocked Will from Facebook, he had no way to reach you to explain that something came up yesterday afternoon. Yeah. That's logical."

Not just any no-good reason, I thought sourly. *My ex-friend Ava.* "I could have been at Hidden Sweets with Bea and Neerja."

"Ah, yes, the friends you see every single day. Is it true you three are physically connected at the hip?"

"Hah, hah."

He moved the chair closer. "You do know, don't you, that Will has a girlfriend out in California?"

"As if I cared." No way would I cop to having seriously

Facebook-stalked him. "Don't we have a project to start?"

"Hey. I'm not the one who forgot." He held up his clipboard and effortlessly switched to homework mode. "Now, since I knew you were going to get all over my case and accuse me of being a leech on society, I came up with a couple of ideas." He checked his notes. "Building models was too time-consuming, so I thought maybe we could use Buzzard's suggestion and do a PowerPoint presentation where we show an element, and flash its atomic weight and one interesting fact about it."

I frowned, trying to pay attention, but I was distracted by the tantalizing possibility that Will did have a reasonable, logical explanation for blowing me off yesterday and that it had nothing to do with Ava. Maybe something had happened to Aidan (tragic, but fortunately recoverable accident?) and he'd had to rush him to the hospital. I could see it now, Will running down the sidewalk carrying a limp Aidan. And maybe Ava happened to be driving by and . . .

"Einstein." Mike snapped his fingers. "Get with it. I just asked you what's your idea."

"I was thinking." I blinked and reached for what I'd written the day before when I was waiting for Will to call. "I thought we could teach the class a system for memorizing the periodic table of elements. Not all of them, just the nonsynthetic ones. That's only one hundred two."

Mike thumbed this down. "Fail."

"No, not fail. It's easy if you know Latin." I smiled in victory. "But, since you don't know Latin, there are some really helpful mnemonic devices."

He closed his eyes. "You're going to tell me, aren't you? It's like an oncoming train headed right toward me and I'm powerless to stop it."

"Repeat after me: Happy Heather Likes Baking But Can Not Open Foil."

"Make it stop." He flung an arm across his forehead. "No. I will have nothing to do with Happy Heather."

"The *h* in *happy* is for *hydrogen*. The *he* in *Heather* is for *helium*. The *li* in *like* is for *lithium*."

Mike covered his ears with his hands and began rocking back and forth in my swivel chair, humming, pretending to be having a fit. He didn't quit until I stopped. "Are you done?"

I inhaled. "Little Betty Bright Child . . ."

"No!" He jumped up. "No Little Betty Bright Child."

I laughed. "What's wrong?"

"We're not in kindergarten, Einstein. You shouldn't just memorize the elements by name. You should know their properties, where they come from, what they're used for. For example, helium, or as you like to think of it, *Heather*, is a noble gas, meaning it's inert and doesn't hook up with other elements, and while it was discovered in space, it's found in the ground, the end product of the radioactive decay of uranium and thorium." He took a breath. "Its atomic number is two and it's most often used in party balloons."

"Wow. That's . . ."

He held up a finger. "Now, lithium, lithium's messed up. It's the only metal besides sodium, number eleven, by the way, to float on water and it's used in everything from pacemakers to batteries and it's found in Bolivia and also in bipolar people who eat it to even out their moods."

He went through five more elements, from beryllium to fluorine. When he was done, I'd had it with Happy Heather and her silly mnemonic memorization. I had just learned more about the elements—at least those seven— than I'd ever gleaned from reading or listening to Mr. Bouchard. "That was . . . amazing."

"Yeah?" He stood by my door, hands on hips, breathing hard, like he was restraining himself from going on to number ten—neon.

"Where did you learn all that?"

He shrugged and frowned at my bureau, every inch of which was covered with boxes of cheap jewelry. "I dunno. I pick stuff up."

I studied him, trying to figure what made this dude tick. On the surface, he was a Man Clan poster boy with his plaid shorts (even on a cold and rainy November day) and red hooded Spartans sweatshirt, his bare, hairy legs leading down to tattered topsiders. He lived for his buddies, lacrosse, soccer, skiing, and hanging out—in that order.

And yet, he knew the elements better than my mother with her MIT PhD.

"Gigi?" It was my grandmother calling me to help with dinner. I yelled back that I would be right there.

Mike took out his phone and raised his eyebrows. "I'd better be going. Sunday night is the one night my dad and I eat together . . . watching the Patriots."

As he got ready to leave, I thought of what Schultz had said about how I shouldn't be so quick to label Mike as simply another jock. "Maybe this project wasn't such a bad idea. You're a lot more intelligent than you seem, Mike."

Crap. That came out wrong.

"I mean . . ."

He smiled, amused. "You know, I don't get you, Einstein. Just when I think you're really smart, you say something really stupid." And snatching his clipboard, he opened my door and left.

Thirteen

I like to think of that weekend as the turning point—the fulcrum, if we were still in ninth-grade physics—when we changed from being nobodies to somebodies.

Even though Neerja didn't get the part she wanted in the play and Will stood me up for the Boston tour and, weirdly, insisted on completely avoiding me in school, our lives suddenly got super-intense.

For one thing, there was the campaign. Turned out jelly beans hadn't been the only reason Bea and Neerja went to Hidden Sweets. They'd also ordered a bunch of watermelon-flavored Pop Rocks, made up tags that read GIGI ROCKS!, attached the tags to the packets of candy, and brought them to school, presenting them to me as a surprise. I was so touched, I was almost speechless.

"Who could forget you after these?" Neerja said, ripping open a packet with her teeth and unscrewing a Coke.

"Don't!" I yelled, since everyone knew that soda + Pop Rocks = exploded head.

"Stand back." She took a swallow and squeezed her eyes shut. We could hear the Pop Rocks crackling in her mouth, even with it closed. Bea bit a nail, worried, while I took out my phone ready to dial 9-1-1.

Finally, she opened her eyes and then her mouth and produced a burp loud enough to set off the fire alarms.

"Wow," Bea said, grinning. "That was awesome."

That's when I decided Bea and Neerja were right—Pop Rocks were the must-have campaign party favors in addition to our hot-pink stickers that said:

I'M

GAGA

4

GIGI!

Will, meanwhile, had his own bag of tricks. Every morning, he greeted the first fifty kids with free donuts, all glazed, some jelly. People were now actually showing up early to make sure they didn't miss out. I had no idea how he could afford it. I mean, I knew he was getting some sort of deal, but still. It had to be setting him back hundreds of dollars.

If that weren't bad enough, Parker Forbes made a video and posted it on YouTube of Ashton Kutcher singing Will's praises. Turns out Ashton had been an assistant coach at Will's school back in California and used to give him rides home or something. Anyway, with Smitty urging everyone not to vote and most of the senior class following his lead, the race was going to come down to Will (donuts + celebrity endorsement) and me (Pop Rocks + sweet stickers).

Right. I was cooked.

Fortunately, I had skiing to take my mind off the campaign. Between running three miles every day after school, lifting weights in the gym, and drylands practice twice a week plus campaigning, I was so exhausted after finishing my homework that I was too tired to lie awake worrying about Will. I was even too tired for the reward of *Bones*.

Bea said it was only going to get worse. Once the temperature dropped, we would have to wake up at the crack of dawn on Sundays and hoof it to Paradise Mountain for downhill practice. This was the pits, in my opinion, since Sunday was my day to sleep until noon and bum around the house. Not anymore.

At least, with a nonspeaking role in *Romeo and Juliet,*

I didn't have to show up every day for rehearsal like Neerja. After moping for a few days, Neerja threw herself into the play, vowing to become the best prompter ever, even going so far as to memorize every line. We're talking all 26,000 words, give or take.

No, that was not normal.

Drew was thoroughly impressed, which only supercharged Neerja's inner overachiever. She and Henry started practicing on their own after rehearsal almost every evening because Lindsay, aka Juliet, had received dispensation to do gymnastics and didn't have time to go over her lines with Romeo.

When she wasn't at rehearsals or practicing with Henry, Neerja was with Justin. As Bea joked, The Jeerja had landed.

Neerja lived for gym, their only class together, and play practice, where they'd grab any opportunity to sit in the back row of the theater, holding hands and giggling. As far as my honed eavesdropping had been able to determine, most of their conversations centered on either how Justin and/or Neerja should do his or her own hair or whether Justin was close to breaking his own record on Angry Birds.

Bea feared for the future of Neerja's brain, even going so far as to suggest an intervention. "Before we lose her forever to the dark side."

We were in the honors lounge eating lunch, alone, while Neerja was hanging out with Justin in the cafeteria. "Give her until the play ends," I suggested. "At some point, she's gotta break."

Meanwhile, Sienna and Maddie seemed to be undergoing a transformation of their own.

It was just another homeroom, nothing special. I was doing my algebra. They were going over Crystal Ball dresses when Sienna turned to me and said, "You know, I could help you with your campaign."

Maddie put down her phone. "She could. Sienna's actually very political. There's no one in this school she doesn't know."

Probably true. Still, I wasn't sure Sienna's offer— as generous as it was—would help since I was running for representative to the school board, not prom queen. "That's okay." I smiled. "Thanks. I'm doing fine."

"Oh, really?" She swung her curtain of glossy chestnut hair. "You have a definite name recognition issue to overcome, Gigi. You didn't even make it on the—"

Please, don't say . . .

"Hot-o-meter."

I cringed. "So?"

"So, where have you been? Where do you go all day? You're not in anyone's classes. I never see you in the halls. Do you see her in the halls?" she asked Maddie.

Maddie shook her curls. "Never."

"I don't even see you in the cafeteria. Do you eat lunch?"

"Sure. I eat with Bea and Neerja in the honors lounge." This did not register. "It's an old office off the library."

"No wonder." She exhaled a sigh at my social ineptitude. "Don't you get it? You're never going to win if no one sees you. I mean, at least hang out at your locker and say hi. Eat in the cafeteria. Actually talk to people, like a normal person."

"I'm a normal person."

"I'm beginning to see that. But how's everyone else supposed to know this if you're always hiding in . . . what's it called again?"

"The honors lounge?"

"Yeah," she said with a snort. "Whatever."

Sienna had a point. I would grant her that. Maybe several points.

The bell rang and she checked her phone one last time. Maddie had IM'd her a toga-style Grecian dress with a high waist banded by a silver rope belt. "That's nice," I said.

Sienna looked doubtful. "You think?"

"It's the best one so far. You'd be awesome in it, especially if you put your hair up and wore those strappy sandals Maddie showed you on Thursday."

She seemed slightly disturbed to learn that I'd been nosing in on their daily dress show, but she couldn't refuse a compliment like that. "You should sit with us at lunch today. We're at the third table down by the windows." She snapped her phone shut. "I'll introduce you around and, uh, you can bring Bea and Neerja, too. Whatever they are."

I half expected Sienna to blow us off in the cafeteria, but when Neerja, Bea, and I approached, trays in hand, she couldn't have been more welcoming. "Hey, guys!" she shouted. "You showed up. Great."

She moved down so there was plenty of room. I plunked my tray on the table and took a deep breath, kind of surprised by my nervousness. These were people I never hung out with. Sienna. Maddie. Janelle. The Thayer twins. And select members of the Man Clan: B.K. Evans, Parker Forbes, and . . . Mike.

Mike, sitting at the end of the table like a king, gave me a wave and returned to arguing about the Patriots lineup with Parker and B.K.

Sienna smiled. "I've been telling these guys how I'm an advisor on your campaign for class president."

"Student rep," I said, peeling off the top of my yogurt.

One of the Thayer twins, possibly April, I never can get them straight, pointed her spoon at Neerja. "Aren't you in the play?"

Neerja swallowed a bite of her apple. "Kind of. I'm a prompter."

"She's memorizing the entire thing," said Bea. "All twenty-six thousand words of *Romeo and Juliet*."

I nudged her. *Too nerdy.* But Bea, who doesn't give a hoot what people think, said, "That's over a thousand lines, for you keeping score at home."

"Oh," said the Thayer twin. "I'm just a lady-in-waiting. I don't have any lines."

Something landed on my tray. A wad of paper napkin tossed by Mike. "Hey, Einstein." He grinned. "Had fun in your bedroom the other night."

I shot a glance at Sienna, who was dipping a chicken nugget into ketchup and chatting with Maddie, oblivious.

"Einstein's running for student rep to save our butts," he said, leaning back in his chair.

I gave him a look. I did not want our cheating brouhaha to get around as the reason I was in the race. That was almost as bad as Smitty Chavez running to protest Mullet's beer bust.

Janelle said, "Who's Einstein?"

I said, "He just calls me that—"

"—because she's smart," Mike cut in. "You remember Gigi, right, Janelle? The pep rally . . . ?"

Janelle said vaguely, "Uh, yeah. But how is she saving your butt?"

"I'll take care of this," Bea said. "There's a stupid

policy that if you're accused of cheating and even if you're exonerated—"

I cleared my throat.

"—found innocent," Bea simplified, "a letter still goes in your permanent file saying you've been investigated for cheating."

"No way!" Janelle put down her water. "That's so unfair."

Mike raised his eyebrows and nodded.

"But that's not the only reason I'm running," I was quick to add. "It's budget season and a lot of staff positions are on the chopping block, including reducing the school librarian to part-time."

Everyone at the table stopped talking and was staring at me expectantly, like they were waiting for me to get to the punch line. Total. Awkward. Silence. So far, they'd been more outraged by the cheating letter.

"And skiing," Mike added. "They might scrap the downhill program completely."

Really?

But even this had no effect. Now, football or hockey, that would have prompted a riot.

"Art," Neerja said, flicking the gold earring she'd made last semester. "That means no jewelry class."

A gasp went up. Janelle said, "I was planning to take

that senior year. Do you know how pissed I'll be if that gets cut?"

"I know," Maddie said. "That course is always closed. I'm like you, senior year."

"Me too," said Sienna. "Seriously, we should protest or something. Jewelry class is the only thing worth taking at this school."

Suddenly they were firing questions: How did I hear about jewelry class? Was it too late to stop the cuts? What about driver's ed—were they going to cut that, too? Because a private course over the summer was, like, five-hundred bucks and already we were down to one teacher and the waiting list was *huuuuge*. Which completely sucked because you couldn't get a license without it. They better not be eliminating that.

I didn't know what to say. So many questions. So few answers. Bea started taking notes for future reference. "Let us do some research and get back to you," she said.

"Maybe I can help."

It was Will. He was standing behind Janelle, hands on her shoulders, massaging them slightly, and looking at me.

I focused on my yogurt, my face going hot. I could tell he knew I liked him—I hadn't exactly been Miss Cool—and he knew my feelings were hurt from last Saturday and being ignored thereafter.

But worse than all that, he was getting ready to show me up. It was hard to choose which disgusted me more.

"From what I know, cutting driver's ed is simply a threat." He coughed slightly. "This is just a bargaining chip, an old negotiating trick. Make a big deal out of eliminating the popular courses as a way of building public support for tax hikes. When I'm student rep, I'll make sure we keep art and jewelry and driver's ed."

Under the table, Bea gave me a pinch that meant, *He's muscling in on your campaigning. Are you going to stand for that?*

What was I supposed to do? Stand and yell, "Objection!"

"But, if you're interested," he went on, "there's a school board meeting coming up Tuesday night. They're going to introduce the student rep candidates. You going, Gigi?"

If he thought I didn't know about the meeting, he had another thing coming. "Seven p.m. Wouldn't miss it."

"Great. How about I give you a ride?"

In his spanking new Saab, I assumed. Will had made quite a splash with this car since so few of us had our own—not to mention a $50,000 convertible. "Actually, I thought I'd walk, thanks."

"Aw, please?" He removed his hands from Janelle's shoulders and clasped them prayerfully. "We really need to talk. I owe you a major explanation about why we couldn't get together Saturday."

He said it in public. Full acknowledgment PLUS an apology.

Bea gave me another pinch, this one so hard my eyes watered. If she kept this up, I was going to be black and blue.

However, it wasn't the wide eyes of Sienna's friends or my throbbing leg that grasped my attention or the way Will was looking at me so intently; it was Mike.

Right then my instincts told me he didn't like Will. Maybe it was the fancy new Saab or the way he had rubbed Janelle's shoulders or that he was buddies with Ashton Kutcher. Whatever the crime, Mike did nothing to hide his disgust of Will's obvious privilege—and the confidence that often comes to those born with advantages.

"Pick you up at six thirty?" Will asked.

I shot a glance at Mike who yawned, bored.

"Sure," I said. "Six thirty's fine."

Fourteen

Whatever cachet I accumulated by being romantically linked with Will, it was hardly worth the grief I got from Bea and Neerja, who went ballistic that I didn't tell them the real reason I bagged out of Hidden Sweets.

Bea rounded on me as soon as we were out of the cafeteria. "That's why you couldn't go with us. You said you were working on the campaign or something. But really you were going out with Will."

"You lied," Neerja said, hurt. "Why?"

How many mortifying moments like this do I have to endure to learn hiding something from my best friends is never worth the grief? "It wasn't a big deal. I was supposed to take Will and his brother, Aidan, to the aquarium. I didn't say anything to you guys because—"

"Because you didn't want us tagging along," Bea said.

"No." Though . . . it was an interesting theory—at least on a subconscious level. "I didn't want you to make more out of it than it was."

Bea went, "Hmph."

"I tell you everything that's going on with Justin," Neerja added.

"But we all know you like Justin and now Justin likes you back. With Will and me it's . . . different. He has a girlfriend in California and . . ."

"He's going out with Ava." Bea closed her eyes, realizing she'd gone too far. "Sorry. I didn't mean it that way. I meant that if you're interested in him, you should realize you're not the only one. Will is definitely taking advantage of his status as the cute new guy. Nice, huh?"

See? I wanted to say. *This is exactly why I didn't tell you about Saturday.* "He *is* nice. You just don't know him."

"I know he's a total flirt!" Bea exclaimed. "Did you see him with Janelle, the way he was massaging her shoulders? It's like he's trying to win this election girl by girl."

"And we *did* see Will with Ava that day you were supposed to be with him and his brother at the aquarium," Neerja said. "Bea kind of has a point."

Bea slung her purse over her shoulder. "Come on,

Neerja. I can't stand people who ditch their friends for guys."

Neerja shot me a sympathetic look and quick-stepped to join Bea, who was practically marching to Latin.

I didn't know why, but I didn't care about Will and California Talia. Ava, on the other hand, really bugged me.

Will was far too preppy and ambitious to be her type. She usually fell for the brooding artists, like Rolf the German exchange student, skinny pale guys in black leather jeans whose pain the rest of us mortals couldn't begin to fathom.

Then again, who was Ava, really? The fun friend who once laughed so hard she blew soda out of her nose? Or the rebel artist who skipped classes?

I was beginning to think no one knew. Not even Ava herself.

Thankfully, there are these random daily events called classes to interrupt the steady stream of drama that is the stuff of high school. By immersing myself in Latin, chemistry, precalc, history, and English, I was able to keep dizzily preoccupied until Neerja forgave me at play practice.

"Bea's coming around," she said as we did our math homework while Drew blocked a fight scene. "I think it's hard for her with me kind of going out with Justin and now you and Will."

"There's nothing between Will and me," I said. "Seriously. Nothing."

"Even so, it's a sign of things to come. I think she's afraid our group's starting to break apart—which it will, eventually. We'll go off to college and get jobs and maybe get married. It won't always be the three of us forever."

But it should be the three of us for now, and I made a private vow to show Bea that she would come before any guy. Friends like her were too precious to lose. I'd already lost Ava and that was enough.

Justin got off the stage and moseyed up to our row. "I'm done for the day," he said to Neerja, leaning over the seat in front of her. "Wanna get out of here? We can go to my house and you can watch me play Halo."

I had to cover my mouth to keep from laughing. Good thing Bea hadn't been here to hear that or we would have lost it.

Neerja tapped her pencil against her notebook. "I can't. Drew might need me for something, and anyway, I've got a ton of homework. Trig. The worst."

"More homework?" Justin scoffed. "You gotta watch it, babe. Do too much of that stuff and it'll start messing with your brain."

"That's the idea," Neerja said lightly as he slid out and

went to pester Henry, who shook his head no since he had homework too.

Neerja watched as Justin sauntered out the doors. "I should have gone with him. He's right. I'm always doing homework."

"Don't be stupid!" I pointed to question number four. "My slope is seventy-five percent. Why is yours eighty?"

And, without giving Justin another thought, she launched into one of her detailed, thoroughly impossible-to-follow explanations so quickly that I decided Bea's idea of an intervention wouldn't be necessary. For now.

At 6:30 Tuesday evening, right on cue, Will pulled up to the curb in front of my house, got out, and came to the door. That simple act of gentlemanly courtesy was enough to win over Marmie, who rushed to the foyer, where she smoothed down my skirt and adjusted my black hairband.

"So many boys lately," she said, her eyes sparkling.

"It's just school stuff." I gave her a kiss on the cheek as she opened the door, hoping to flee before she could harass him with questions. No such luck.

Where were we going? When would we be back? What grade was he in? How was he enjoying the crisp New England autumn weather? Was that his car? His *own* car? Was it new? Did he drive it to school?

"We have to go, Marmie," I said, clutching the door handle.

"*Cœur qui soupire n'a pas ce qu'il désire,*" she answered with a knowing wink.

"Ah. 'The heart that sighs does not have what it desires.'" Will shoved his hands into the pockets of his trench coat and smiled to himself as Marmie closed the door behind us. In his button-down shirt and red tie he looked extremely J.Crew. And extremely handsome. My stomach did that flip-flop thing again—even though I was still kind of pissed about Ava and the weekend.

"Is that just a phrase you happened to have picked up?" I said. "Or are you fluent?"

"*Je parle couramment.*"

"Just what I need. Another one."

Will opened the shiny black door for me and I got in, attaching my seat belt, inhaling the new car smell and the white paper floor mats and wondering when—if ever—I'd sat next to a guy who had his own car. And who was my age.

"You don't speak?" he asked, inserting the key into the ignition.

"I like to say that it's a conspiracy between my grand-mother and mother, who wanted to be able to gossip in French without me eavesdropping. So . . . they made me take Latin. Which will be incredibly helpful if we're ever invaded by centurions."

He laughed, checked his mirror, and pulled out. "Look, I wanna explain—"

About Ava?

"—about this car. I'm not the kind of jerk who comes into a new school with a brand-new Saab to win friends and influence people. I just want you to know that. It's a bribe from my father. I guess he thought if he gave me a Saab I'd be okay about leaving California and Mom and Harvard-Westlake."

And Talia, I added mentally, since I felt she deserved an honorable mention. "Okay."

We stopped at a light, its red glow illuminating his fine features, the perfect profile, the strong jaw and effortless hair. He swallowed, his Adam's apple bobbing up and down as he kept his eyes straight ahead on the road. "And I owe you an apology about Saturday."

Finally!

He pressed the gas. "Here's the thing. The other night when I was taking you home, I mentioned my girlfriend, remember?"

"I *think* so," I said, pretending like I hadn't been thinking of this 24/7.

"The thing is, Talia's always been there for me, including during my parents' separation and a lot of other stuff. She's pretty cool and extremely smart. I think you'd really like her."

"Uh-huh." I found it totally obnoxious when guys you liked claimed you'd like their girlfriends.

"Lately, we've been talking about how we can be closer and she was looking into transferring to a boarding school nearby, maybe Andover." He took a deep breath. "Anyway, we realized this weekend it wasn't going to work. On Saturday, while I should have been out with you, Talia and I were having The Talk. Her parents don't want her to live that far away and so we're wondering whether to break up. When I finally got off the phone, it was after four and too late for the aquarium."

But not too late for Ava, apparently. That girl was a one-woman convenience store, open at all hours.

I focused on the passing houses filled with couples who'd somehow survived this teenage craziness of he-likes-her-but-she-likes-another-guy-who-likes-somebody-else. How did they do it? How did they end up in their golden, warm, and cozy living rooms with their 2.3 children and dogs and cats? Because getting from where I was to where they were seemed millions of light-years away.

He turned right into the school parking lot. One set of windows revealed a lit room with people at tables. The meeting was already underway.

Will parked and turned to me as he slid his arm along the back of his seat. "I told you all that because I want you to know I didn't stand you up on purpose. I guessed that's what you must have thought—you immediately unfriended me on Facebook."

I was so dying to call him on this lie that I almost said, "Um, except you were out with Ava." Though that would have definitely placed me in stalker territory, and then I would have had to explain that Bea and Neerja saw him in Harvard Square, which would have meant we were talking about him, which would have been pathetic.

"We better go," I said. "The meeting's already started." And got out.

"You're still mad at me, aren't you?" He caught up to me as I crossed the parking lot.

At the door to the school, I stopped and said, "Look, Will. You don't owe me anything, except maybe a Saturday afternoon that was wasted waiting around for you and Aidan. That's a mistake I won't make again. In the meantime, let's just be friends."

"But . . ."

"But . . ." I opened the door. "Come on."

To me, schools at night feel like an amusement-park fun house gone awry. The bathroom doors are propped open for airing. The janitor's silently waxing the floor. It's quiet and smells weird, like cafeteria meat loaf and mashed potatoes mixed with Lysol. Creepy.

Will and I made our way to the conference room,

signed our names on a clipboard, and grabbed a couple of agendas before finding seats in the far back.

I could sense Will trying to catch my eye as I pretended to pay attention. According to the agenda, there were three items of interest, all of which had to do with the budget that was due to be approved by the end of the calendar year, mere weeks away.

Across the room, looking extremely tense, Mrs. Greene, the librarian, was sitting with Drew and Jerry, our ski coach, and Dr. Schultz, who was next to Felicity McKay, our much-adored art teacher who taught jewelry making; she was the only teacher at Denton who insisted on being called by her first name. Possibly because she didn't seem that much older than us.

Clearly they were here for one reason: to save their jobs.

"Smitty didn't show," Will observed, checking around.

"Why would he? He's running to protest Mullet's punishment."

"And you're running to protest *your* punishment."

A bit snarky. "That's not the only reason I'm running."

He folded the agenda into a paper airplane. "That's what Mike said."

"Mike doesn't know bubkes." I paused to see if Ava's favorite word elicited any reaction and was glad to see he remained unfazed. "There's also the upcoming budget cuts. I don't want our jewelry class cut or driver's ed, or

Mrs. Greene taken down to part-time."

"Might be necessary if you want Denton High to be the kind of place Ivy League colleges take seriously. Jewelry's fun and everything, but this isn't summer camp, Gigi. It's high school."

Oh. No. Please, do not tell me Will is one of those, I thought as the school board president shot us a darting look to shut up. Folding my hands, I scooched an inch away and smiled at Mrs. Greene, who waved her pinkie in return.

Summer camp, indeed.

Finally, the meeting was almost over with, as far as I could tell, nothing resolved. They scheduled a couple of public hearings about the budget cuts and discussed re-shingling part of the roof that had been damaged in a September windstorm. Also, something about hiring an energy consultant to make the high school more efficient and approving a series of the superintendent's proposals and we were done.

"Before we adjourn," the school board president, Mark Occum, said, leaning into his microphone, "it has come to our attention that we have two students here who are running to replace the student representative position vacated by Jim Mullet, who, as previously reported, resigned after making a bad choice that has rendered him unable to serve."

Mark cleared his throat as several members on the board shifted in their seats uncomfortably.

"I'd like the candidates, if they wouldn't mind, to stand and please state their names, their year at Denton High, and why they're running." He waved toward Will and me.

Everyone turned to us. A photographer from the local newspaper snapped our photos. Will asked if I'd like to go first, and since already my palms were sweating and my throat was clenching at the prospect of approaching the mic, I graciously offered to let him do the honors.

Will got up and with his customary self-confidence approached the microphone, stuck one hand in his pocket, and proceeded to introduce himself, making excellent eye contact with nearly every person in the room, his voice deep, clear, and even.

"Finally, I'd like to close by saying it's good to see the board is willing to make tough decisions with regard to our education. As a student transferring from a private school in another state, I can testify firsthand to the fact that Denton High, while a great institution with lots of potential, could set the bar higher."

The tips of my fingers gripped the underside of my metal folding chair, as I fought a flurry of powerful impulses to leap up and grab the microphone from him. If their self-satisfied smiles were any indication, the board members were lapping up his every word while Mrs. Greene sat stone-faced, the words *tough decisions* no doubt striking her with horror.

"In conclusion, all I want to say is, I look forward to serving."

The board broke into applause, Mark Occum actually standing and giving Will a salute as he returned to his seat. I was not surprised to see that the teachers whose jobs were on the line clapped tepidly—if at all.

"Next?" Mark Occum raised his eyebrows as if expecting that I, too, would play suck-up.

Yeah. Right.

"Thank you," I said, taking the mic from its stand. "I'm Gigi Dubois, sixteen, a sophomore like my opponent." Bea had taught me that, in politics, you try to avoid referring to the other candidates by name. "But unlike my opponent, I have very, very different views on the proposed cuts."

Reflexively, my hand flew to my abdomen, as if ready to calm the butterflies. Surprisingly, the butterflies had yet to appear even though the school board members were already studying their pens and looking like they wished I'd just shut up and sit down.

I persevered. "Jewelry making and driver's ed, drama and a full-time librarian might seem superfluous to you, but to us students they are really important. Mrs. Greene is way more helpful than Google could ever be and, with all due respect to the other teachers here, jewelry is the one class everyone fights to get into."

Mark Occum rudely turned to the pages of his notes, flipping loudly. Normally, something like that was enough to unleash the first waves of nausea and dizziness. Soon my legs would be quivering and I'd be practically begging to sit down. But then I saw Mrs. Greene had tears in her eyes and, ever so subtly, Schultz nodded for me to go on.

I cleared my throat and took a deep breath, willing myself to calm down and stay on point. "So, what I'd like to say in closing is that after I'm elected, I look forward to finding a way to make sure Denton High can be all things to all students, a place of great learning and a place to learn other stuff too, like acting and jewelry making and how to drive." Okay, that last part sounded a little dumb. "Thank you."

My hand began to shake as I fumbled to get the mic in the stand. Great. *Now*, I was breaking down.

Suddenly there was Will taking the mic out of my hand and placing it neatly in its holder.

"Come on," he said into my ear. "Let's get out of here."

Will led me out of the school, taking me by the hand into the refreshingly brisk night air. It was gradually hitting me what I'd done, that I'd managed to get up and speak in public without choking on my words. It'd been because I cared, I decided as I stepped into his car. I cared so much about getting my point across that for once I was able to push past my nervousness.

I could do it again. *I could!* I'd do it in a heartbeat if I had to.

It wasn't until we were out of the parking lot that Will relaxed behind the wheel and said, "I completely disagree with most of what you just said. You're one hundred percent wrong about schools needing to teach arts and crafts. You don't know what you're talking about and . . ." He smiled. "You were awesome."

I laughed out of relief. "You were awesome too, even if your head's up your butt."

"Oh, really." He leaned back. "Because why? Because I happen to have high standards? I guess that makes me ignorant."

"That makes you pig-headed. You don't even know Mrs. Greene or Drew or Felicity, our art teacher. How can you say the school will be better if they go?"

Will just shook his head. "I don't want to argue."

"Well, I do." Already we were only a block from my house. I usually loved living so close to the school. Not tonight. "I want you to listen to me and agree. I want you to say, 'You know, Gigi, after listening to you, you're right. I concede.'"

"Never." He pulled up to my house and parked the car. "Unless . . ."

I reached for my purse. "Unless what?"

"Unless . . . this." And before I knew what was happening, Will's lips were on mine.

A kiss. Not a kindergarten slobbery post-office kiss or our fifth-grade graduation party when we played spin the bottle and I was forced to press my lips against the wet pair belonging to Robert Bonatello, who didn't even go to our school anymore and was rumored to be in Canada on a commercial fishing boat with his dad. This was not the awkward eighth-grade fumbling during my two-day Cape Cod fling with Dave Kirstin, the son of my mother's friend from MIT. No.

This was a real kiss. Slow and sweet and . . . wow. No slobber. Nothing chapped. No awkwardness—in fact, Will seemed to know exactly how to do it, which is to say, well.

When we broke away, he smiled shyly and said, "I concede."

All I could do was manage a weak grin before I got out of the car, ran into the house, and went upstairs.

To throw up.

Fifteen

Will did not call, write, or Facebook me. (To be fair, that would have been hard since I refused to re-friend him for the sake of my own sanity.) Nor did he acknowledge my presence in class or between classes or at lunch, even though I was now eating in the cafeteria every day and hanging out in the halls, trying to get votes.

It was like the kiss never happened. Every day that passed, my expectations for us, my excitement over the prospect that he really liked me, grew fainter and fainter, until I finally decided the only thing to do was give up. It was horrible. *Painful*, even. Had I been the victim of some cruel prank? Or was he too embarrassed to face me after I freaked when he kissed me?

"Typical," was Bea's conclusion as we rehashed Will again while standing in the atrium handing out pink I'M GAGA 4 GIGI! stickers. "Of course he's completely ignoring you. That's the way *they* are."

I love how while Bea has never had a boyfriend, she knows all about guys.

"It's been scientifically proven. The male of the species is focused only on what he sees in front of him at the moment. Out of sight? Out of mind. It's not that he's just not that into you." She stuck a sticker on B.K.'s backpack. "It's that he simply forgot who you are."

Neerja mouthed, "No way."

"It all goes back to the jungle," Bea said with a sniff.

"Well, well, well." Mike came up the hall with Sienna and Parker Forbes. "If it isn't Candidate Barbie. And where's Candidate Ken?"

"Say what?"

"The photo in the newspaper," Bea said. "Of you in your headband and Will in his tie. They're calling you Barbie and Ken."

I reddened. So that explained why Will was distancing himself from me. We must have looked like a couple of wonks.

"Sorry you were put off by my fashion sense, Mr. Ipolito. Next time, I'll call you before I go out to make sure I meet with your personal approval." I handed him a sticker.

Mike took it, examined it, ripped the backing off, and stuck it on his T-shirt. "There. How do I look?"

"Pink." Bea laughed. "Though what's your buddy Will gonna say when he sees you've joined the other side?"

"Frankly, my dear, I don't give a damn." Mike's eyes flashed as he wheeled toward me, adding with odd seriousness, "He's not your friend either, Einstein. He's your enemy. Keep that in mind."

I was startled. Mike didn't let anything bother him—not even being accused of cheating. So how come he suddenly had a bug up his butt about Will? Having witnessed Mike's reaction in the cafeteria when Will bragged about his new Saab, it had to be pure jealousy. I didn't know much about Mike's family, but he clearly didn't have Will's bucks. None of us did. But you didn't see the rest of us going around making snarky comments.

"It's only an election for student rep, Mike."

"That's what you think. Wolves like him eat lambs like you for breakfast." Then, switching back to his old carefree self, he said to Sienna, "I feel like skipping health. You want to miss fourth period and go hang out?"

Sienna said she couldn't, that she was already in trouble for skipping a class last week.

"How about you, Einstein?" He wiggled his brows.

He reminded me of Ava, who was always trying to get

me to break the rules. "As if I've ever skipped anything in life."

"Oh, right. I forgot. Barbie." With that, he spun on his heel and ducked into the staircase that led to the roof.

Sienna watched him and rolled her eyes. "Mike's got issues."

"No kidding."

Ava, meanwhile, seemed to be going out of her way to avoid me.

If I was sitting at Sienna's table, she sat with Lindsay. But if we were sitting with Henry and Lindsay—who, as Romeo and Juliet, were becoming something of a couple—she would sit with Sienna. The person I never saw her with was Will.

Never.

It even crossed my mind that Bea and Neerja might have been mistaken about the Harvard Square sighting. However, they swore up and down that not only had they seen Will and Ava, but they'd seemed super close.

Anyway, with play rehearsals and running three miles every morning, not to mention the election and the periodic table presentation just days away, I didn't exactly have the luxury of sitting around eating bonbons and musing over other people's love lives. My stress level was already at the max.

Mike and I met once more in the library to run through the PowerPoint presentation, and I was glad I'd insisted we scrap Mike's idea of going element by element because we would have taken up an entire class, maybe two. Instead, our presentation categorized the elements by metals, metalloids, etc., and we threw in some fun examples, like the fact that chlorine in small amounts saves lives by disinfecting, but that in large quantities has been used as poisoned gas to kill thousands, even though most of us eat it every day as salt (NaCl).

That's the kind of trivia I love.

"This should satisfy Buzzard," Mike said, powering down the laptop. "You going to be able to handle this Tuesday? Or will I have to do all the talking?"

"I'll be fine," I said, packing up. "I think I'm making progress in that area, actually. At the school board meeting I spoke at the mic and did okay."

"Maybe it was the hairband."

I stuck my tongue out at him.

He returned the gesture, shoved his laptop into his backpack, and sat on the table with his hands between his knees. "Seriously, what happens to those letters in our files if you don't win?"

"Thanks for the confidence."

"I'm just saying. Will seems like the type of jerk who'll get off on being in power, even if it's only being a member of a school board. I can just see him sticking by the cheating policy, telling us it was our own fault for being falsely accused."

"Gee," I said, somewhat surprised by Mike's open hostility. "Why don't you tell me what you really think?"

"You gotta admit, he's a piece of work. Been in school all of a month and suddenly he's the big man on campus, running for election, flashing his daddy's cash." He glanced away. "When you come from a family like mine, where you better get a full scholarship or you're not going to college, a pretty boy from California with a fifty-grand convertible is a little hard to take."

I'd never thought about it before, how crucial those athletic scholarships were for him. Here I'd been resentful when really I should have been understanding. Though I still didn't get why putting a little white ball in a net was so freaking important.

Mike slid off the table and slung his backpack over a shoulder. "Bottom line is, you better win, Einstein. Or I'll be spending my life on construction sites. If I'm lucky."

What happened at the ski swap didn't exactly do much to improve the situation.

The ski swap was held in the gym every year the weekend before Thanksgiving and was a great way to get quality used ski equipment cheap—as long as you didn't mind waking up before dawn and waiting in the gray November cold for a couple of hours. In addition, a few stores set up booths displaying their brand-new, crazy expensive skis just to make you feel bad for being poor.

Bea and I had no business drooling over the new Rossignols and Dynastars since we were using our own (meager) savings, but we couldn't resist. They were gorgeous.

"Oh my god. Check out these Nordicas." Bea ran her hand over the smooth, twin-tipped skis with the sexy red flames. "Me. Want."

I examined the price tag. "A thousand bucks before bindings. You. Not. Have. Cash."

"Me. Rob. Bank?"

Coach Jerry came up and shooed us away. He was a relatively short and muscly guy who wore a blue skullcap and sweats, like all coaches, I supposed. I can't say he was thrilled to learn I hadn't skied since the after-school program in sixth grade. But with me on board, the women's team was now eligible to race and, besides, I'd stuck up for him and the other teachers at the school board meeting. There wasn't much I could do wrong.

"I'll get to you later, Gigi. First, Bea needs two pairs of skis, rock and racing. Plus boots."

Bea rolled her eyes. "I only have four hundred and

fifty bucks, Coach. Give me a break."

You could tell Coach did not think this was enough. "Can't hit up your parents?"

Bea and I exchanged guilty looks. The truth was, Bea had yet to tell her parents, which was why her liability forms weren't in. "Um. My brother's in college and money's kind of tight right now."

"Okay. Okay. We'll work something out." He patted her on the back and led her toward the cheapest stuff.

I was following behind when I saw exactly what I was looking for: books.

A whole stack of secondhand books and DVDs about skiing. Most were ridiculous extreme skiing videos, skiers with death wishes being dropped off by helicopter on massive mountains, or memoirs by Olympic athletes. But a thorough perusal turned up my heart's desire, a book entitled *Teach Yourself How To Ski Like a Pro!* by someone named Gunther Humboldt *and* an accompanying DVD, *Going from Blue Circle to Double Black Diamond the Gunther Humboldt Way.*

Gunther had *a way.* I knew because I'd already watched some of his videos on YouTube and read a few articles he'd written about skiing out west. Yes, like my mother, I'm a geek who loves research.

Unfortunately, researching online is like finding your way out of the woods blindfolded. You can never tell if you're on a path that's going to lead you to safety or plunging into a ravine. How many times have I stumbled across the perfect source for a history paper, only to find it was written by another high school student just like me, who probably ripped it off another kid who got it from another. . . . Well, you get my point.

Anyway, I was happily paying for my purchase—a whopping total of $4.50—when I saw Mike strolling by, zeroing in on those awesome Nordicas. I gave him a wave and he back-stepped.

"Einstein? What are you doing here?"

"I'm on the ski team." I pocketed the change from my five bucks. "Didn't you know?"

Apparently he didn't. "You mean, you're the one who signed up at the last minute so the girls can race?"

When he put it that way, I felt almost heroic. "I did it mostly for Bea. She needed support and I thought, how hard can it be to learn?"

Mike's eyes bugged. *"You don't know how?"*

"Well, that's not entirely true. I know how to pizza-wedge." I pointed my toes inward. "My french fries are kind of shaky, though. Unless I'm on a bunny slope. Bunny slopes with perfect conditions and plenty of hot chocolate breaks and I'm okay."

This revelation rendered him speechless.

"That's why I bought these." I showed him Gunther

Humboldt's book and DVD.

He scoffed. "You can't learn skiing from a book."

"Maybe *you* can't learn skiing from a book, but I can." I headed to the other end of the gym to find Bea. "I've learned lots of things from books and not just school stuff. I taught myself how to drive—in theory—and how to make a cake from scratch. I learned all about raising basset hounds and how nuclear fission differs from nuclear fusion. I even taught myself how to knit. I'm sure old Gunther here"—I patted Gunther's book—"will set me straight."

Mike smacked his forehead. "This is a disaster in the making."

"Don't be so dramatic. I'll be fine."

"We're only getting in a couple of hill practices before our first race in two weeks."

A race so soon? "We don't have any snow yet."

"Vermont does. On the double-black-diamond slopes." He cut his eyes in my direction. "Of course, it'll be icy up there. And the bigger rocks will be exposed at the drop-offs."

Ice? Rocks? Double black diamond? *Drop-offs!*

I focused my attention on Bea stepping into a pair of ski boots as I clutched Gunther a little tighter. *For Bea*, I reminded myself. *She needs you.*

Besides, she'd absolutely murder me if I chickened

out. "Whatever the challenge," I said, lifting my chin, "I'm sure I can handle it. I have confidence in confidence alone." Cue Maria dancing off the bus in *The Sound of Music*.

"Hold on." Mike jogged over to Coach, who was kneeled over Bea's boots, adjusting the buckles. "Hey, Coach. Are you aware Einstein here hasn't skied since she was a kid?"

Coach glanced over his shoulder. "You mean, Gigi? Um, yeah. How are these, Bea? Too loose around the ankles?"

Bea walked back and forth in her black moon boots. "They're fine."

Mike tapped him on the shoulder. "But the first race is on Organ Grinder."

I must admit, I did not like the sound of a slope called Organ Grinder.

"Look, Mike." Coach stood and put his hands on his hips, exasperated after a morning of fitting ski equipment. "I think I know what I'm doing. I've been coaching for twelve years. Gigi's fit. She's skied before. She might not be the fastest . . ."

"She's only been on green slopes."

"I'll be fine!"

Coach gave me a nod. "There. You see? Now, if you really want to help the team, why don't you find Gigi a pair of skis and boots before all the good ones are taken."

I couldn't figure out Mike's problem. What did he care

how good a skier I was? Wasn't like my speed was going to ruin *his* team. He seemed almost insulted that I'd had the audacity to join.

"Okay, Einstein. Let's look at what we've got here." He picked out a pair of shorter skis that would be easier to control, even if they were slower than the kind Bea was trying on. "We can upgrade you as you get better. *If* you live that long."

I pointed to a pair of sleek, dark purple boots. "Love. Those."

"It's a ski slope," Mike said. "Not a catwalk, Einstein." Twenty minutes later, fitted with two pairs of cheap, short skis and those stellar boots, he was helping me carry my haul to the cash register when who should step into our path but Will.

Holding the Nordicas.

Mike let out a low whistle. "Don't tell me you're *buying* those."

"Bought," Will said, stroking the tips. "Aren't they sick?"

"The sickest." Behind my new skis, Mike rolled his eyes. "But you're going to ruin them on this East Coast terrain, dude. Tell him, Gigi."

I had no personal experience with East Coast conditions, though according to my online research, compared to the Rockies, New England skiing sucked. "Yeah. The hills here will eat those to pieces."

"That's why I'm saving them for Breck," Will said.

Short for the über-tony Colorado ski resort town of Breckenridge. That much I knew.

"Nordicas. New Saab. Breck." Mike smirked. "Whatever Will Blake wants, Will Blake gets, huh?"

Will shrugged. "Guess I'm pretty lucky, yeah. How about you, Gigi?"

It was the first conversation we'd had since the kiss, and I was still kind of miffed that he'd been ignoring me in school, so I'll be forgiven, I hope, for what happened next.

"Oh, sure. These are my East Coast rock skis." I rubbed my thumb over their worn edges. "My good stuff I save for out west."

Mike gave me a slight nudge; I nudged him back.

"I'm not one for the chatter on this East Coast hardpack when, with a discount red-eye to chutes at Breck, I can bomb around the moguls on a nice, wide fattie." I had no idea what I was saying. I was only parroting what I'd read on extremeski.com. "I don't like to brag, but I'm something of a ripper on the pow."

Desired effect achieved. Will regarded me with an open expression of awe as Mike stifled a laugh. "Whoa!" Will said. "I had no idea."

"Yes. There's much about me you don't know, Will.

And on that note, I've gotta pay for these or I'll have nothing to ski on when we hit the hill for practice next week."

"You're on the team too?" he asked, even more impressed.

"*And* running for student rep," Mike reminded him. "Most likely winning."

"No doubt." Will stepped aside to make way for Bea, who, seeing Will, immediately shot me a questioning look.

"What's going on?"

"Einstein here was just telling Will how she likes to ski out west bombing around moguls on her fatties." Mike somehow managed to keep a straight face. "Apparently, she's something of a ripper on the pow."

"Is she, now," Bea said, her lips twitching in amusement. "More like a bragger on the fly."

"Seriously, guys, this stuff is heavy." I moved one step closer to the cashiers at the folding tables.

"Hey, before you go," Will said, taking the boots from my arms, "what are you doing tonight? Thought maybe you and I could catch a movie in Harvard Square or get coffee."

My heart dropped. Although he hadn't spoken to me in days, memories of that kiss lingered and I felt the disturbing rekindling of a flickering hope. "Um . . ."

"You're opponents!" Mike exclaimed. "Whatever happened to healthy competition, checks and balances and all that stuff?"

Will grinned. "We're just making it more interesting. So how about it, Gigi? Pick you up around six?"

Sure! I wanted to say. Though I didn't, because there was Bea looking somewhat forlorn, the sting of my lie about why I didn't go out with her and Neerja the other weekend as fresh as the hurt of being stood up by Will. I'd vowed then to put my friends first, and that wasn't a promise I intended on scrapping simply because the cute new guy at school was asking me out.

"Thanks, but I'm sleeping over at Bea's house tonight."

"Gigi . . ." Bea started. "You don't have to. . . ."

"I *want* to." We inched closer to the table, now only one customer away. "Maybe some other time, Will?"

"That might not be until after the election, but I don't know if we'll be speaking to each other then."

Mike intervened. "So, wait. You're only asking her out *before* the vote? What's up with that?"

Will shrugged. "Like Don Corleone said in *The Godfather*, 'Hold your friends close and your enemies closer.' That's a joke, by the way." Plunking my boots on the cashier's table, he grabbed his shiny red new Nordicas and walked off.

"Wow," Bea said. "*The Godfather.*"

"Actually, Sun Tzu," Mike corrected. "Chinese general who wrote *The Art of War* around the sixth century BC. I'm surprised he didn't know that."

"I'm surprised *you* did," I said.

"Why? Because you still think I'm a dumb jock, Einstein?"

"No, I . . ." Oh. Why did I always end up accidentally insulting him?

"That's okay. I don't mind being thought of as stupid. Lowers everyone's expectations and makes it just that much easier to win in the end." He leaned on my skis and watched through the doorway as Will got into his Saab. "Or as Sun Tzu said, 'All warfare is based on deception. Pretend to be weak, that the enemy may grow arrogant.

"'Then crush him.'"

Sixteen

I was beginning to learn that the things you dread most turn out to be nothing in the end—which would be great if the opposite weren't also true.

For all my complaining about the periodic table project and worry over whether I'd be able to pull it off with my schedule, Mike and I had fun putting it together, and even standing up in front of the class wasn't so bad. People actually laughed when I described inert noble gases as the "snobs of the atomic world."

When Mike and I finished our PowerPoint, we opened it up to questions and answers. Mike sat on Mr. Bouchard's desk while our crusty teacher clicked his pen from the back of the room, where he sat scratching notes. None of my fellow students, bless their dark little hearts, had questions, so Buzzard directed one at me: "Ms. Dubois. Could you explain how the periodic table came to be?"

It was an obvious question and the answer I knew off the bat. It was right on the tip of my tongue. Only, my mind went blank as the door opened and in walked Schultz, who quietly took a seat behind Amanda Bleskoe, a girl renowned school-wide for her mindless humming. I'd been fine until then, but there was something about the principal being in the room that triggered my old public-speaking phobia.

I could feel the blood draining from my upper extremities.

"Ms. Dubois?" Buzzard prompted.

Right. Where were we? Periodic table. Origin.

Neerja raised her hand. "Weren't you telling me, Gigi, that while several people came up with the idea of organizing the elements, it was the Russian scientist Mendeleev who got around to it, and that the cool thing was he left room for future elements yet to be discovered?"

"Yes! Yes!" So grateful she'd come to my rescue. "It was his idea to arrange them by atomic weight and still he didn't win the Nobel Prize, even though he definitely should have. Lost by one vote."

Oh god. I hoped that wasn't prophetic.

The bell rang and the torture was over. "You kept it

together, Einstein. Good for you," Mike said, patting me on the shoulder. "Did you see Schultz come in?"

As if I could have missed her. We waited for Buzzard to stroll up the aisle, loudly announcing to the class that while Mike and I had "treaded dangerously close to cheating" on our exam, we had redeemed ourselves by "enlightening the class with an excellent lecture" that required a lot of research and effort on our part, "but, since when did more work ever harm inquisitive students?"

Behind him Schultz nodded with approval. So Mike had been right—again. This project had had nothing to do with the two of us. All along, it had simply been about saving face. *Buzzard*'s face.

"I'm sorry I didn't catch more of it," Schultz said. "But from what I saw, it seemed very thorough and complete. And you two worked on it equally, is that right?"

I nodded. Mike hung his arm over my shoulder and said, "She was slacking off at first, but I got her to knuckle down."

Cute. "Mike was fine," I said. "Helpful, really."

Mike went, *"Helpful?"*

"Okay, more than that. He came up with the idea of finding unusual properties of the elements and making it fun. If it'd just been me, I would have been teaching straight memorization."

"Nothing wrong with memorization," chimed in Buzzard.

Schultz clasped her hands. "Well, at any rate, I believe all of our goals for this assignment have been met, don't you think, Mr. Bouchard?"

She was so obviously pressuring him to drop his case against us.

Buzzard's thin smile tightened. Pushing up his steel-frame glasses, he said, "You'll be pleased to know the A's you earned on today's presentation will replace the zeroes on your midterms. Perhaps this was a hard lesson to learn, but it is always best to take the high road. Cheaters never prosper."

"Except in baseball," Mike said. "Not that I'm saying steroids had anything to do with the Sox winning the 2004 World Series. I'm just saying sometimes cheaters do prosper—and they get bazillion-dollar contracts."

Lying on the cold, hard, smooth back of ARTHUR JAMES LITTLE, I stared at the stars through the bare branches of the towering oaks that put the shade in Shady Acres Cemetery. The nightmare of the cheating scandal was over—except for the letters in our files—and now it was Thanksgiving vacation. A chance to relax.

Already it felt like so much had changed since finding Parad's yearbook. Sienna's advice to quit hiding in the honors lounge and eat lunch in the cafeteria, to hang out instead of doing homework, had been more helpful than I'd have expected. Almost everyone knew my name or said hi when they passed me in the halls. I'M GAGA 4 GIGI! stickers were on tons of lockers, along with VOTE FOR GIGI posters in all the bathrooms and in strategic places near the water fountains.

I was no longer a nonentity. I was actually *participating* at Denton instead of standing on the sidelines like an outsider.

As Sienna would say, I was becoming a "normal" person.

Even Ava had made a comment a few days earlier when she found me, feet up, in the atrium shooting the breeze with the Thayer twins. "Look who got herself a life all of a sudden," she said, doing nothing to cover the not one but two YES, WE WILL! buttons on her jean jacket.

She was looking a little better lately, I'd noticed. Not so heavy with the eyeliner. And the tweed coat was gone, replaced by the jean jacket over a tight black tank. With a touch of pink lip gloss, some mascara, and her hair neatly brushed into a flattering half chignon, Ava was actually pretty—again.

She nodded at the Thayer twins. "How's it going?"

The Thayer twins responded with their own nods, but otherwise focused on their phones. I reached into my bag.

"You need a bright pink Gigi sticker."

"No one gave me one."

Was that metaphorical for our failed friendship or what? Peeling off a backing, I plastered it across her portfolio. "There. Now I'm a work of art."

"You always were a piece of work." She admired the sticker. "Not bad. But you could have done without the sparkles."

Those sparkles had kind of bothered me, too. "It's supposed to make the Gigi stand out."

"It makes the Gigi seem girly and frivolous whereas the Will"—she ran a jet-black nail under Will's name on her button—"is in dark red. Like he means business."

"Hmm." Okay, I had to ask. "You two have become pretty good friends, huh?"

"*Friends?*" She cocked an eyebrow, a smile playing on her lips. "Yeah, I guess you could say we're good *friends.* Will gets me. Being from L.A., he appreciates someone who's not afraid to express her creative self. He's not all caught up in . . ." She rolled her hands, searching for the words, and finally waved toward the twins in their matching Madewell skinny jeans. ". . . *that.*"

For days, I'd been wondering what, exactly, *"that"* was and whether I, too, was caught up in "that."

Meanwhile, Bea was psyched for our first hill practice Friday even though we were leaving at 6 a.m. to pile into the coach's van to New Hampshire. Me? I was scared spitless, but I wasn't letting on. There was something to be said for Marmie's favorite expression: *"Feignez afin d'être!"* Or, to put it in cruder English, "Fake it to make it!"

My attitude was, get on the hill and see what happens. Hey, if Gunther said I could ski like a pro with his program, then I could. Anyway, how hard could it be? Turn. Go. Stop. Tiny little Nordic children did it without thinking all the time.

Yup, it was all going to turn out fine. Just fine.

God, I hoped so.

"I don't know what to do about Lindsay. She's missed so many practices 'cause of gymnastics that Drew's getting really pissed," Neerja said from her tombstone, where she was being cuddled by Justin, who deftly kept one hand around her waist while playing Angry Birds with his other. "This weekend, she's gotta practice with Henry or me or something bad's gonna happen. After we get back from break, the play will be only days away."

Bea said slyly, "Maybe Drew will realize the error of his ways and replace her with you."

Neerja let out a snort. "As if." Then, "You think?"

Poor Neerja. She so wanted to be on that stage. "You *do* have the whole thing memorized."

"Yeah, but Lindsay has star power." Neerja poked

Justin. "What do you think? You think Drew will make me Juliet?"

Justin pumped his fist. "Score! Got a pumpkin. Die, you piggies."

"I was talking about the play," she said, insulted.

"The play?" He lifted his head briefly. "What play?"

"Oh brother." She stood abruptly, and though it was leaves she brushed off her arms, it was almost like she was brushing off Justin's callousness. Three weeks going out with the love of her life, the boy she'd pined for since kindergarten, and already the magic was fading.

For his part, Justin didn't even seem to know she'd moved away, so eager was he to level up.

"Let's go," she said. "I've gotta help Mom with . . ."

Shuffling of leaves. Footsteps. We went silent as two figures came up the hill from Neerja's street. There'd been reports of vandalism up here lately, and cops were leery of teenagers hanging around the tombstones. I didn't want to get busted for trespassing, nor did I want to get beat up by thugs.

"Henry?" Neerja said into the dark.

"Aha," he said. "My calculations were correct. I knew we'd find you here."

Oh, please. Not Lindsay, too. I was just not in the mood to tolerate her effervescent chatter.

"How many times have I told you, young lady, not

to come up to the cemetery after dark?" It was such a dead-on impersonation of Neerja's mother that all of us—except for Justin—froze.

"Parad!" Neerja screamed and hugged her big sister. "You weren't supposed to get back until tomorrow."

"My last class was canceled and I got on standby. I wanted it to be a surprise, so I called Henry to pick me up at Logan since Karla's not home yet."

"We would have made it earlier, but I sort of got lost on the way," he said. "My sense of direction sucks."

"No problem," Parad teased. "I've always wanted to see Cape Cod this time of year."

Neerja gave him a push. "You didn't! You went to the Cape?"

"Just the wrong way on the Southeast Expressway. But it was worth the hassle," he said. "Can't celebrate Thanksgiving without my favorite Indians." The three of them cracked up.

"Dudes." Justin finally looked up from his phone. "That's so racist. They're not Indians. They're *Native Americans*."

Neerja had to sniff back tears of laughter. "No. You don't understand. Parad and I, we're Indians. From India. When Henry was . . . Oh, you tell him, Henry."

"Can't. It's too embarrassing."

"It's not. It's cute!" Parad said. "When Henry was in

second grade, his teacher asked him to draw a picture of the first Thanksgiving and he had all these Pilgrim white guys sitting around with women in their saris and men in their jodhpuri suits drinking tea."

"Because when he heard 'Indians,'" Neerja said, "he thought of us, his next-door neighbors. Those were the only Indians he knew." She paused, expectantly. "*Get it?*"

Justin thought about this. "No. See, there weren't any Indians at the first Thanksgiving. That's what I'm trying to tell you guys. Geesh, what do you guys think I am? A moron?"

Naturally, I would have preferred my mother being home for Thanksgiving, but since the Swiss celebrate things like Berchtold's Day instead of Thanksgiving, the industrious nerds at the Large Hadron Collider didn't have an excuse to flip the off switch and call it a holiday. I would have to wait until Christmas to see Mom.

In the meantime, I saw Harry and Alice Honeycutt and the extended Honeycutt clan, and that, believe you me, was excitement enough.

For the past two or three years, my grandmother and I have spent Thanksgiving this way, with Bea and her parents (both lawyers), and her brother (pre-law), and uncles (lawyers), aunts (ditto), and cousins (many aspiring to the legal profession)—arguing.

Marmie disagrees with this term. She says the French argue while never raising their voices. The Honeycutts argue by basically clobbering each other over the head with thick verbal clubs.

Either way, I find it very entertaining, especially when Mr. Honeycutt gets up from the head of the table and, wielding the long silver turkey-carving knife, demands that his brother (said uncle) recite the Bill of Rights if he's so gosh-darned in awe of the U.S. Constitution.

Inevitably, Bea's uncle can't (partly because Bea's father is clutching that knife) and next thing you know, relatives are packing up and leaving and assuring Bea's mother, Alice, that they had a lovely time, only they must be getting home early to watch the game and/or avoid bloodshed.

But this year, there was an added twist. This year, when we were getting ready for a game of Scattergories after doing the dishes, Alice went to look in Bea's backpack for pens and returned holding the USSA ski form. She held it gingerly, by the corner, like it was a dead rat.

"Beatrice Rachel Honeycutt." There was a sharp intake of breath as Bea's mom tried to control her emotions. "What. Is. This?"

This was a rhetorical question. We all knew it was the membership form for the United States Ski and Snowboard Association, the one that had to be signed before you could race on the ski team. Everyone in the Honeycutt family knew it too. Only my grandmother was clueless. Thanks to an opportunity after her second glass of Bordeaux, when I slipped it in with a bunch of meaningless forms, she had actually signed it!

"Um . . ." Bea flashed me a look of panic.

"It's mine!" I shouted, lunging and missing as Alice dangled it out of reach.

Marmie, sitting in the wingback chair with a cup of coffee, frowned. "Now, you know very well, Gigi, that I signed a form exactly like that last week."

This was the problem with my grandmother. She was always more on top of things than she seemed.

Bea put down the Scattergories timer and removed the paper from Alice's pinched fingers. "It's mine, Mom. You might as well know. Gigi and I are joining the ski team."

From the other room, where the whistles and cheers of the football game surely would have drowned out this mild announcement, Bea's dad yelled, "What?"

He and Bea's brother rushed out. "Tell me I didn't just hear what I think I heard," Harry said.

Alice slumped into a chair. "We've been over this, Bea. It's just not worth the risk."

"Give me the form." Harry held out his hand and Bea dutifully submitted it as her father ran his finger down the waiver to the pertinent paragraph. "Always read the fine print. You too, Gigi. And you too, Helene."

Helene, aka my grandmother, put down her coffee and took the seat he held out for her at the table. Over her shoulder we read:

> *I understand that skiing . . . involves many RISKS, DANGERS, and HAZARDS. . . . I know that the risk of SEVERE INJURY and even DEATH exists. . . . With full knowledge and understanding of the RISK OF SEVERE INJURY AND DEATH involved in ski and snowboard training and competition, I FREELY AND VOLUNTARILY ACCEPT AND FULLY ASSUME THE RISK THAT I MAY SUFFER TEMPORARY, PERMANENT, OR EVEN FATAL INJURIES. . . .*

Marmie rested her cheek on one hand. *"La jeunesse est gaspillée sur les jeunes."* Youth is wasted on the young. "There is nothing we can do, Harry. These girls, they will do as they will. What is to be done?" She punctuated this with a Frenchy *"Boop."*

Harry couldn't believe she wasn't more upset. "I'll tell you what is to be done. What is to be done is to rip up this form! Look at George." He gently cuffed him above the ear. "I'm not sure he's not still slightly brain damaged from that snowboard accident."

George rubbed the spot where he'd been smacked. "I can't believe you would do something like this, Bea. I didn't think you had it in you."

Bea's eyes turned into fireballs. "You didn't think I had it in me? I'll tell you. . . ."

"It's a compliment," I said, reaching for her arm. "He's trying to say he's impressed."

She hadn't thought of that. "Oh."

"Yeah, I mean . . ." He shifted his feet awkwardly. "I've been feeling really bad about this. You were an awesome skier, Bea, and who knows how far you could have gone if I hadn't overshot a half-pipe. It didn't make sense, didn't seem fair, that you had to pay the price for my accident."

Alice bit her knuckle. "I had no idea. Harry . . . did you know that's how George felt?"

Harry grumbled something unintelligible under his breath, though it must have meant something to Bea because she gave a hop and screamed, "So you'll sign then?"

"I'll take it under advisement."

"You better take it fast because we have our first down-hill practice tomorrow morning." Bea winced. "Don't be mad."

Harry cocked his head warningly. "How can I not be mad? That's hardly any notice."

"She would have brought the form to us sooner,

Harry, if she didn't think you were going to react this way." Alice tapped her fingers on the table.

There was a long pause as we all waited for the verdict. Finally, Bea's father said, "Give me the pen." And that was that.

We were headed to the hills.

Seventeen

Bea slept over at my house because it was so close to the school, and Coach offered to pick us up on his way to New Hampshire for our first downhill practice. Not that door-to-door service made waking at 5 a.m. during school break any easier. We basically tumbled into his van and collapsed in the back, trying to get in a few extra z's amidst the skis, poles, and boots. I couldn't believe some of my friends actually chose to get up this early just to grab a few Black Friday bargains. Ten percent off Steve Madden ballet flats was definitely not worth it.

The temperature plummeted as the van crossed the New Hampshire border and climbed into the piney mountains. I'd had my doubts about finding any snow on Thanksgiving weekend but, sure enough, Paradise Mountain was open, albeit with limited trails.

Paradise wasn't exactly a resort—more like a 1950s wooden lodge where you could hang inside by the fire and warm up. But it was cheap and so it was packed with college and high school students who came for the discounted preseason tickets and the chance to return to school on Monday and boast that they'd already been skiing.

As Mike had predicted, there was only one lift running and it led to the top of the mountain where the snow was. I didn't have to look at the map to know the only trails open were black diamonds.

"Where is Mike anyway?" I asked Bea as she snapped me into my boots. A chalkboard over the service counter warned: CONDITIONS: POOR. ADVANCED AND INTERMEDIATE SKIERS ONLY. KNOW YOUR SKILL LEVEL!

Great.

"I guess Mike's out of town." Bea had to practically stand on a buckle to close it. My foot cramped in protest. "Then again, half the team's not here 'cause of Thanksgiving."

I was glad for that. This way, I'd only embarrass myself in front of the senior girls and B.K. Evans. And I definitely did not care what B.K. thought.

"All right, everyone suited up and ready to go?"

Coach clapped his hands once. He was wearing a bona fide DENTON HIGH red-and-black ski jacket. "I want to be on that mountain by oh eight hundred."

Military time. Another bad sign.

"Just remember," Bea said. "Don't panic."

"Don't panic," I echoed as we left the crowded lodge and its inviting smells of wood smoke, hot chocolate, and french fries. For one fleeting, desperate instant I hoped that maybe I'd break something. Nothing major like a leg or my neck. Just enough to land me on the DL. Then I'd get to stay inside by the fire reading a good book, never having to set foot on skis again.

Then again, that was not the Gunther Humboldt way.

I'd come to love Gunther Humboldt, his apple cheeks and Teutonic can-do 'tude. I loved the robust way he urged me to "lean your knees, yah?" as he zigzagged down a hill without his poles, touching only his outside leg. He would say, "I see you've got it. Good for you! That's the way." And I'd feel sort of guilty because there I was, propped against a bunch of soft pillows in my bedroom, stuffing my face with Raisinets, when really I should have been on the hill, making Gunther proud.

Under the gray November skies threatening rain, we found our skis. I clicked into mine, grabbed my poles, and tried shuffling toward the lift on a thin strip of man-made snow between brown grass and even a few rocks.

"Like this," Bea said, pushing off one ski and then the other.

I tried it and fell flat on my face. Ow.

Bea swung around and gave me her pole to pull up on. I stood, unsteady and shaking. If this was how I behaved on a level surface, what hope would there be for me on a hill?

She lifted her goggles to reveal those emerald-green eyes. "You gonna be okay?"

"Yup," I lied.

"Good!" She slipped on her poles. "Now, all we're going to do is ski a little to the chair lift and get into position. When the chair comes, remove your poles, hold them in one hand, and reach out for the chair back when it comes up behind you. I'll take care of the bar."

"I remember." How could I forget? This was the part that gave me chills, the merciless march of the chair lift that would instantly whisk me into the air so that I dangled twenty, maybe fifty, feet above the ground with a flimsy bar to keep me from sliding out.

Bea effortlessly glided toward the chairlift before turning and waiting for slowpoke me. I did as Gunther instructed, toggled between making a wide pizza wedge (taking care not to let my knees touch) and straight french fries. It reminded me of that wooden universe game we used to have where you rolled a metal ball up and down so that it ideally landed in the perfect spot, like Mercury instead of Pluto.

"Excellent!" Bea exclaimed, as if I were a child.

I gave her a look. "Don't patronize me."

"Just trying to be encouraging."

I somehow managed to join her at the red line under the ice, remove my poles, and grab the chair as it swung around. Bea lowered the bar and we zoomed up the hill. Suddenly the terrain below us turned snow-covered as we zipped to the top. I gripped the edge of my seat for dear life.

"That wasn't so bad, was it?" She gave me a hug. "You know, I wouldn't be here if it weren't for you, Gigi. I swore I'd never ski again. As for the team? No way. But now, because of you, here I am and . . ." She looked down. "Holy . . . Is that . . . ?"

The red flares on the brand-new Nordicas were unmistakable. Will was on the slope below us, expertly negotiating the moguls on a black diamond. Oh God. And here I'd told him I could ski. That I skied out west. On *pow*!

Please don't let him see me, I prayed, trying to make myself smaller.

"Will!" Bea shouted.

"*Bea*," I hissed. "What are you doing? Don't you remember the ski swap?"

"Huh?" Bea asked, flaking out.

Will lifted his goggles and waved. "Hey! Is that you, Gigi?"

She lifted my hand and made me wave like a puppet. Seriously, I could have killed her.

Will shouted, "See you on the hill!"

Bea gave him the thumbs-up and then let out another gasp. "And look who else is here." She pointed to a girl stopped on the hill behind Will. "Ava!"

"I had no idea she could ski," I said, since Ava detested anything smacking of outdoors and/or sports.

"I had no idea she owned a coat that wasn't black. Well, if there's any doubt about the two of them being a couple, this should take care of it. Whoops! Ski tips up!"

We were at the top already. My pulse racing, I raised my ski tips, arranged my poles, and braced for the short drop off the lift. Bea pushed up the bar. I made eye contact with the guy in the little hut to let him know he might need to rescue me and then that was it. Skis down. Stand up. Ski.

Skkkkk. The sound of my edges against ice set my teeth on edge as we slipped down the mound to join the rest of the team waiting at the top of a trail entitled, much to my heart's distress, Terminator. Fortunately, it was marked by a blue circle—intermediate—which was a far cry better than a black diamond.

"Listen up, everyone," Coach began. "I know you guys are excited about your first ski of the season, but let's take it slow today. Let's try to ease ourselves into the groove."

Oh, okay. If I have to.

"Now, as you veterans know, each year I start off by assessing your technique. So I want you to form a line single file on the side of the hill and then you'll go off one by one. Gigi, I'd like you to go last."

Yes, I expected that, I thought as I shuffled to the end. One by one, each team member took off and immediately I knew I was way out of my league. B.K. effortlessly swished like a pro. Parker bombed down without taking one turn. Bea turned and did so gracefully.

"She's going to hug those gates," Coach said, impressed. "All right, Gigi, you're up. Now listen, I know you haven't skied in a while, so let's try to concentrate on form over speed. Keep your knees bent, feet together, lean forward. Pretend you're squeezing oranges at your ankles. Pull yourself in tight."

Nothing about trying not to kill myself. He might have wanted to mention that first.

Lowering my goggles, I gripped my poles and gave in, trying not to be shaken by the ninety-degree drop and the ice glinting under the pathetically thin layer of snow. Having calculated slope + speed + momentum = instant death, I decided to take the prudent approach and ski *across* the hill.

Coach wasn't buying it. "When I said slow, I meant somewhat faster than a crawl. For example, I've always found that when you're racing, it helps to direct your skis down the hill." Not that he was being sarcastic—*much*.

"Oh, okay." Like going down the hill hadn't occurred to me. "I'll try."

Which is when Will cruised by, right as the coach was lecturing me for being a scaredy-cat.

It might have been my paranoia, but Will seemed to be showing off, barely turning as he zipped past wearing only jeans and a dark gray coat to match his dark gray helmet. Perhaps Ava told him I couldn't ski. Or perhaps he was like a bear and could smell my fear. Whatever, I knew then that he knew I was a big fat liar.

"Don't worry about the other skiers, Gigi," Coach was saying. "Just concentrate on getting to the bottom of the hill."

Twenty minutes later, I did just that. And I was ready to collapse from fighting gravity every inch of the way.

"Finally!" B.K. said. "What took you guys so long?"

"It's Gigi," answered one of the senior girls. "She doesn't know how to ski."

Bea snapped around. "Our team wouldn't qualify if it weren't for Gigi, don't forget."

That shut her up.

Coach gathered us in a circle. "Look. We're a team, all of us, boys and girls. And that means, number one, we support one another no matter what. We'll all have bad days, some of us more than others." He chose that moment to pause and slap me on the shoulder. "That's okay. Just give it your all, help one another, cheer one another, and be the kind of team that everyone wishes they were part of."

Our overall mood improved somewhat after that pep talk. Coach gave each of us tips on how to perfect our form and then we went back to the top of the hill and did it again. Whenever I reached the bottom, the whole team let out a cheer—since I was always the last. And with each run the cheers got louder and louder, until one of the ski patrol guys nicknamed us the Screaming Meanies.

That was the first time I really understood why people make such a big deal about being a team player. I got as excited about B.K. improving his time as I was about overcoming my fear of losing control. I high-fived a senior when Bea came in as the fastest girl, and the senior hugged me when I arrived as the slowest. I knew they wished I'd speed up but hey, like Bea said, if it hadn't been for me they wouldn't have qualified.

We ended up going down the hill for twenty runs. With each one, I refined my technique and tried to go faster. Bea even wheedled her way into making me ski the mogul trail Will had been attacking when we were on the lift. It was called Rumble, which was a deceptively modest name for a nightmare of rocks, unexpected drops, annoying moguls, and ice.

It took forever, but we did it, toasting our success with paper cups of hot chocolate that we sipped on the deck outside the lodge as we split an order of wonderfully greasy fries. The air was crisp and clean. My cheeks were rosy from exercise and my muscles were tired in a good way. That night, I knew I'd sleep like a log.

In fact, the day would have been perfect if it hadn't been for Will periodically surprising me on the hill, cutting too close for my comfort, skiing backward or in and out of the woods. Nibbling on our fries, Bea and I tried to figure out if his behavior was meant to impress or taunt.

"Impress," Bea concluded, as we watched him take off his skis from our hidden vantage point on the deck. "Because here you are and here he is and I haven't seen Ava since this morning. If he didn't like you, he would have gone off with her long ago. I'm sold."

Eighteen

When I woke the next morning, I realized everything hurt. My muscles ached like I'd been stretched on some medieval torture device. My knees throbbed and were slightly swollen. Even my bones were sore. It was all I could do to gingerly step out of bed and make my way to the shower, which definitely helped. As did the Advil.

Clearly it was a day to lie by the fire reading, as a stiff rain whipped against the windows. But none of my books fit my mood. Having finished *Jane Eyre*, I was done with Gothic for a while. What I needed was hard-core chick lit. Pink covers. Catty girls. Cute boys. Maybe a beach or two.

So, braving a sleeting rain, I zipped up my hoodie,

took the 73 Waverley bus into Cambridge, and slogged down Mass Ave. to Harvard Book Store. Upstairs it's just a regular bookstore. Downstairs, Used and Remainders, it's different. And cheaper. Tons of books, from serious academic stuff to graphic novels, cramming shelves peppered with newspaper clippings and cartoons. An impoverished bookworm's paradise.

In fiction, I searched for my favorite authors, women I have trusted to reassure me that not all teenage guys are total ditwads, that the archetype of the noble cute hero who devotes himself to the girl he loves has not gone the way of the rotary phone. That all I had to do was be myself (smart, hardworking, funny) and be patient and kind and he and I would find each other.

As Bea would say, this is why they call it fiction.

I moved through the rows snatching every book by my favorite authors until I had a stack that would carry me through next year if all went . . .

Smash!

My brand-new precious collection lay scattered on the floor, a fan of pastel covers, thanks to some nerd who was so lost in his book that he walked smack into me while reading.

"Oh, sorry." He knelt and began awkwardly fumbling through my pile. I studied his dark green canvas coat and long dark hair, slightly damp and disheveled, and thought,

This is who gets into Harvard?

"Here you go," he said, handing me *Boy Meets Girl.*

Our eyes locked and I couldn't believe it. "Mike?"

He checked the book again. "Einstein. I would have expected to run into you in a bookstore—literally. But not reading trash like this!"

"It's not trash." I snatched it out of his hand. "It's Meg Cabot, and you don't know what you're talking about."

He rifled through them all. *"Anna and the French Kiss?* Ooh la la!"

"Stop!" I whispered as he started to laugh, making me even angrier. "At least they're better than what you're reading, *The History of the Red Sox* or whatever."

I must have struck a nerve because he slid the book into the pocket of his coat, though he could not hide the telltale red cover. I had that exact same edition in my bookshelf.

"The Scarlet Letter?"

Mike stood and smiled sheepishly. "Came in to get out of the rain and figured I might as well start on Smullen's reading for next quarter. You know . . . until it lets up out there."

I didn't recall *The Scarlet Letter* being on her list for the next quarter. Oh well. "That's based on a true story, you know."

This, perhaps, is my favorite local trivia.

"Nathaniel Hawthorne used to work at the Customs House by Boston Common and he'd take his lunch to the cemetery near there. One day, he was strolling through and there was this A on a tombstone and . . ."

Catching sight of someone or something over my shoulder, Mike's eyes widened in alarm. "Gotta go." He took off.

"Where? Why?" I asked, gathering my books and tripping after him.

"No reason. Just, uh, I remembered I gotta be somewhere." Mike checked over his shoulder. I checked over mine. Behind us, a store clerk, several books under his arm, moved toward us very swiftly.

"Sir!" He held up his index finger. "Sir!"

Shoplifting. Mike's hand concealed *The Scarlet Letter* as he negotiated the maze of bookshelves. Now, intrigued and alarmed, I felt compelled to keep up, to defend his character if necessary, to defend his right to read a great American classic or—worse!—bail him out of jail.

"Mike!" I hissed, as he took the stairs two at a time. "Don't do it!"

"Sir! Please, stop!"

"Stop!" I yelled, not caring if the whole store heard. "If you don't have money, I'll pay."

That did it. Mike stopped.

The clerk behind us, a thin, pale man with glasses,

caught his breath. "Thank you. I was afraid you'd leave before . . ."

I waited anxiously.

". . . I could give you these." He thrust a stack of books toward Mike. Not just any stack. A stack of poetry.

My mind went blank. None of this was on our assigned reading list. Walt Whitman. Anne Sexton. What was going on?

Mike looked mortified, as if he'd just been shoved into the girls' bathroom or pantsed in public. His cheeks were flushed and he didn't respond, just nodded, while the clerk prattled on about other poets Mike and he had apparently discussed. William Carlos Williams. T. S. Eliot.

That's when I remembered his reference to *The Wasteland*: "*April is the cruelest month. . . .*" So it wasn't just a random line of his after all.

Was Mike a . . . *closet intellectual*?

When it was over and the clerk rushed off to help someone else, Mike set the books aside on the counter. He looked down at me. I looked up at him. The proverbial ball, the way I saw it, was in his court.

"How about we go check out that cemetery?" he said. "I gotta see where this so-called scarlet woman is buried."

We paid up and shoved our books into Mike's ratty backpack before heading into the rain. Far from having let up, it had only gotten heavier. And colder.

Was that snow?

We're nuts, I thought, as we ducked into the T station and down the stairs through the red-tiled underground. We passed a bearded guy playing a Bob Marley song on his guitar, the case open at his feet and littered with coins and dollar bills he'd probably put there himself to give the impression that people routinely paid him for his serenading. Even though I knew they hadn't, I still felt guilty for passing by without giving him something.

Mike bought my ticket from the machine and said, "Don't think he should give up his day job."

I said, "I think this is his day job."

Then we slid in our tickets, went down another set of stairs, and hopped on the red line that would take us over the "salt and pepper" bridge that spanned the Charles River to downtown Boston. I desperately wanted to say something to Mike to put him at ease, to let him know his secret was safe with me, but I didn't know where to begin.

Finally, after sitting side by side, swaying in the train, and not saying anything for a bit, Mike studied his shoes and said, "It's the anniversary of my mother's death. Five years ago to this day. She, um, was kind of a poetry freak."

I had no idea. I didn't even know his mother had died, though thinking back, I vaguely recalled a winter in sixth grade when he'd been missing from school for a while and some kids said his mom was sick.

I tried looking at him through a fresh perspective, as if we hadn't known each other since the days of snack time and Legos. And what I saw was not the laid-back goof, the jock who took nothing seriously except scoring goals and hitting on girls. That casual act of his, it wasn't apathy.

It was grief.

I reached out and covered his hand with mine. After a while, Mike gently tightened his grip and we sat that way until Park Street.

"I always forget which one it is," I said as we moved our way past the thin, old headstones of King's Chapel Burying Ground.

Mike was reading the inscription on John Winthrop's tomb while I looked for the crooked black grave, the one with the *A* in the corner. My mother being her weirdo self had first showed it to me when I was six and couldn't understand why I was far more interested in Mother Goose, who was buried down the street. Then I saw the stone sinking into the ground.

"Here it is! Where's your copy of *The Scarlet Letter*?"

Mike zipped open his backpack and fished it out and I flipped to the end, searching for the exact reference Hawthorne made to this headstone. It's always so cool to think the thing you are looking at today is something other people have been looking at for centuries. It's the closest I've come to touching immortality, by reading the words of dead people.

"Elizabeth Pain," Mike said, squinting at the barely detectable *A*.

I read from the end of the book:

> *And, after many, many years, a new grave was delved, near an old and sunken one, in that burial-ground beside which King's Chapel has since been built. It was near that old and sunken grave, yet with a space between, as if the dust of the two sleepers had no right to mingle. Yet one tombstone served for both.*

"So he's buried here with her?" I asked.

"Guess so."

Mike seemed to know who I was talking about. "You mean you've already read it?"

"I told you, Einstein. I pick up things. Hey, here's a thought." He rested his elbow on my shoulder. "All these upstanding Puritans are buried here, right? They followed the law. Didn't sin. Went to church for hours every Sunday. But who's the one who's the most famous?"

Interesting observation. "The woman who committed adultery."

"Exactly. Come on. Let's go down to Faneuil Hall and get a slice. I'm starved."

We ended up bypassing Faneuil Hall and heading straight to the North End, the Italian section, figuring if you're going to get pizza, you might as well go to the source. Mike insisted on Pizzeria Regina, a small place on the corner that was packed with people sick of leftover turkey sandwiches. We grabbed several slices, a can of Coke each, and ate standing on the sidewalk under the dripping awning.

Maybe it was the cold rain or that I'd been hungrier than I realized, but that was the best pizza ever, chewy and cheesy. Mike folded his and consumed it faster than I thought humanly possible, wiping the grease onto his coat sleeve and going back for seconds.

"You're a pig," I said, laughing.

"You sound just like Sienna." He smiled, showing not a hint of guilt or regret.

"What's she doing today?" Figuring, if he was with me on a Saturday, she had to be out of town.

"Beats me. Probably what she always does. Shopping . . . Hey, you want some cannoli?" He wiggled his brows. "Can't say no to cannoli."

And though I was absolutely stuffed, he took my hand and dragged me past the redbrick buildings of Prince Street to Mike's Pastry, which, like Regina's, was crowded; the staff was shouting orders as we worked our way down the line, past the glass cases filled with cakes and éclairs, tarts, and a bazillion cookies in all different colors, plus every kind of cannoli you could imagine— including chocolate chip.

"I can't," I said, clutching my full stomach.

Mike ordered two chocolate chip. "You must."

I did take a tiny nibble as we made our way out of Mike's. It was getting dark and the gaslights flicked on, lighting the old neighborhood with what I imagined was a European kind of feel. Golden light spilled onto the sidewalk as restaurants opened their doors to entice passersby with their aromas of garlic and herbs. Couples walked arm in arm, heels clicking on cobblestones, as greetings were exchanged in shouted Italian. In the distance, the faint strains of a violin wafted from a window.

Despite being chilled to the bone, I wanted to stay, to drink in all the sounds and smells of a Saturday evening in the North End.

Or, maybe, I just didn't want to leave Mike.

He might have felt the same way because he was strangely silent as we walked through Faneuil Hall and made our way toward Park Street. "So," he said, tossing the cannoli box into the trash, "any word from your opponent?"

Again, the slight tinge of sarcasm. "Saw him yesterday

during ski practice. How come you weren't there?"

"I was driving home from Maine." Mike wouldn't get off Will, though. "I'm surprised he wasn't in California visiting his girlfriend."

"You know about her?"

He adjusted the backpack on his shoulder. "Guy talks about her constantly. Her name's Talia and I guess she's pretty hot."

I didn't know if Mike was trying to help or hurt me. "I know!" I said, maybe a tad too quickly because he shot back, "You do, huh? So there's some truth to the rumor that you're really into him."

I bristled. The way he'd put that made me seem so desperate.

"We went to a school board meeting. That's all." And then, on a whim, just to see how he'd react, I added, "He kissed me."

"Ah."

"Ah?" I wheeled around to read his expression. But it was too dark and he kept his head down, trudging.

"What do you mean by 'ah'?"

"What I mean is a kiss doesn't mean that much, Einstein. At least not for guys like Will. For girls like you, it's like getting engaged."

"Is not!"

"Then why did you bring it up? Why did you say it

that way—*he kissed me*—if it didn't mean anything?"

"Are you implying I'm some sort of *nerd*? I suppose to you I'm a cloistered nun who spends her life locked in a tower reading and . . ."

He reached out and caught me as I stumbled slightly onto Park Street. "Whoops. You almost walked into that car."

Oh God, I did, I thought as the driver leaned on the horn loudly, made a couple of rude gestures, and pulled away. Typical Bostonian.

"No. Not a nerd at all." He kept hold of my hand as he crossed the street, like I couldn't be trusted. "Nerds never fall off curbs."

I gave him a slight punch. "You're it." And I took off toward the T station, where I ran down the stairs and through the gates. He chased after me, annoying several people in our path, I'm sure, as he slid down the metal railings and weaved through the underground maze of stops.

The train was waiting and I got on just as the doors were about to close. For one brief scary second, I was afraid Mike would get his arm caught and be dragged to death, but, turns out, there are safety precautions for that kind of thing and he managed to slip in.

"Nice try." He dumped his pack. "Ditching me like that."

"I figured you'd be faster."

"I figured you'd be slower."

It was too crowded and noisy to continue our conversation about why guys didn't make a big deal out of a kiss. This was not the kind of subject you could just shout across a subway with little old ladies listening and college kids making out.

It wasn't until we were on the 73 bus and leaving Harvard Square, sitting next to each other, that Mike said, "I hate to tell you this, but most guys our age are jerks."

This was not what I wanted to hear.

"I mean, it's not like we choose to be jerks. We don't wake up in the morning and say, 'You know, I think I'll be a jerk today.' It's just, there's so much going on with us. So much in our heads that we do one thing and mean another and vice versa." He turned to me. "You understand."

Mike's eyes were very brown. *Soulful* was the word they use in books. I thought of him losing his mother and buying poetry in her honor and how that was so heartbreaking. "Not all guys. Look at you and Sienna. You've been going out since eighth grade."

"Right. About that. You seem to be under the impression that—"

Ding! Ding!

A text alert. Which was odd since I'd already texted

Bea and Neerja that I was out in Boston with Mike and even that we were on the bus home. I'd been sending them frequent updates, actually.

Ding! Ding!

"Aren't you going to see who it is?" Mike asked.

Ding! Ding!

"Sounds urgent."

On some instinctual level, I already knew who it was, and my suspicion was confirmed: Will.

where r u?
U pissed abt ystdy?

Ding! Ding!

hey—I miss u

Mike must have seen the texts because he opened his pack, pulled out the Walt Whitman, and began flipping through it, sending signals that he wanted to be left alone to read. I muted my phone and looked out the window and wondered what it was Mike was going to say about Sienna—and why I cared.

Nineteen

With one week until the election, it was perfectly normal to be focused on my opponent. Only, how many candidates flit between flirting and ignoring one another? Whatever Will and I had going on, it was weird.

Despite a night of texting me repeatedly, the next morning he *again* passed me in the hall like I didn't exist. Not a smile, a nod, not even a wave of acknowledgment.

Nothing new there. I was used to being ignored—by my classmates. However, that wasn't true now either.

Handing out Pop Rocks at the front door Monday mornings had made me extremely popular. Plus, Bea had gotten word out that I'd joined the ski team, which really scored big with the jocks—my toughest demographic. In fact, it looked like the jock vote might put me over the top, which was great for me, not so great for Will, and a downright bummer for Smitty.

Or so I discovered when he accosted me in the hall on the way to play practice.

"Five minutes. That's all I need," he pleaded from a corner by the trophy case where he'd been lurking. "Alone. In the box office so no one sees us."

I wasn't so sure about that. I didn't know Smitty that well aside from seeing him in the halls and hanging out with the Man Clan, though he seemed harmless enough.

"I'm late, so . . ."

He lifted the corrugated-metal window and climbed over the counter into the booth. "Come on," he said, waving me in.

Against my better judgment, I scrambled into the box office, whereupon he flicked on a light and closed the window. We were alone. Smitty ran his hand through his dark fro and said, "You gotta quit the race."

Instinctively I'd been afraid of something like this when he mentioned the ticket booth. I reached for the window. "No way!"

He kept the window shut. "Look, you've been screwed by the school on this cheating thing. You were innocent, so was Mullet. He was holding a beer for a friend—*me*. That's why I ran as a protest candidate, to raise awareness that the administration is out of control."

"And you've done that. No one who likes Mullet or thinks what happened to him is fair is going to vote. Can I get out now?"

"Except . . . you're going to win."

Was he messing with me? I studied him, searching for a hint of sarcasm, but he seemed totally legit. "Get out."

"Seriously. We've been doing informal polls. If an election were held tomorrow and we told everyone who'd planned on sitting out this election to switch tactics and vote for me, you'd still win."

Wow. I couldn't believe it. Will had impressed so many people with his celebrity endorsement and, of course, all the seniors were behind Smitty and Mullet. "That's great!"

I guess me being thrilled wasn't the right reaction because Smitty frowned and said, "No, it's not. You should be just as pissed as Mullet and I are, Gigi. Don't you see? If you join the board, then you become part of the problem. You become The Man, man."

"I'll never be a man. And if I'm on the board, I might be able to get the cheating policy rewritten. But if I drop out of the race like you want, then Will will win. Or you!"

"Yeah, but I'll immediately resign. That's the secret plan."

This was news. "But I thought . . ."

"You thought I didn't want anyone to vote, right? That's what we *wanted* Schultz to think. That's why we didn't put up any posters or do any campaigning. If she knew I wanted to win so I could quit and embarrass her, she'd disqualify me ASAP."

This was dizzying.

"On election day, we *were* going to send out a massive text telling those who were going to protest the vote to vote for me instead. That would have worked three weeks ago, when I would have won. Now, with your constant campaigning and whatever, you're going to beat Will and me, combined. So if you drop out, I'll win because I can beat Will. No one liked that Ashton Kutcher promo. A lot of people were put off by it."

I had to puzzle this through. "And then what happens?"

"Then I'll immediately step down and it'll make the local news that the high school held an emergency election for student rep and the winner resigned out of protest. Reporters will ask what this is about and we can tell them that Mullet got framed and the administration is run by a bunch of Nazi control freaks who don't trust their own students. Only, it won't work if you win. If you win, our plans are screwed."

Drew's voice came over the intercom: "All cast members to the auditorium. Dress rehearsal begins in ten minutes."

"I gotta go," I said, reaching for the window again.

"Think about it," Smitty said. "If we don't send a message to the administration now, Gigi, there's no telling where this insanity will end."

Insanity appeared to be the theme for the day.

Granted, Drew's fits near dress rehearsal were legendary, even to newbies like us who'd never been involved in drama. This one, however, could have made the record books, complete with hair pulling (his own), foot stomping (ditto), and screaming (at us).

It started with Lindsay's disastrous performance in the garden scene, the same one she'd aced and Neerja had bombed during auditions. She skipped lines, forgot crucial words, dropped the Bluetooth piece that was constantly affixed to her ear, and called Henry *Henry*.

"Romeo," Neerja prompted from the sides.

"Oh, right." Lindsay smacked her head. "Duh."

"Lindsay," Drew barked, calling her over, "walk with me. Everyone else, five-minute break."

Neerja left the stage to sit with Justin, who patted the seat next to him and then took out his phone for another scintillating game of Angry Birds. "You wanna go outside and get some air?" she asked.

He grunted.

Henry tapped her on the shoulder and nodded to the

door. "Gigi and I are going out for a soda. Wanna come?"

"Sure."

Fortified by Mountain Dew and fresh air, Neerja didn't beat around the bush. "Parad says I should break up with him. What do you think?"

This is one of those impossible questions, the kind that would have stumped the Sphinx. If I told her the truth—that she should have broken up with Justin on day one—and then they stayed together, our friendship would turn craptastic. If I lied and said, "No! He's awesome!" what kind of friend would I be?

Thankfully, Henry came to the rescue. "It's simply a question of logic," he said, scratching behind one of his oversized ears. "If you don't like him, break up. If you do like him, stay. So which is it?"

Neerja glanced off. "I'm not sure."

"Maybe it's just physical," I said, trying to be positive. "That's okay. He's super cute and everyone thinks he's hot."

"It's not physical." She ran her finger around the top of her green plastic bottle. "I mean, I don't know if it is. We haven't . . ."

Henry and I leaned forward. What hadn't Neerja and Justin done? Or rather, what would I have to remember to hide from her mother that she and Justin hadn't done?

". . . kissed. I know. It's weird. I don't understand it myself."

I focused on my Mountain Dew, trying not to scream, "YOU HAVEN'T KISSED?"

Henry, in his utter male daftness, blurted, "That's not what Justin says."

Neerja looked up, alarmed. "You're kidding."

"Don't worry. I didn't take him seriously." But the tips of Henry's ears had gone bright red, as they often did when it came to stuff like girls/love/kissing. "Anyway, there's more to a relationship, I guess, than *that*."

Not when it comes to Justin, I thought. With no brains and zippo personality, all he had going for him was *that*.

The door opened and Justin stuck out his head, the phone still glued to his hand. "Dudes. Drew says to come back. He wants to, like, start the scene or something."

He let the doors close on him and Henry said, "Yeah. Dump his ass."

I returned to my math homework. Henry got onstage. Neerja took her usual seat in the sidelines, and Lindsay, her eyes red rimmed as if from crying, tried the garden scene again.

We got as far as "O Romeo, Romeo! Wherefore art thou Romeo? / Deny thy father and refuse thy name. / Or if thou won't—"

"Wilt!" Drew corrected.

"'Or if thou wilt be sworn my love.'"

Drew clenched his jaw. "'Or if thou wilt NOT, be but sworn my love.'" He tucked the script under his arm. "Don't you see that, Lindsay? It doesn't make sense otherwise."

Lindsay fiddled with her Bluetooth, which, in my opinion, Drew should have asked her to remove. Maybe he thought it was a hearing aid.

"Once more." Drew rolled his hand and Henry gave Lindsay the cueing line.

Lindsay said, "But I thought we were leaving off at 'wilt'?"

That was it. Drew ripped his script and kicked a metal folding chair. Henry took a protective position near Neerja, leaving poor Lindsay to fend for herself, alone.

"We are mere days away from our first performance and you can't even get through the most famous scene in all of Shakespeare, one that every child who's ever watched *The Simpsons* knows. . . ."

On it went. We were disorganized. We were unprepared. We were automatons. "As if all this weren't enough of a debacle," he yelled, pausing slightly before uttering The Magical Words, "there is a *massive winter storm* moving up the coast and we're going to have a *snow day*."

"Snow day?" Justin clicked off Angry Birds. "For real?"

A few of the guys in lighting let up a cheer that was stifled when Drew kicked a cardboard tree. "One to two feet at least. Maybe more. We could lose two days of practice."

"Whoo-hoo!" Justin raised his fist.

The snow, it seemed, was all anyone could talk about.

"Did you hear?" Bea asked as we changed in the girls' locker room for dryland practice. "We're getting a nor'easter. Three days of solid snow."

I quickly slid on a pair of sweats and wiggled into my sports bra. "I heard. Drew dropped the bomb in drama."

"Are you not thrilled?" She was prancing around the benches on tiptoe. "No school and we get to race on Saturday. Coach says it's all but confirmed. We're even getting our GS suits."

"Bea, I . . ." Huh? "What's a GS suit?"

"You know. Those super-tight bodysuits you wear to reduce wind resistance. Like Lindsey Vonn."

Until that moment, it had not occurred to me that I might have to wear a body-hugging polyester suit that showed *ever-y-thing* and made me go faster. But sure enough, after we returned from our run, there they were in a cardboard box, in fetchingly ugly black and red.

"Yes!" Mike picked out his. "It's on." He and B.K. high-fived and then high-fived Bea, who high-fived the four senior girls and the other guys who hooted and hollered, jumping around like Zulu warriors preparing to spear the British.

"We are so wasting Belmont," B.K. said.

"And those stuck-up WMSA jerks," Mike added. "With their ten-thousand-dollar equipment and private trainers."

"Settle down. Settle down." Coach assumed the usual position: foot on chair, hand on hip. "Now, I know we haven't had a chance to get in much hill practice, which means we're gonna eat ice on Saturday."

Eat ice?

"But don't be discouraged. Look upon Saturday as a test run, a way to try out the course that we won't see again unless we make the All New England championships, which is why every other high school ski team from New England's going to be there too."

"We'll see it again, Coach!" B.K. shouted.

Mike yelled, "Booyah!" He was in max jock mode, hardly resembling the sensitive poetry reader I'd run into on Saturday.

Coach went on. "Are we gonna wipe out? Sure. Are the conditions going to be perfect? Not at all. It's the beginning of December. It's ice, people! Is the Organ Grinder course a double black diamond? So what?"

So what? I wanted to yell. *So what?* I'd barely survived

Rumble and I'd had all the time in the world.

"Isn't this exciting?" Bea let out a little squeal. "Like I was telling you on the lift last week, I'm so glad you talked me into joining, Gigi. I feel like it's changing my whole life, getting in shape and doing what I love again."

"Bea, I, uh . . ."

"What I can't get over is, if you hadn't joined because of *me*, our girls' team wouldn't qualify. It's, like, so karmic."

And before I could confess that karma wasn't going to keep me from breaking a leg, she wrapped me in a hug, saying I was the best friend ever.

Seems I had no choice but to light a few candles and pray for a miracle.

That night, as I watched Gunther's skiing DVD again to get pumped for the race, something or someone hit my window. I checked my laptop clock. It was after midnight.

Thwack!

Putting Gunther on pause, I slid out of bed and went to the window, where I found melting snowballs sliding down the glass. The good news here is that burglars generally don't announce their presence with snowballs.

Thwack! Thwack!

I opened the window and peeked out. Someone was

standing in my yard, his jet-black hair recognizable under my light.

"Will?"

He was getting ready to toss another.

"Don't you dare."

"Come down then."

"I can't." I was in my pj's. Besides, he wasn't exactly my favorite person at the moment.

He tossed the snowball so hard it rattled the shutter. He was going to wake up Marmie if he didn't knock it off. "Stop it!"

"No. Come down. But leave Petunia. I'm out of hot dogs."

Oh, all right. Grabbing a ski-team sweatshirt, I covered a snoring Petunia, slipped into a pair of my faux Uggs, and tiptoed outside, this time remembering to unlock the door before I closed it.

Will was entirely underdressed in just jeans and a couple of shirts. "Isn't this the best?" He held out his arms and lifted his face to the falling snow. "I've never seen this before."

"You were on snow just last Friday."

"Yeah, but I haven't seen it fall. It's so cool. I love looking up and watching each flake."

It was freezing. Rubbing my arms, I kept a decent distance in case he tried to work his J.Crew looks to my disadvantage, which I knew he would.

"You've been avoiding me." He winged the snowball at the apple tree. "Haven't you?"

"Hah!" I scooped up a handful and patted it. "It's *you* who's been avoiding *me*."

"What? I repeatedly tried to get your attention on the hill and you kept ignoring me."

"Because I was at practice." *Smack!* My snowball landed square in the middle of his chest.

"Hey!"

"Shhh." I thumbed toward the house. "Don't wake my grandmother. Besides, how come in school you act like I don't exist?"

He stepped out of the light, brushing off the snow. "You didn't answer any of my texts, even after I begged you. You ignored my calls, and you still haven't re-friended me on Facebook."

"You're avoiding the question." I tucked my cold red hands under my arms and kept my gaze on my boots, where I knew it'd be safe from his sparkling dark blue eyes and those lips of his that could . . . *Stop*, Gigi.

He came closer. "Okay, you want the real answer?"

"No. I want the lie." *Snort*. "But let me spare you the trouble of inventing an excuse by providing some oldies but goodies. Pick one. You don't want people to think you're friends with the competition. You need to maintain professional conduct in the workplace. You're a free bird and this bird you cannot . . ."

"I'm falling for you. There. That's the truth."

Well, that certainly shut me up.

Will got close. So close, I could detect the faint smell of flannel and soap and some spicy deodorant. "And," he added, "that's really, really bad."

"Thanks," I said. "I'll try not to be insulted."

He closed his eyes, as if gathering his thoughts. "I don't want this to come out wrong, though I know it will. But I *like* you."

"Not seeing the problem."

"But I'm technically still going out with Talia and . . ."

"Ava."

He blinked. *"Ava?"*

"Yes, Ava. Don't even try to deny it. You two are a thing."

"We're not a thing. We're just friends."

"With benefits?"

His lips twitched. "A gentleman never tells."

That old cop-out. I scooped up and packed some snow. "What would Talia say if she knew?" I threw the ball at the apple tree, hitting the trunk dead on. "And I'm assuming she doesn't."

"Ava and Talia aren't in the same ballpark. You, however, are a definite contender."

Why did that rub me the wrong way? "I've got news for you, Will. This is not spring training and I am not hoping to come up from the minor leagues. Either you like me or you don't. Either you want to go out with me or you want to keep the coast-to-coast thing going with Talia." I packed some more snow and held the ball threateningly. "But I am done playing games."

He picked the ball out of my hand. "All right. That's fair. Then how about you go with me to the Crystal Ball?" He tossed it at the tree and missed. "By then, Talia and I will have officially called it quits. We're almost over, anyway, since . . ." He took a deep breath. ". . . I told her I was going to ask you."

Okay, here's my dirty little secret about the Crystal Ball: For all my eye rolling at Maddie and Sienna, it has been bugging me a teensy tiny *leeeetle* bit that while they had dates, I had no one. Not that I'm one of those girls who dies if she doesn't have a guy to go with to the prom. It's just that all through middle school, Bea, Neerja, and I went to those dances together. And we left together. Ditto for the eighth-grade graduation bash.

But here was the Crystal Ball, the first big prom of high school, and, once again, I was in the same situation. Only this year it was worse. This year Neerja was going out with Justin, which meant if I went with Will—as cool as that would be—Bea would be on her own.

And that, to use the phrase so loved by our gym teacher, Sgt. Seidel, was simply unacceptable. I am not a woman who drops everything when a guy calls. I stick with my friends.

"No more games," Will was saying. "Okay?"

I took a deep breath. *Bea, you owe me major!* "Thanks for the offer, Will, but I can't. I'm already committed." *More like I should be.*

He took a step back, obviously hurt. He'd really stuck his neck out and I'd swiftly swung the ax.

Crap. Could my life get any more screwed? "I'm really sorry. I really would have loved to. . . ."

"It's okay, Gigi. You don't have to explain. It's not like I'll cry myself to sleep at night because you can't go with me to this stupid dance. I'll live."

He mounded another handful of snow and chucked it at the tree, this time hitting it hard before shoving his hands into his jeans pockets and heading through the snowfall toward the street.

With him went my favorite fantasy. You know the one: hot boy adored by all the "It" girls goes not for them but for the quirky, smart chick with a heart. Yeah, that's me. Asks her to the big dance. She gets a makeover and arrives finer than Cinderella and everyone oohs and ahhs as he takes her in his arms and shows the world that it's character that counts, not superficiality.

Except, I kicked this fantasy to the curb—*I turned down Will Blake.*

And for what? For a friend who, in the end, would probably understand and think I was a fool for not going with him.

Yup. And I'd do it again in a heartbeat.

Twenty

Four thirty in the morning is a nasty hour to wake anyone on a Saturday. When you're a workaholic like me who relies on the weekends to catch up on sleep, it's cruel and unusual punishment.

But that's what I found myself doing, stumbling around Bea's house in the dark, gathering my skis, boots, shin guards, helmet, goggles, and poles and piling into the Honeycutts' Canyonero.

I don't know if it's officially called a Canyonero. That's the nickname Bea and I gave their oversized SUV because it's *huuuuge*. Her parents bought it with the idea that when Bea learns to drive, nothing could kill her, though I'm afraid the same can't be said for those unfortunate cars/pedestrians in her path.

Being our former Brownie leader, Alice Honeycutt had packed the car with essentials based on her detailed analysis of how to fuel young athletes for maximum efficiency. Every hour on the hour she'd tell us to open the cooler in the back and help ourselves to orange juice/nuts/Luna bar/Gatorade, when all we wanted was sleep. It was three hours to Vermont and when we arrived at the ski area I was so charged with electrolytes I could have lit up the lodge Christmas tree.

We reconnoitered in the parking lot with our team members just as the sun began to do battle with the brittle Vermont cold. The four senior girls had driven together by themselves, which I thought was way cool as there was something babyish about being chauffeured by Alice. Mike and B.K. had come up in the beater car owned by B.K.'s older brother, J.J. (One wonders if the parents were so ADD they couldn't be bothered with bestowing on their sons full names.) The rest were piled into Coach's beat-up red van.

Yawning and shuffling around the lot dressed in our pj's and sweats, the Denton High Alpine Team was a pretty ragtag bunch, but never more so than when the super-deluxe, heated, chartered bus pulled up next to us and out marched, in uniform procession, a line of skiers in spiffy yellow GS suits.

Bea and I chewed on bagels and stared in awe as the underside of the bus was opened and each kid was handed his or her set(s!) of skis. Skis that made Will's brand-new Nordicas look like rickety Popsicle sticks.

"Who," I said, swallowing the last of my bagel. "Are. They."

Mike, who'd been lounging against Coach's van, made a sound of disgust. "WMSA. Sixty-grand-a-year tuition."

"The White Mountain Ski Academy," Bea translated. "Where Mom and Dad were thinking of sending me before . . . you know."

Before you know was before George's accident, when Bea was such a hotshot skier coaches from places like the White Mountain Ski Academy would hand her parents business cards and beg them to enroll Bea ASAP if, for the Love of All That Was Holy, they cared about the future of the U.S. Olympics.

All these kids *did* was ski. Classes were kind of squeezed in on the side, like we fitted in the ski team and drama.

Mike said, "What bugs me is that they have a totally unfair advantage over us. The only reason they're here is to race the course that'll be used for the New Englands. The rest of us don't stand a chance of placing now."

Who cared about placing? I just cared about surviving.

Still, seeing how bummed it made Mike and Bea had me equally upset, even though Coach reminded us, again, that this was just a test run and we shouldn't be spooked by WMSA's times. But it didn't seem to help. Everyone was low.

"I've been thinking," Bea said once we were alone in the locker room of the lodge. "I know how you can get through this today. Now that we know for sure the WMSA's here, you can ski as slowly as you want. Our team time won't mean squat."

Every team, apparently, would be led through the course together to familiarize us with the flags, etc. "And everyone goes super slow for that, so don't worry," Bea said.

But when each of us raced alone, her advice to me was to immediately go the wrong way around the flag. "The minders on the side will tell you to hike up the hill and go around it the right way, but you'll only have a few minutes until the next skier comes down. It'll be an instant DQ."

DQ meant disqualified. My times wouldn't count, but my presence would. As long as we entered the race with six girls and four did both runs without being DQ'd, the team could qualify.

Sounded like another one of her perfect plans.

Bea helped me zip up the back of my GS suit and I

helped zip hers. Then we regarded ourselves in the full-length mirror, two slick red-and-black aliens in catsuits.

"Teenage Mutant Ninja Turtles," I said.

Bea clarified. "Teenage Mutant Ninja Martians."

We trudged through the lodge packed with high school ski teams from at least four states. As Bea and I snapped on our heavy boots, I decided to pretend I was like them—fearless, worried not about the steep hill or how scary it would be at the top, but about simply getting down to the bottom as fast as possible.

Outside in the bright morning, surrounded by blindingly white snow, we found our skis. I clicked into mine and grabbed my poles, and we pushed off to the lift. Mike was waiting for us at the end of the line. Under his helmet, his longish mane was tamed, though a few strands peeked out the back. "You gonna be okay?"

"Bea thought up a plan."

Mike nodded. "You're a good friend. She's really glad you're here. I can tell."

It was sweet of him to say. I didn't think guys noticed those kinds of things.

We sat on the lift three across, Mike and Bea making an extraordinary effort to keep the conversation light as they discussed mundane things like what was the best chocolate after a ski and whether they should hock a loogie on the cocky snowboarder below. At one point, I glanced down and saw each had a hand on my knee.

"Your first race, Einstein," Mike said. "Just wait. You'll get to the starting gate and you'll get that burst of adrenaline and I bet you eat up that hill."

"Better than the hill eating me," I replied.

"Ski tips up!" Bea announced as we got to the top.

We joined the team and formed a line like ducklings, Coach in the lead, Mike in the rear. This duty was handed to the best skier and, apparently, that was Mike, even though he was only a sophomore. I was in front of him, behind Bea.

"Take it nice and slow," he said. "No rush."

That sounded good until we got to the top of the slope and I nearly had a heart attack. Gates—more like orange flags—were set up down the hill. Our job was to zigzag around them as fast as possible, which shouldn't be too hard because . . . it was the steepest drop-off I'd seen. Ever!

"*Ohmigod*," I whispered. "*Ohmigod.*"

Mike rubbed my shoulder reassuringly. Bea turned around and said, "Follow me and keep your eyes on the backs of my skis."

Okay. Okay. Suddenly we were moving, everyone in line talking and laughing as Coach led the way around the course. I concentrated on Bea's skis, as I bent the tips of mine inward, leaning so heavily I thought my knees would break, leaning on the left when we needed to go left, leaning on the right when we needed to go right, and crossing my fingers when we had to go straight.

Which was a lot.

"You're doing great," Mike shouted. "See if you can go a little faster." I don't know why he said this. Possibly because Bea was fifty feet ahead.

Summoning my will, I let myself go slightly. Okay. I had control. As long as I ignored the steepness, as long as I focused on Bea's skis and the flags, I was okay.

And then we were done. Thank God!

"Great. All we have to do now," Bea said to Mike, "is do that again—super fast."

"Right," I said. "Super fast."

"Atta girl," Mike said. "Just turn your brain off for once and follow your gut. In case you don't know where that is, that's right here." He poked me in my stomach and laughed. "When you're in the moment, the gut rules."

At ten o'clock the race began, with the girls going before the boys. Supposedly, this was because the course would be newly groomed and in better shape, the implication being that boys could handle tougher conditions. Yeah. Right.

Since this was the first race of the season and no one was seeded, there was no particular order. We all got numbers on our bibs—mine was a lucky #13—and then lined up at the top. Bea was #12, so again I was right behind her. The last in the team.

Over a loudspeaker, an announcer named each racer by name and school. We were given ten seconds after the "Go!" to pass a spring-held wand. If we lingered longer, it was an automatic DQ.

I could tell Bea was getting into race mode the closer we got to the starting line. She flexed her knees and shoulders and slid her skis back and forth watching the competition intently. So far, the fastest skier was from New Hampshire. She zoomed straight down, like a rocket, punching the gates out of her way as she zigged and zagged.

"Sara Connors from Concord," the girl behind me said snarkily. "Didn't get into White Mountain. So . . . she's not that great."

I dunno. Sara Connors seemed pretty great to me. The girl who'd made the comment was in the trademark WMSA yellow suit, and I realized, with slight vindication, that she would be stuck behind me as I disqualified myself at a gate.

It's the little things in life that give you pleasure.

Bea was next. "You can do it!" I said. "Just reach inside of you and bring out that old Bea."

She swore like a sailor, which is what Bea does when she's stressed.

The gatekeeper asked if she was ready to go. I studied the course, now lined with spectators behind blue plastic snow fences. Cowbells rang noisily, almost drowning out the shouts. The air was filled with the smells of hot chocolate and ski wax, Vermont snow and adrenaline. It was incredibly thrilling and frightening and ultimately super cool. I got what Mike meant about the adrenaline.

"Number Twelve!" the announcer began. "Beatrice Honeycutt. Denton High, Denton, Massachusetts."

The countdown had begun. ". . . Five, four, three, two, one. Go!"

Bea froze. I panicked. She had only ten seconds after "go." *Go,* I thought. *Go!*

Finally, I blurted, "Chicken!"

That did it. She hopped past the wand and flew down the mountain. I was so proud of her, I was about to burst.

"You ready?" the gatekeeper said.

Who, me? "Sure." I kept my focus on Bea, who was making wide circles around the red gates. Gunther would probably say too wide, but at least she was getting down pretty fast. *That's my girl,* I thought. *My baby is back.*

"Too slow," Miss Ski Academy scoffed. "And her form is off."

My eyes narrowed. This was my Bea she was talking about.

"Gigi Dubois. Denton High, Denton, Massachusetts."

"Denton will be so easy to beat," she murmured.

The countdown had begun. I swung around and there she was, waiting with her arms folded. "Hey. Do you know what else is yellow?"

"Go!"

No time to finish that crack, I didn't even stop to think as I flew past the wand. Every muscle, every bone in my body was crouched and taut, determined to crush that ski academy witch. If I raced only once in my life, this was it. Fear had no place. Worry, begone! With Gunther as my guide, I leaned left and hugged the first gate, my skis rattling over the hard-packed snow.

Keep your eyes on the next gate, I heard him say. *Ya?*

Ya!

I leaned to the right. Crowds were cheering. Cowbells were ringing. Someone shouted, "Go, Gigi!"

Cut in with your outside ski, reminded Gunther. *Looking good!*

I punched the gate. It snapped back and hit me on the butt and I didn't care. Continuing to crouch, I hurtled to the next and got around that, too.

I was going with my gut and found Mike was right. With my brain dialed down to "hum," I was actually racing. And I was racing well!

Then I did something you should never do, not in life, not on a double black diamond going thirty miles an hour—I checked behind me to see if Miss Ski Academy was gaining.

That's when my edges caught.

Here's what I remember about that moment: I remember wanting to go one direction and my legs heading in another. I remember the sensation of being carried along at full speed toward the crowd behind the blue snow fence and a spike of panic and thinking, *Uh-oh. I so DQ'd.*

And then, because I did not want to crash into the crowd and ruin their whole day, I shifted and went straight downhill, tumbling in slow motion so violently, both my skis snapped off as I slid, face-first, toward the finish line, where I came to a dead stop.

Everything hurt and everything, I was sure, was broken. An air horn blasted. There were shouts not to touch or move me. Someone in their infinite wisdom threw around the phrase "spinal cord injury."

"Gigi."

A face appeared over mine and I looked up into his brown eyes filled with concern. *He didn't say Einstein*, I thought vaguely. Since the wind had been knocked out of me, all I could do was smile.

"Stay still. Don't move."

Yeah. Like I could.

He stroked my cheek. "You scared the crap out of me, but you did it, Einstein. You went with your gut!"

At the corner of my vision, red curls bobbed. "Oh, Gigi. Oh, this is my fault. I told you to DQ, but not like *this*!" Bea was almost crying. "The ski patrol's coming. I'll go with you."

No. She couldn't. She had to do the next run. Squirming to my side, I managed to get up on one elbow, then . . . owww!

"Don't move," Mike said.

Coach came over and told everyone to back off. Then a couple of ski patrol guys in red coats came and felt up and down my legs and asked me to move this or that. I could move everything, right down to my toes.

They helped me up and I stood, barely. Everyone applauded. Bea raised a fist and Mike threw back his head and said, "Yes."

It was only when they touched my elbow that I wanted to scream. Nothing was dislocated, but ski patrol guessed my elbow might be chipped.

Bea's mother was so hysterical at the idea of me with a chipped elbow that Coach suggested she go home now, and save herself the agony of watching her daughter's second race. Coach could fit Bea and me in his van.

Alice agreed, much to Bea's immense relief, because the last thing she needed was her crazed mother running around panicking about broken elbows.

Turned out that I'd been very lucky. No major bones

broken (aside from the chipped elbow that required putting my left arm in a sling) and no head injury, thanks to my sturdy new helmet.

The ski patrol guys said I'd be sore the next morning. And bruised. But I got to watch the rest of the race from the top floor of the lodge, next to the fire, with bottomless cups of hot chocolate, which was A-OK by me. My dream come true.

Bea, having heard what the ski academy witch said, pushed herself to get the best race time on our team—although she was still a good ten seconds behind the slowest WMSA girl. It didn't matter. Bea was a total hero and the whole team lifted her on their shoulders after she went up to get her award for coming in tenth.

Mike skied beautifully, flowing around each gate with strength and precision, his hair flying from under his helmet. He was almost artistic. I sipped my chocolate and thought about how it was too bad his mother wasn't there to see that her son had grown into such an amazing athlete, that he read poetry in her honor, and was the first to rush to my side when I crashed.

That night, after the race was over and the Denton High team came in eleventh—not bad, considering—we dragged our sorry carcasses to the parking lot, exhausted beyond belief. Mike insisted on carrying all my stuff down to the van. And then he insisted we go home with B.K. and him.

"This van's too crowded with your skis and Bea's skis," he said, keeping it practical.

"Shotgun!" Bea called. With B.K. driving and Bea in the front, Mike and I squished together in B.K.'s dinky backseat.

B.K. turned on some tunes, and Bea, still pumped from her amazing debut race, quickly objected to his taste in music. They argued about that for a good half hour, until we were on the interstate, and then they argued about the Yankees versus the Red Sox, Bea absolutely appalled that a Yankees fan was in her proximity. Soon they moved on to which colleges were better and why and at what temperatures you should use red wax versus yellow.

I found myself drifting off to their banter, my head falling on Mike's shoulder. He shifted his body so I could lie on his chest, careful to cradle my elbow so it wouldn't get bumped.

"Hey, Einstein," he whispered. "You did great back there. You're my hero, you know that?"

"Hmm?"

He planted a gentle kiss on the top of my head. "You heard me."

He was right, I had. I just wanted him to say it again.

Twenty-one

I didn't set out to start a small riot on election day, it just kind of happened, and the odd thing was, until I jumped on a cafeteria table and called for a revolution, everything had been going so smoothly.

Will and I faced each other mutely as we stood by the front doors, holding up our respective YES, WE WILL! and I'M GAGA 4 GIGI! signs, though Bea had to hold mine because of my elbow injury.

"Good luck," Will said rather tersely.

"Back atcha."

Smitty, on the other hand, breezed through the door with about a second to spare until the first bell. "Oh, was I supposed to be doing some last-minute campaigning?"

He let out a laugh. "My bad." To me he said, "It's not too late to change your mind, Gigi. Voting doesn't start in homeroom for a few minutes yet."

Will snapped out of his funk to flash me a questioning look.

When I said nothing, Smitty shrugged and said, "May the best *man* win," before strolling off, humming a vague tune.

"I don't trust him," Bea said. "He's up to something."

Had Bea known about Smitty's proposition, Lady Justice would have been in Schultz's office demanding his disqualification, which was why I hadn't told her. I'm a big believer in letting things work out naturally. Besides, I was kind of curious to see what Smitty would really do if he won.

In homeroom, we were handed ballots with the list of candidates: William Blake, Smithers (his real name!) Chavez, and Genevieve Dubois. The "Genevieve" had been an oversight. What if voters didn't know that Genevieve = Gigi? Darn.

"Genevieve, huh?" Sienna checked off the box next to my name. "People sure do call you lots of things. Gigi. Genevieve. Einstein."

"As long as they don't call me stupid," I said, folding my ballot. "Anyway, Bea says I'm like a Russian novel." I paused, realizing she wouldn't get that. "The characters have lots of nicknames."

"I know," Sienna replied, defensive. "I read *Anna Karenina*."

"You *did*?" Then, remembering how insulted Mike got when I acted surprised, I readjusted my tone and added, "Me too."

"There are definitely boring parts, like all the talk about agriculture. Yuck." Sienna slipped her ballot in the box. "But I couldn't put it down. And what was up with that freaking Count Vronsky? I mean, what a bro!"

Had I only known Sienna felt this way about Vronsky we could have had so much to talk about in homeroom besides prom dresses. I nodded vigorously. "What did Anna see in him?"

"Are you kidding?" Sienna acted like the answer was obvious. "Look who she was married to."

"Seriously," I said.

Maddie came up and dropped in her ballot. "What're you guys talking about?"

"*Anna Karenina*," Sienna said.

Maddie shook her curls. "You and that book. By the way, Gigi, everyone I talked to says they're voting for you. You are so definitely going to win."

Sienna and *Anna Karenina*. Me winning! Things were definitely looking up.

* * *

Drew decided that the chorus could live without me standing onstage in a sling so I was excused from the matinee, and for that I was extremely grateful. Not to be harsh, but if that play was any indication, the evening show was doomed.

Think *Titanic*. Only faster sinking, with no violins.

It wasn't just that Lindsay continued to botch the garden scene or that you could hear Neerja hissing her cues from the sidelines. Justin's sword also snapped in two during the duel. Halfway through her speech, Marissa Brewster, the nurse, got such a case of stage fright that she had to run to the wings, where we could hear her gagging. And the crew forgot the dagger, so Lindsay had to improvise with her thumbs.

Only Henry managed to emerge in one piece, though we all agreed that the chemistry between Lindsay and him was nonexistent. You know it's bad when Romeo and Juliet are found dead and the audience applauds.

Afterward, I went backstage to boldly lie that it was "Great! Really, really great!"

Neerja was with Henry and looking mighty pale. He was holding her hand while she leaned her head on his shoulder. "Drew's going to kill us, you know. It'll be just like the dress rehearsal, but worse. I tried with Lindsay. I really did. She just couldn't get it."

"It's okay," Henry said. "At least you were perfect."

He squeezed her hand. "As always."

"Aw, Henry. You're so sweet." Neerja sighed. "I don't know how I would have gotten through this play without you. It would have been so stressful."

I thought: *Justin?*

Henry's ears went red. "I'm just being a good friend."

"Where's Lindsay, anyway?" I asked since she and Henry were something of a thing, and I was thinking she might have a problem with her old gymnastics buddies running to each other for comfort.

Henry nodded to the door. "She's at lunch. Said she didn't want to stick around to hear Drew rip her a new one."

"And Justin?" I asked. "Also AWOL?"

Neerja shrugged. "I dunno." Then she sat up and let go of Henry's hand. "He's here."

Drew sauntered in carrying an open bag of Tootsie Pops and looking . . . *weird.*

"Congratulations, everyone." He tucked the bag under his arm and applauded lackadaisically. "Super, super effort. I'm so thrilled." Then he picked out a cherry lollipop, tossed the bag to the stage crew, and collapsed on a metal folding chair.

"Drew?" Neerja said, her eyebrows furrowing. "Are you . . . okay?"

"Okay? Okay? Of course, I'm okay." He removed the

wrapper and gave the lollipop a lick. "Never better."

"But we sucked," one of the guys who played a musician yelled.

"That's true but, you see, it doesn't matter, because after our last performance of *Romeo and Juliet*, there will be none other. The final curtain is closing on our little drama department, people. The lights are dimming for eternity."

His pronouncement caused a mild uproar, until Drew explained that he had it on "good information" from Mrs. Greene that the board had outlined its upcoming budget and had decided to ax the position of a drama teacher to save $30,000 a year. Any plays—if there were any plays—would be directed by volunteers, i.e., parents.

Soon the drama geeks were competing to see who could throw the best hissy fit. There was lots of crying and pounding of walls, though others chose the more restrained approach. Two tears silently rolled down Marissa's cheeks. Lilla Dimarco rewrapped the scarf around her neck, double crossed her twiggy legs, and meditated upon a spot on the floor, pained, as if she'd just lost her best friend.

I raised my hand. "Look, Drew. Are you sure?"

"Ah yes, the student rep candidate." Drew crunched his candy. "Well, I hope you can do something when you're elected, Gigi, but from what I've been told, it's a lost cause for me and Felicity, since they're scaling back the art department, too."

Another gasp.

"But you'll be pleased to know that sports, those sacred cows, have been spared," he said bitterly. "God forbid athletics should take a backseat to the arts."

So skiing survived. And I was glad to know Mrs. Greene's job was safe. Still, a high school with limited drama and art was a lifeless place. How could the board be so clueless?

Because they didn't have a student rep, I thought. With Mullet out of the picture, they'd passed these cuts without our input. If he hadn't been busted for beer holding, or whatever, he could have told them that jewelry making really mattered, not just to me, but to most of the school. And that if it weren't for a drama department, a lot of kids who might otherwise be outcasts would have no place to hang.

This gave me a brilliant idea.

"We need to get down to the office," I said, whipping out my phone and texting Bea. "Henry, you know Mrs. Greene's copier password, right?"

"I know everyone's copier password." He reached over his head and scratched his other ear as if it contained the answer. "The library's is two-two-five-three."

"Great. I'll get Bea."

"What for?" Neerja asked.

"We're going to save drama and jewelry while we still can."

It took Bea no time to draw up the petition:

> *We, the undersigned students and parents of Denton High, greatly object to proposed budget cuts that would eliminate a drama instructor and reduce our only art teacher to a part-time position. Art and drama enhance our education and are as vital to learning as math, science, history, and English. We respectfully ask the Board to find other means to balance the budget.*

"Too gentle?" Bea asked as we huddled near the library photocopier.

"I think it's much improved by eliminating your previous ending, 'or else you'll be in a world of hurt,'" I said, drawing my pencil against the ruler to create signature lines. "No one appreciates being threatened."

The prototype finished and only minutes to go until the last lunch period was over, we punched in Mrs. Greene's number and ran off a hundred petitions. Then we divided them among ourselves and ran down the hall.

Will was outside the cafeteria, talking to Ava. "Hey," he said, reaching out and touching my bad elbow. I flinched.

"Oh, sorry. Just want to tell you the results are in and Schultz is gonna make an announcement at any moment."

My heart did a little flutter, and I was glad for more pressing issues to occupy my obsessive mind. I handed him and Ava each a petition. "Read this. If you support it, sign it and pass it around."

"Hot damn," Ava said. "They're cutting art? That blows. Art's the only thing in this school that's decent."

"You can't have everything," Will said practically. "Not in these tough economic times."

"Well, that's true," Ava said, purposely avoiding my startled glare since, supposedly, art was her raison d'être. Did she agree just to score points with Will?

Mike hook shot a cup into the trash. "What would you know about tough economic times, Blake?" he said, apparently having overheard.

Will smirked. "I know that it's making some people into jerks."

"Got that right." Mike held out his hand for a petition. "What is this, Gigi?"

"Read it and weep."

He read it and nodded. "That sucks. How about skiing?"

"Sports, allegedly, is spared. Including skiing."

"Sweet." He held out his hand. "Give me a few more. I'll get these suckers signed."

The first bell rang. Everyone was getting up to go.

At that moment, I knew what I had to do—school rules or not. And let me just say here that I was really, really glad I'd chosen this day to wear jeans because standing on top of a lunch table in one of my short pleated skirts exposing my pink-and-purple FRIDAY bikini underpants would have definitely attracted a different sort of attention.

I marched to the nearest table and tried to get on, which was hard since I was holding a bunch of petitions and one arm was in a sling.

"Here," Mike said, lending a hand as I stepped up.

"Thanks." I squared my shoulders, preparing myself for the possibility that what I was about to do could hand me three days of detention.

Up here, I had a bird's-eye view of the cafeteria. I could see everyone looking at me—including the nasty cafeteria ladies and Joe the Janitor and Mrs. Greene, who was monitoring. This was my total nightmare come true.

Summoning my courage, I said, "Excuse me!"

Most everyone kept talking and moving out, the cafeteria humming like a beehive.

"Excuse me!" I tried again.

Mike put his fingers to his lips and whistled. Loud. Everyone stopped. "Yo! People." He pointed at me on the table. "Gigi has something to say."

Now all eyes were on me. My stomach twisted. Will had folded his arms, keeping his expression neutral. But there were Neerja and Bea, looking up at me with admiration, and Mike, who said in his low voice, "Do it, Einstein."

I began at the most logical place. "Hi. I'm Gigi and I ran for student rep and if you voted for me, thanks, and if you didn't, that's okay, but that's not why I'm here."

A bunch of kids yelled they had. Someone whistled and a few guys in the corner shouted, "Gaga for Gigi!"

"Here's the thing." My throat went dry. Mrs. Greene was talking to Joe the Janitor and telling him to close the doors, probably so the principal wouldn't find out. "Unless we do something, two teachers we love are going to lose their jobs and drama and art are going to get cut by the school board next year. That means no more plays. No more jewelry making."

There was more murmuring.

"So we've printed up over a hundred petitions and we're going to pass them around. We hope you and your friends sign them, that you'll take them home and give them to your parents, neighbors, whomever, to sign, and then bring them back and drop them off at the office. There's a mailbox just for the school board. Mrs. Wently will show you. Or give them to Bea, Neerja, or me. Because no way are we going to let our school become a place without art or drama. Not without a fight!"

"Yah!" the Man Clan shouted in unison.

"After all," I asked, my heart pounding like the hooves of a racehorse, "who goes to this school? The school board? Or . . ." I threw out my arms. "Us?!"

The cafeteria erupted in applause and thunderous stomping. Mrs. Greene was on the phone, probably explaining why a riot was happening on her watch.

Mike gave me a hand down and said, "Good on ya, Einstein. Way to get your butt in trouble again." But he was smiling and I knew he was proud that I'd taken the chance. Sienna actually gave me a hug.

"Look at you!" she squealed.

"Oh my god!" Bea grabbed me. "That was awesome. Do you know how awesome that was? All my petitions are gone."

Neerja said, "We've got to get you out of here. The doors are open and Obleck's on his way. Maybe we can . . ."

"*Attention, students!*" Schultz's voice erupted over the PA system. "*The results of the emergency election for student representative to the Denton High Board of Education are in and we have a winner.*"

Bea stood on one side of me, Neerja on the other. Mike winked.

"*William Blake garnered ninety-three votes. Smithers Chavez, two hundred seventy-one. And Genevieve Dubois, eighty-two.*"

My stomach dropped. Not only hadn't I won, I hadn't even taken second place! But what about Smitty's informal polls?

Mike shook his head and mouthed, *No way.* In my ear, Bea whispered, "Fraud. You must have gotten more votes than Will."

"However, due to a technical error, Smithers Chavez has been eliminated as a viable candidate. Therefore, I am pleased to announce that the new student representative to the school board is William Blake. Congratulations, Will!"

But Will was gone.

If he had any decency at all, he'd be in Schultz's office demanding an explanation.

Twenty-two

"Four hundred and forty-six votes out of a school of, what, a thousand kids?" Bea asked for the umpteenth time as we walked home from school that day, our boots sliding through the melting snow. "It doesn't make any sense. If Smitty didn't want anyone to vote, then how come he got the most?"

Bea kept saying this.

"It's not possible."

She kept saying that, too.

"I voted," she said. "Gigi, I know you voted. Neerja, you voted."

"Duh," Neerja said. "So did Justin."

"No, I didn't."

Neerja let go of his hand. "Get out!"

"So what?" He checked his phone. "Not like one vote's gonna make a difference."

"Yes, it does. It *did*," Neerja said. "It's Gigi we're talking about here."

"Yeah?"

"So she needed every one of our votes, obviously. She only lost by eleven."

"If I'd voted for her, it would have been ten. Still would have lost."

Neerja clasped her arms in disgust. Justin didn't seem to care.

Bea said, "Did you ever find out what the so-called technical issues were, Gigi?"

"Nuh-uh." Though I had my suspicions. Either Smitty resigned on the spot and Schultz refused to give him the satisfaction of embarrassing her by letting him do so publicly. Or, she'd learned about his plan and deep-sixed him before he could quit.

Either way, the election didn't make sense. I was supposed to win. Smitty himself said so. And Bea was right—what *was* up with that low turnout? It would have been understandable if Smitty's supporters hadn't voted, but since his supporters voted for him, something seemed off.

Luckily, with Christmas break right around the corner,

there was so much going on that I didn't have time to wallow in my loss. Plus, there was a lot to celebrate, including the petitions. According to Mrs. Wently, over two thousand parents and students had signed them—enough for the school board to table its vote on the budget cuts until the new year when, um, Will could add the student input.

Hmm. I'd have to bring him around to our way of thinking. As for the cheating policy, right now the budget cuts were more important. Mike and I had two years to get those letters out of our files before colleges saw them.

In gratitude for my petition effort, Mrs. Greene left homemade blueberry muffins for us in the honors lounge with a note quoting Anne Frank: *How wonderful it is that nobody need wait a single moment before starting to improve the world.* I didn't know if saving art and drama was exactly "improving the world," but I do know those muffins were delicious.

Also, on my response to a literature paper for *The House of the Spirits* by Isabel Allende (awesome read!), Mrs. Smullen circled a quote I'd used from the book— *Can't you see how far I've come? I'm the best now. If I put my mind to it*—and in red pencil added in the margins, *This is you, Gigi, when you put your mind to something!*

I have to say, her comment and the Anne Frank one definitely got to me.

Anyway, with the play on Friday and a Crystal Ball

shopping trip planned for Saturday, my loss quickly faded into the background as an interesting chapter in my high school experience. Not one that I'd wish to repeat necessarily, but illuminating nonetheless.

Life, as they say, goes on.

And then, while waiting for lunch, Mrs. Wently pulled me out of line and said Schultz wanted to meet with me in her office. Bea raised her brows in concern when I was led away. As my consigliere, she preferred to be present when her client was interrogated.

"We're not to be disturbed," Schultz said when Mrs. Wently closed the door and I was back in familiar surroundings. I took my regular seat and noted that the zen garden had a new sand pattern—and a teeny tiny beach ball. Cute.

"Genevieve, I must say it's gratifying to see how far you've come since we first met." Schultz offered me a basket of candy canes.

I took one and unwrapped it, my stomach groaning since I was missing lunch.

"You seem to have blossomed over the past few weeks, working so well with Mike on that periodic table project, accepting the gamble in running for student representative, and then, of course, petitioning your peers for such an admirable cause." She sucked on her cane. "I could imagine you going into politics some day. If not as a politician, then as an activist. Being a Latin student, you're familiar with the phrase *Quis custodiet ipsos custodes?*"

"Who will guard the guardians?" A question posed by Plato, a Greek, to his teacher, Socrates, also a Greek, which was why I never could understand why it was most famous in Latin.

"Yes, exactly. Government is only as honest as its watchmen."

I bit on my candy cane and crunched. "Dr. Schultz, if this is about me standing on the table in the cafeteria. . . ."

"This is not about you standing on the table in the cafeteria. However, it is about honesty, which is how you first came to see me, isn't it?" She stood, folding her arms and going to the window that overlooked the soccer field. "It has been brought to my attention, Genevieve, that the voter turnout for student representative was not as low as I previously feared. Allegedly, several boxes of collected ballots were set aside and subsequently destroyed."

I quit sucking, stunned. "Are you saying I would have won?"

"I wish I could answer you definitively. Alas, without the votes in hand I cannot say, though I can surmise that, yes, such was likely the case."

I knew it. The candy cane fell from my mouth onto my jeans. I tossed it into the wastepaper basket and said, "What makes you say that?"

"Because Jim Mullet's friends, who procured the voting boxes, intentionally removed your ballots so Smithers would win." She turned from the window. "Their actions were inexcusable and I promise you that when I pinpoint the culprits, I will impose the harshest penalties. But until then, you should know that as far as I've been able to determine, William had no part in this."

Well, that was a relief. I guess.

"Fortunately, one of Jim Mullet's friends came to me with this information. I had already disqualified Smithers, of course, when I learned that he planned to resign if elected. When questioned, he readily admitted that he was prepared to relinquish his post in a most public way to bring attention to what he considered to be an unfair punishment of his friend. But he had no knowledge of the stolen ballots. And I believe him."

I was tempted to tell Schultz about Smitty and how he tried to talk me into quitting the race. But that would make me a snitch and, besides, it was remotely possible that he was innocent. *Remotely.*

"Unfortunately, they didn't bother to count all the ballots to determine if the victor would have been you, though logic dictates you would have won. Otherwise why steal and destroy such proof? The question going forward is, what do we do now?"

To my way of thinking, this wasn't much of a debate.

"You get on the intercom and say there was a mistake and Gigi Dubois is the new student rep."

"Ah, if it were only that easy I would do it like that." She snapped her fingers. "But those ballots are bonfire ashes. And let me be frank. In light of the cheating scandal last year, do we really want Denton High to be dragged through the mud again and so soon?"

I thought about Mr. Watson losing his job after the cheating scandal. The same might happen to Schultz if it became public knowledge that a group of seniors had stolen the ballot boxes. This had to be why she wanted to keep it under wraps.

On the other hand, because I'd lost out as student rep, I wouldn't be able to get the cheating policy changed. And that meant the letter of referral would still be in my file and in Mike's. So, in the end, we'd be the ones who'd be ultimately punished—not Smitty or his friends. Not Schultz.

Which is when I devised the perfect solution. What if Schultz removed the letters of referral in our folders if I agreed not to make a big stink about the ballots? Wouldn't that solve everyone's problems?

"Dr. Schultz," I said. "I just might have a compromise."

Friday night's performance of the play was a notable improvement over the matinee.

No one applauded when Romeo and Juliet were found dead, and a few members in the audience even cried. Lindsay's acting continued to be lackluster, though mysteriously she didn't forget a single line, uttering each word in almost robotic perfection.

It was Henry who stole the show, receiving a standing ovation for his passionate portrayal of a teenage boy madly in love, dueling with impeccable footing, and, finally, throwing himself on Juliet as he downed the poison.

For a minute, even I had a crush on him. Or maybe it was that outfit.

"He was quite something, no?" Neerja's mother said to me as we met in the lobby after the play. "Why doesn't he take Neerja to the Crystal Ball?"

"Because Henry's taking Lindsay and Neerja's going with Justin." *Her boyfriend*, I wanted to add. *Remember him?*

Dr. Padwami just sighed.

Afterward, Neerja, Justin, and I went out with the Padwamis for dessert in Waverley Square. At the last minute, Henry had to bow out because Lindsay wanted him to go with her to Marissa's party—a change in plans that seemed to send Neerja into a mild funk.

"Don't you think Henry is super-talented?" Neerja asked, dreamily twirling her spoon around the whipped cream. "I had no idea he had it in him."

Neerja's mother glanced at me over her tea. "Oh, yes. I thought he was the best Romeo ever, and I have seen *Romeo and Juliet* acted in the original Globe Theater."

"Where's that?" Justin asked.

"England," Neerja's father replied with little patience. "You know? Shakespeare's own theater?"

Justin frowned, impressed. "Dude. I had no idea Shakespeare owned a theater. A megaplex?" He grinned.

It was supposed to be a joke, but the Padwamis obviously took it as more evidence of their daughter's boyfriend's idiocy because they didn't laugh and Neerja's mother quickly changed the subject. "I thought Lindsay was having trouble. But she didn't miss a line."

"Because of the Bluetooth in her ear," Neerja said. "I don't know why it didn't occur to me sooner. She kept her phone in her bra, hidden, while I dictated lines to her over mine."

"Brava!" Her father clapped madly, too loudly for the small ice cream shop. "It is like that old ditty, if you can't be biggest tree on the hill, then be the biggest shrub in the valley."

Poor Neerja. Always being relegated to shrub status. "What did Drew think about your trick?"

Neerja scooped up the last cherry. "He had his doubts at first. If Lindsay lost her Bluetooth it would have been a disaster. But tonight he said I'll win the drama award for single-handedly saving the play."

More applause from Neerja's dad. His wife gently placed a hand on his arm and asked him to keep it down. I was really proud of Neerja. She'd set out to be the best prompter ever and, amazingly, she actually *was* the best prompter ever.

"He's even talking about giving me the lead in the spring musical, *Beauty and the Beast*. Me as Belle." She swallowed the cherry and smiled.

Whoa! That was huge. Her parents had no idea that everyone wanted to be in the spring musical, and that Belle was *la prima* part. Far bigger than Juliet.

"That's awesome, Neerja!" We slapped high fives.

Justin pushed back his plate, bored. "Hey, are we going to Marissa's party or not?"

I knew the Padwamis would be horrified by Marissa's pre–cast party because they were horrified by all parties that did not begin at noon and end at four with party favors and balloons.

"This late?" Dr. Padwami checked his watch. "It's almost ten."

Justin was unfazed. "So . . . are we?"

Neerja shot a look at her mother, who was sending every possible signal besides Morse code and semaphore flags that the answer was no. "I can't. I'm getting up early tomorrow to go shopping for Crystal Ball dresses with Bea and Gigi."

Justin sighed. "Yeah, all right. See you, then." And, without so much as a "thanks," he left the coffee shop, leaving Neerja in total devastation. You could tell her dad was ready to pop his top.

"I know what you're thinking, Bapa, but he is really, *really* sweet," Neerja said hurriedly.

Dr. Padwami went, "Hmph."

"And he is taking me to the Crystal Ball, so . . ."

"There will be other balls, Neerja. Other boys." He added to his wife, "Why can't she go with that nice boy next door?"

Henry? I started to laugh, but Neerja shot me down with a glower. "I can't go with Henry because he has a girlfriend."

"And you have a boyfriend," I reminded her. "A pretty cute one, too."

"That's true," Neerja said. "Besides, I can't back out now. It wouldn't be fair to Justin."

The Padwamis were nothing if not polite. "Okay, okay," her mother said. "As long as you get home in time and safe, it's okay with us if you go with him."

Neerja might have won a small victory, but she wasn't happy. If she hadn't been going out with Justin, I'd have pegged her as heartbroken.

* * *

Crystal Ball dress shopping was a lot more fun than I'd expected. To tell the truth, I'd been kind of dreading it, mostly because, unlike Neerja, I didn't have a date and I couldn't quite see the point of spending my hard-earned allowance on a ridiculous gown that only Bea would admire.

Bea's attitude was that going solo was better than going with a guy because you weren't obligated to stay with your date. This made no sense to me since the only guys I might be interested in already had girlfriends and I planned on keeping as far away from them as possible.

"What we have to do is look hotter than everyone else so every guy kicks himself for not asking us instead," she said from the adjoining dressing room. "Are you with me, Gigi?"

"I'm with you, Bea!" I zipped up a white dress with white roses at the waist and curled my lip. Yuck. Bridesmaid meets grandmother.

Next was a one-shoulder deal that, while gorgeous, I had to reject because it had been Maddie's choice for Sienna. Too bad, because the whole Grecian goddess thing definitely worked for me, I thought, running my hand over the beaded strap.

Mike would love it.

Geesh. Where did that come from?

"Gigi? How about this?" Bea was outside the door standing on the short stool in front of the three-way mirror in a short, strapless dress that showed off her long legs. She was gorgeous, except . . .

"Is that black?" The Crystal Ball dresses had to be either black, silver, white, or gold. Anything smacking of a holiday—like, um, Christmas—was strictly forbidden because it was a school-sponsored affair.

"Are you blind? It's green." She twirled and the dress went out. It really was something.

"You can't wear green."

"No, I can't wear white because it makes my freckles pop and I can't wear black because with my pale skin I look like a corpse. But I can wear green because with my red hair I look amazing."

They were never going to let her through the door.

"I will not let myself be a victim of redhead discrimination," Bea said. "My people have been through too much already. Sunburns. Nicknames! When will it end?"

"Try it," a voice said.

Behind me, Ava was in a white Grecian gown just like mine.

And she was totally blond.

"Ava?" I drew closer. The kohl under her eyes was completely gone, replaced by a tasteful shading of brown. She'd morphed—again. This time into a preppy blonde.

Bea said, "You're back to normal."

"I was always normal."

"What happened?" I could barely formulate the direct question. "*Why?*"

"I dunno. I thought I'd try something different." She checked her back. "I've done the brunette thing. Now I thought I'd do the blond thing."

Bea put her hand on her hip and smirked. "Don't BS us. You did it for Will."

My God, she was right. Talia. Me. Is this what Ava hoped, that by transforming herself into another Talia, Will would upgrade her to a bona fide girlfriend?

"You did change for Will," I said. "Just like you went all Euro artist for Rolf the German exchange student."

Ava's expression soured and I could tell we'd hit the bull's-eye. There was an awkward pause as she smoothed down her skirt, preparing her comeback. "I just ran into Neerja, who says you two are going to the ball together."

"And . . . ?" Bea asked.

"Don't take this the wrong way, but that is really sad. You two are actually kind of pretty in a certain way, yet the guys just never seem to go for you, do they?"

It took every ounce of reserve not to blurt that she'd been second choice, that Will had asked me first. But, as that would have only hurt Bea, I returned to my dressing room and shut the door.

"What's sad," Bea said, hopping off her stool, "is a girl who claims to be a creative free spirit, but really she's just a chameleon who changes her colors to please the latest guy. Artist? Preppy blonde? Check and check. What's next, Ava? Athlete? Lumberjack?"

"What do you care?" Ava shot back. "It's not your life."

"No, but you hurt someone I love. You dropped her as a friend because she got in the way of your image as the über-cool *artiste.*"

I held my breath. Bea was talking about *me*!

"So, yes," Bea said. "I care very much."

"Well, at least I'm not so desperate that I'd go to the Crystal Ball with another girl." Ava went back to her room too and slammed the door, sliding the lock.

That's when I knew Ava wasn't to be despised but pitied. Ava had no concept of friendship. She only wanted me to skip school with her so she'd feel better about skipping school. She wanted me to drop out of honors and be impressed by her supposed sophistication, her partying, her whole edgy shtick. All she wanted from me was validation.

It had always been about her. Never about us. And she was too clueless to realize how truly sad that was.

Twenty-three

The evening of the Crystal Ball, Parad came home from the New Jersey Nerd Tank called Princeton and my mother came home from the Swiss Nerd Tank called the Large Hadron Collider.

I was upstairs in my bedroom painting my nails Bazooka Pink when I heard a door slam and lots of French being spoken. Leaping out of bed, Petunia at my heels, I rushed downstairs and, sure enough, there was Mom in her familiar black coat and black pants and, as if she couldn't be European enough, a gold striped scarf knotted at her throat.

"Mom!"

"Gigi!" She wrapped me in a big motherly hug. It was so wonderful to have her home, to smell her trademark lavender perfume and feel the brush of her graying blond curls against my cheek. It was such a relief knowing I wouldn't have to be the only one responsible for dinner.

When we were done hugging, I said, "Who's making sure the universe isn't being destroyed?"

"Ah, we got the kid next door to house-sit." She laughed and held me at arm's length. "Gee, Gigi." (Bad family joke.) "You seem so . . . different. So grown-up."

Which is when Marmie went, *"Vooley vous vous jajaja."*

And Mom went, *"Vooley vous vous jajaja?"*

"Oui, oui." Marmie nodded.

Look, I loved my mother. I loved my grandmother. But this kind of blatant French code malarkey had to end. Maybe I needed to sneak in one or two of those crash courses so I could get the skinny.

Marmie heated up some hot chocolate, and I built a fire in the fireplace as Mom kicked off her boots, unwound her scarf, and launched into excruciating detail—as intercontinental travelers do—about a flight delay in London and Christmas crowds and airport security. Then, when that was done, she said, "I thought you hurt your elbow."

"I only had to wear a sling for a week." I stuck out my tongue at Marmie, who'd sworn she wouldn't tell Mom that I'd been injured.

"Good. Because I thought for old time's sake we could

go down to the pond and go ice skating tonight. Remember when we used to do that when you were little? We'd buy a Christmas tree and make some cookies and take them with us along with a Thermos of—"

"Gigi's off to the Crystal soiree," Marmie said, using the French word for *ball*.

"Oh." Mom kept her lips in a perfect oval. "With anyone I know?"

"A lovely young man named Bea Honeycutt."

Mom blinked as if stalling to form the most sensitive response, and I realized she had leaped to the wrong conclusion. "What I mean is, Bea and I are going together as friends since Neerja's going with a guy."

"Henry?"

"Believe it or not, no." And I explained about Henry and Neerja's plan to do the school play so Henry could hook up with Lindsay and Neerja with Justin, though it wasn't that much of a hookup, as far as hookups go, because they had yet to kiss.

Mom frowned. "That's odd. And how long have they been going out?"

"Six weeks or so."

"Oh dear," said my mother, turning to Marmie and going, "*Ce Justin, est-il gai?*"

Marmie handed her a hot chocolate and shrugged. "*Qui sait? Je ne suis pas sa petite amie.*"

Laughing, Mom translated, "Who knows? I'm not his girlfriend."

Then I told her about Will asking me out and me turning him down because of Bea, and Mom put her hand to her chest and said that my sacrifice for friendship made her very, very proud. "Men will come and go. Trust me."

I was living proof of that.

"But girlfriends, ah." Tears sprang to the corner of her eyes. "They are forever."

"That's nice, Mom," I said, sipping my hot chocolate. "Exactly how much sleep have you had, by the way?"

She held up her hand. "Four hours."

"Since when?"

"Thursday."

It was now Saturday. "Right. Maybe you should take a nap."

And soon I was leading her upstairs. I was running the water in her tub so she could soak off all the international grime and trace radioactivity or whatever, when she popped her head into the bathroom and said, "What are you wearing?"

"The usual." Which is to say a little black dress Marmie bought me for my sixteenth birthday, claiming that no woman should be without one. It was very plain and very functional, as well as expertly cut and *trés* French. It wasn't going to knock off any socks, but I wouldn't be laughed off the dance floor either.

"That's no good." She returned with a garment bag that she hung on the bathroom door and unzipped. "This would work, right?"

I couldn't believe what was inside. A full-length strapless white evening gown ruched at the top and edged by shimmering rhinestones.

"Mom! I had no idea you MIT wonks had this kind of taste." It was gorgeous! Elegant and slim and slippery.

"Well, you know, I bought it for a special occasion once and that special occasion never came to pass." She sighed at it regretfully. "Anyway, it's just been wasting away in my closet. Try it on."

I did not need to be asked twice. In a flash, my clothes were off and that dress was on. I held up my hair. "How does it look?"

Mom's hand went to her mouth and those tears popped into her eyes again.

"Seriously, Mom. You need some major z's."

The game plan was that Bea would stop by my house around seven. We'd shove down some food, do our hair and makeup, get dressed, and then her brother would drive us to the ball at the Oakmont Country Club. Bea's dad would pick us up, and we'd do a sleepover at her place.

But that never happened. Instead, Bea hadn't been at

my house more than fifteen minutes when Neerja called.

"Guys?" Her voice was thick and weird like she was sad and angry. "You won't believe what just happened."

I held up the phone so Bea could hear.

"Justin . . . That ditwad broke up with me. He and Marissa hooked up at her party last weekend and now they're together. I just . . . got . . . dumped."

Which was ironic since Parad had been telling her to dump *him*.

Bea snatched the phone. "Where is he? I'll call Henry and we'll track him down and beat the daylights out of his Bieberish head."

I punched the air. Yes!

"Henry's already here."

Henry got on and said, "She needs you. I've gotta get ready to go pick up Lindsay."

"Gotcha," Bea said, screwing the cap on her mascara. "Tell her we'll be right over."

My dress, my lovely, gorgeous dress, hung limply in its garment bag. "I guess this means the ball is off."

"Yeah, right!" Bea tossed makeup into her bag—mascara, blush, liner. "Listen, Gigi, don't announce this to the world, but I intend to make my move on B.K. tonight."

My lower jaw unhinged. "But he's a member of the Man Clan!"

"So what? I had a really good time with him driving back from Vermont, and since apparently he's not going out with anyone and I do look sizzling hot in this dress"— she twirled—"I'm going for it."

I didn't say anything because I was stunned—in a good way—though Bea immediately assumed the opposite.

"Oh no! Now you're mad. Don't worry," she said, clutching my arms. "I promise not to leave you in the lurch. We'll still do the sleepover and everything. Only, we'll have more to talk about."

"Darn straight," I said, "because guess what? *I* turned down a guy for *you*."

"Who, Mike?"

"What?"

"Don't act like this is a shock. You don't think I saw what was going on in the backseat of B.K.'s car? You lying with your head on his chest. Him stroking your hair."

He was stroking my hair? "Nothing was going on," I said, my cheeks growing hot.

"Oh, and so that's why you're blushing."

My hands flew to my face. "Anyway, it was Will. He asked me to the ball."

She gave me a shove. "Shut. Up!"

"No, YOU shut up!" I pushed her back.

She shoved me back. "No, YOU shut up!"

"You shut up!"

"Both of you shut up!" my mother called from her bedroom. "Some of us are trying to sleep."

Parad answered the door to Neerja's room when we got upstairs and found her lying on her four-poster bed, staring at the ceiling. Neerja's beautiful black dress with the gold trim was on the floor, her strappy sandals lay at either end of the room.

"I've tried telling her that guys are scum, but she won't listen." Parad sat on a chair and folded her arms over her Princeton sweatshirt. "I never went to the Crystal Ball and look how I turned out."

Bea cut her eyes in my direction. "Thanks, Parad, we can take it from here."

Slowly, reluctantly, Parad got up and inched toward the door. "You know, Neerja, you got a lot farther in high school socially by sophomore year than I ever did. I never even had a boyfriend—so think about that."

"Bye-bye." Bea eased her out to where Thing One and Thing Two were eavesdropping, their ears against the wall. "You too," she threatened.

Neerja's little sisters screamed and ran downstairs. When they were gone, Bea shut the door and said, "Take a shower, Neerja. Do your hair. Put on the dress and let's go."

"I can't." Neerja blinked.

"You cannot let Justin do this to you. You cannot put your life on hold for a boy."

"It's not Justin." Neerja propped herself on her elbows, the rims of her eyes swollen from crying. "It's Henry."

"Henry?" we both exclaimed.

Bea fell into the chair and I sat on the edge of Neerja's bed. "What about Henry?" I asked.

"I can't stand to see him at the ball with Lindsay."

This was so confusing. Bea and I looked at each other, baffled. Henry and Neerja were friends. It was common knowledge they didn't like each other *that* way.

"But you wanted him to get with her," Bea said.

Neerja swung her legs around. "I *thought* I wanted him to get with Lindsay just like I *thought* I loved Justin. But once I was with Justin for more than a day, I was bored out of my brain. And seeing Henry get closer to Lindsay was pure torture."

She grabbed a pink pillow and placed it over her lap. "Do you know why I memorized all twenty-six thousand words of *Romeo and Juliet*?"

"To be the best prompter ever!" I said.

"Or, you hoped Drew would ask you to sub for Lindsay if she continued to screw up her lines," suggested Bea.

"Exactly. Though I did want to be the best prompter ever too." She sniffed and Bea threw her the box of tissues. "Does that make me a ditz?"

"It makes you in love."

We hadn't heard the door open or Neerja's mother come in. "You're in love, Neerja. Do you know that?"

Neerja nodded at her mother. "I think I am."

"So all you can do is be your own beautiful self and let love win. But," she added, closing the door a little behind her, "don't tell your father I said so. Now, go get ready for that dance. I'll even let you drive Dad's Mercedes."

Incredible. Dr. Padwami never let anyone drive his Mercedes.

It took some doing, but we managed to get Neerja into the shower, get her out of the shower, and dry her hair so it was beautifully sleek. Bea did her makeup and then my hair so it hung loose and bouncy. I put up Bea's in a twist and then we got into our dresses, stepped into our shoes, and regarded our reflections.

We were beautiful.

"Three goddesses," Neerja said.

"Three friends," I said.

Bea, in the middle, squeezed us to her. "For-*ever*."

Twenty-four

The Oakmont Country Club at the top of the hill was lit up like a castle when we stepped out of the Padwamis' Mercedes and Neerja's mother drove off. We linked arms, giggled, and walked to the door together, not caring one little bit what anyone else thought.

We were the smart girls, yes, and we were *awesome*.

"Um, there's a dress code," a senior girl at the door said as she took our tickets. "White, black, silver, or gold."

Bea frowned. "Really? Is that a law? Is it written somewhere? If so, show me the rules. And who's to say in some other universe this green isn't black?"

The senior rolled her eyes and snatched the ticket out of Bea's hand. "Oh brother. Just go already."

Bea pumped her fist as we made our way inside.

The ballroom was decorated with ice sculptures and billions of tiny white lights. The theme was supposed to be out of a Russian fairy tale in winter—without the trolls.

Except for one.

"Justin!" Neerja gasped. We held her steady. Justin was standing in the corner with Marissa, who was glancing about the room, yawning, as he checked his reflection in a darkened window.

"He's with her," Neerja hissed.

"Correction," I said. "He's with himself."

I scanned the room crowded with our classmates. There was Sienna with Maddie, talking to B.K. and Parker. The newly blond Ava was with Will near the stage, where a band was playing some really bad old Nirvana. The room was thick with a haze of cologne, hair spray, body odor, and, for some reason, the smell of fried shrimp.

It was really, really loud.

"Hey, guys." Henry approached holding a simple white rose. He was even more handsome than with his cape. All washed up, his hair smooth to one side, in a suit and tie. No white socks. "How are we doing?"

By *we*, I knew he meant Neerja. Neerja inhaled and smiled. "Much better, thanks."

"You look fantastic, Neerja. Really, really pretty."

Did he have any idea that his best friend was madly in love with him?

"I got you this." He handed her the rose.

Neerja cupped it gently. "Oh, Henry. That's so sweet. But it doesn't have a pin."

"Because it belongs here." He gently brushed back her hair and placed it behind her ear. Her face lit up, her eyes sparkled. "There. How's that?"

She fingered it delicately. "It's lovely. Thank you."

"Wanna dance?"

Bea ever so slightly stepped on my toe. Seriously, she had to stop stepping on me and pinching my legs under tables. It was getting painful.

"Sure." Neerja beamed.

"Come on," he said, taking her hand. "Let's show Justin what he's missing."

Bea sighed as they went off, Neerja practically skipping with happiness. "I never thought of it before, but they are truly the perfect couple. They're both kind of dorky, they love their inside jokes, they're best friends, and even their parents want them to be together." She sighed again. "Don't you think, Gigi?"

"Could you get off my foot?" My toe was throbbing.

"Oh, yeah. Sorry." She laughed nervously. "Uh-oh. Don't look now, but someone's coming for you. I think I'll go stun B.K. with my amazing beauty."

Sienna bustled toward me in the white one-shoulder dress that Maddie had chosen.

"Hi," I said, admiring her gown. "Great choice."

She glanced down. "You think? Maddie picked it out. Did you find Mike? He's looking for you." She glanced around, smiling and waving in her Sienna style, working her gum like it was 8:15 a.m. in homeroom.

"Isn't he with you?"

She sucked on the straw in her soda. "No. Why would he be with me? I'm with Parker."

"Oh." So Ava had been right after all. Mike was a free agent—a thought that suddenly lifted my hopes. "Then what does Mike want?"

"I don't know. Maybe he needs something."

Of course, I realized, my hopes fizzling. Why should I be surprised that Mike was looking for me because he *needed* something? "Let me guess," I said, forcing a smile. "He needs to borrow my notes from Tuesday's history class he skipped?"

Sienna was staring at me in astonishment. "That's not what I meant. Do you really think Mike only wants you for your . . . *notes*?"

"Oh, no. Not just my notes. He also wants my homework and maybe a few answers on a quiz. Mike's not picky that way. He's very accepting." Frustrated, I rearranged the top of my dress, which kept slipping.

"You really need to get over yourself, you know that?" She folded her arms. "You have no idea what Mike's done for *you*, going to Schultz about those stolen votes even though he's friends with Smitty and Mullet."

Hold on. Mike was the one who ratted to Schultz?

Will was heading toward us and Sienna dropped her voice. "Don't tell anyone—especially Mike—that I said anything, okay?"

"He could have told me himself."

"Yeah, right." She rolled her eyes. "I'm sorry, Gigi, but you're not the easiest person to deal with. How many weeks did you sit next to me in homeroom before you deigned to speak to Maddie and me?"

I was about to set the record straight when I felt a tap on my shoulder and there was Will, dashing as always, in a classic tux.

"Hey," he said gruffly, all business.

"Hey," I repeated dully, still reeling from this latest revelation. "What's up?"

"How do you feel about getting onstage with me for a sec? Schultz is going to do the principal thing and then I'm supposed to say a few words, and I want you to be there with me, if that's all right."

"Um, sure. What's this about?"

"Let's just say I have to do something I should have done a long time ago."

"Sounds mysterious."

"Not that much. By the way, you look freaking incredible. I mean, really. Just . . . wow." He slapped his hands over his heart. "Good thing you turned me down because if you were here with me looking like this, Talia would *not* be a happy camper."

I deciphered his line of code. Mike was right about Will. He could really sling the BS. "So, I guess that means you two are still together."

"Yeah. We're gonna try to give it our best shot. We'll see each other over Christmas break and then I'll go back to California next summer and who knows." He paused. "Anyway, you know what they say, distance makes the heart grow fonder. At least, that's what I'm hoping."

My gaze shifted over to Ava, twirling her hair mindlessly as she studied the two of us. What could she be expecting from this night? Because if she was expecting Will to fall for her, she had another thing coming. "And Ava?"

He followed my gaze and nodded. She blew him a kiss. "She's, you know, Ava."

"Yeah, and she deserves better." If there was anything lower than ditching your friends for guys, like Ava, it was treating girls as if they're disposable razors, like Will. "She's not some loaner car for you to test drive while your luxury model is shipped cross-country."

Will made a sound that was halfway between a cough and a swear. "That's harsh."

"No, that's the truth." I tapped him on the chest. "See you onstage. I've got to find someone first and apologize."

I sailed off to find Mike, not bothering to check back to see if Will was standing there, gaping.

Though I knew he was.

Mike was leaning against the doorway, his hands in the pockets of his khakis, his longish brown hair still delightfully messy. I don't know if it was his thoughtful expression or the way he was finally out of his plaid shorts and in a crisp white shirt, navy blazer, and green striped tie, but I saw him in a whole new light.

When he saw me, everything about him changed. He straightened slightly and took me in, top to bottom, drinking in each detail—the pearls at my ears, the way the dress hugged my body, my bare shoulders, my hair. His eyes met mine and I saw that he was just as nervous.

He clasped his hands behind him. "Hello, Einstein." For a charmer who used to throw his arm around me on a whim, he seemed suddenly very stiff and proper. "What happened to my nerd who fell off the curb?"

He called me "my" nerd! "Why didn't you tell me you were the one who went to Schultz?"

He looked over at Sienna who was, I suspected, intentionally keeping her back to us. "Did my ex tell you that?

Don't believe her. The girl's a pathological liar."

"Yeah, right. What I want to know is why?" My hands landed on my hips, demanding. "What do you want in return?"

A corner of Mike's mouth turned upward. "You really do have an incredible knack for putting the nicest spin on things, Einstein."

I winced. Crap. I'd inadvertently insulted him again. "Sorry. I didn't mean it that way. Sometimes, I think one thing, but then what comes out of my mouth sounds really *dumb*."

"Then let me answer your question with another question." He bent his head toward mine so we were nose to nose. "Did it ever cross your brilliant mind that I might actually *like* you?"

As soon as he said this, something inside me clicked and I thought, *Yes!*

"Aha. For once, I have rendered the genius speechless." He smiled, almost in victory. "By the way, I think your boyfriend's calling you."

Will was onstage, shielding his eyes against the lights. The band had stopped playing and everyone was waiting for me.

I turned back to Mike. "Where'd you get the idea that he's my boyfriend?"

"Gee, I don't know. 'Cause he kept asking you out in

front of me and, don't forget, he kissed you, didn't he?"

"Gigi Dubois! Come on, Gigi. Don't leave me hanging," Will was saying. The crowd was chanting, *"Gigi, Gigi, Gigi!"*

"Stay right there." Hiking up my dress, I twisted my way to where Will was waiting at the microphone. The stage lights were really bright. I couldn't see anything except a sea of blurry faces. I couldn't see Mike.

I felt Will take my hand and hold it tightly. "Okay, guys. I have an announcement to make."

Will pulled me toward him just as I found Mike in the crowd—right when he was heading out the door.

"As you all know, I won the emergency election for student rep." Will held up a finger before anyone could applaud. "However, it recently came to my attention that there was a screwup in the vote counting."

What was he doing? "No," I whispered, covering the mic. "Schultz and I made a deal."

"Don't worry. It's cool." He brought the mic up. "Therefore, it is my honor to present to you the person who really got the most votes. Give a big shout-out for our new student rep, Gigi Dubois!" He raised my hand and immediately the place went wild.

At first, I didn't know what was happening. Then the pieces fell into place. Will was stepping aside. I'd won. It was official. And everyone knew it! I looked to Schultz to see if she was okay with that. She smiled and mouthed, *Say something.*

Will handed me my old enemy. I took one look at that stupid mic and thought, *You don't scare me anymore.* There were no butterflies. No waves of nausea.

"A friend once told me," I began, as the crowd settled down, "to not be like a boxer and keep it brief."

A round of laughter.

"So, all I want to say is, thank you to all of you who voted for me and thank you to Will for being such a stand-up guy." I covered the mic and whispered, "Most of the time."

Will grinned halfheartedly at Ava, who gazed adoringly from the front row like a groupie.

The Man Clan let out a cheer in unison. "We're Gaga for Gigi!"

"But I also need to thank my friends, Bea and Neerja, for watching my back since kindergarten, for always making me laugh, and for being the best friends *ev-ah*!"

"Woo-hoo!" Bea stuck her fingers in her mouth and whistled above the applause. Neerja jumped up and down so hard the rose fell out of her hair.

"And to everyone here, have an awesome time tonight. You deserve it, because Denton High rocks!"

The band struck up "We Will Rock You." Will took the mic and joked, "Not bad. Have you ever considered a career in politics?"

A photographer pivoted to the front, crouching to get a shot. "For the yearbook!" he yelled, clicking madly.

"No, wait!" I reached down and brought Bea and Neerja onstage so the photographer could get a shot of the three of us.

"And who are these girls?" he asked, taking out a pad to write our names.

"Beatrice Honeycutt and Neerja Padwami. Skier. Actress. My campaign advisors. They're pretty rad."

The photographer cracked a smile. "Pretty rad, huh? I don't know if that will fly with the yearbook staff, but I'll try to get you in."

Mike! I'd almost forgotten.

"Gotta go," I said, giving each of them a hug and then jumping off the stage. If Mike left because he got the wrong idea when Will put his arm around me, then I would simply have to hunt him down and explain, I decided, squeezing and sliding my way through the throng.

I found him outside the door. "Mike Ipolito!" I yelled. "Where do you think you're going?"

He spun around. "What's it to you?"

"Come on." I reached out and took his hand, searching for a room, someplace to escape where we could be alone to talk, finally settling on the courtyard.

It was cold out there, a shock compared to the

stuffiness of the ballroom. Flurries had begun to fall, illuminated by the lights surrounding the covered swimming pool. The doors closed behind us with a click and we were alone. At last.

"It's freezing." He shrugged off his blazer and laid it over my bare shoulders. "There are warmer places, you know."

"Yeah, but no place where we can talk without being overheard." I found myself feeling slightly dizzy, like I used to when I had to get up in front of the class. Only this was different.

With Mike inches away, those brown eyes of his so curious—so warm and deep—and with me about to say what I'd wanted to say since forever, the sensation coming over me was almost like vertigo. As if at any moment I might simply fall into oblivion.

"Are you okay? You seem kind of pale." He stepped closer, sending my heart fluttering.

"Mike." I licked my lips, which had suddenly become very dry. "Look, I want to apologize. Like Sienna says, I'm not the easiest person to deal with and, like I said, sometimes I say one thing when I mean another."

"Einstein." He got even closer. "Is this your long-winded way of saying you like me too?"

Was this a joke to him? Did he take anything seriously? "I'm trying to say that I misjudged you. When you used to ask me for favors, I thought you were using me. And, for that, I'm sorry."

"I was."

What? *"You were?"*

"Well, not using *you*. Using those excuses. It was the only way I could get you to talk to me." He was so near me now, I could smell the faint scent of soap on his skin, the spice of his aftershave. That dizziness again. "You were always out of reach or attached to those two friends of yours. You wouldn't give me a second look."

"But . . . that's not true."

"So," he went on, "I had to come up with a legit reason to get next to you. It's not like I needed to copy your homework or get the math assignment."

"You mean, you had that stuff all along? You were just faking?"

He shrugged. "For all the good it did me. You'd throw me whatever and then walk off."

That was so untrue. "It was *you* who walked off, Mike."

"If I did—and I doubt it—it's because you didn't give me any reason to stay. Like tonight. You walked off again, this time to be with Will. So why should I stick around?"

He straightened the blazer while I searched for the right words, though there was nothing I could say that would change his mind.

There was only one solution.

"How about this?" I said, reaching up and pulling him toward me. "Is this reason enough to stay?"

Before I could think, I kissed him full on the lips as his hands slid over his jacket on my shoulders and down around my waist. My mind raced as time hit the brakes. I was kissing Mike. *I was kissing Mike.* He wasn't pushing me away or politely turning me down. He was kissing me back.

And it was *awesome*.

We kissed so long that our classmates spotted us and started pounding on the ballroom windows. When we finally broke away, he gave his head a shake. "Einstein. Where did you learn to kiss like that?"

I laughed. "Would you believe books?"

"No. I would not believe books. Let's try that again. I want to see what you've been reading." He covered my smiling mouth with his.

I'd never felt this way before, so excited and charged and just plain happy. Because not only was Mike cute and funny, but he was smart. *Really* smart. And that was the best part.

Like they tell you in health class, the biggest sex organ in the human body is the brain. And you know what that means . . .

Poor Justin!

Harry, if she didn't think you were going to react this way." Alice tapped her fingers on the table.

There was a long pause as we all waited for the verdict. Finally, Bea's father said, "Give me the pen." And that was that.

We were headed to the hills.

Seventeen

Bea slept over at my house because it was so close to the school, and Coach offered to pick us up on his way to New Hampshire for our first downhill practice. Not that door-to-door service made waking at 5 a.m. during school break any easier. We basically tumbled into his van and collapsed in the back, trying to get in a few extra z's amidst the skis, poles, and boots. I couldn't believe some of my friends actually chose to get up this early just to grab a few Black Friday bargains. Ten percent off Steve Madden ballet flats was definitely not worth it.

The temperature plummeted as the van crossed the New Hampshire border and climbed into the piney mountains. I'd had my doubts about finding any snow on Thanksgiving weekend but, sure enough, Paradise Mountain was open, albeit with limited trails.

Paradise wasn't exactly a resort—more like a 1950s wooden lodge where you could hang inside by the fire and warm up. But it was cheap and so it was packed with college and high school students who came for the discounted preseason tickets and the chance to return to school on Monday and boast that they'd already been skiing.

As Mike had predicted, there was only one lift running and it led to the top of the mountain where the snow was. I didn't have to look at the map to know the only trails open were black diamonds.

"Where is Mike anyway?" I asked Bea as she snapped me into my boots. A chalkboard over the service counter warned: CONDITIONS: POOR. ADVANCED AND INTERMEDIATE SKIERS ONLY. KNOW YOUR SKILL LEVEL!

Great.

"I guess Mike's out of town." Bea had to practically stand on a buckle to close it. My foot cramped in protest. "Then again, half the team's not here 'cause of Thanksgiving."

I was glad for that. This way, I'd only embarrass myself in front of the senior girls and B.K. Evans. And I definitely did not care what B.K. thought.

"All right, everyone suited up and ready to go?"

Coach clapped his hands once. He was wearing a bona fide DENTON HIGH red-and-black ski jacket. "I want to be on that mountain by oh eight hundred."

Military time. Another bad sign.

"Just remember," Bea said. "Don't panic."

"Don't panic," I echoed as we left the crowded lodge and its inviting smells of wood smoke, hot chocolate, and french fries. For one fleeting, desperate instant I hoped that maybe I'd break something. Nothing major like a leg or my neck. Just enough to land me on the DL. Then I'd get to stay inside by the fire reading a good book, never having to set foot on skis again.

Then again, that was not the Gunther Humboldt way.

I'd come to love Gunther Humboldt, his apple cheeks and Teutonic can-do 'tude. I loved the robust way he urged me to "lean your knees, yah?" as he zigzagged down a hill without his poles, touching only his outside leg. He would say, "I see you've got it. Good for you! That's the way." And I'd feel sort of guilty because there I was, propped against a bunch of soft pillows in my bedroom, stuffing my face with Raisinets, when really I should have been on the hill, making Gunther proud.

Under the gray November skies threatening rain, we found our skis. I clicked into mine, grabbed my poles, and tried shuffling toward the lift on a thin strip of man-made snow between brown grass and even a few rocks.